©Noboru Kannatuki

8

GOBLIN SLAYER

"...You, sir, are the worst."

Contents

GOBLIN SLAYER

 VOLUME 8

KUMO KAGYU

Illustration by
NOBORU KANNATUKI

New York

GOBLIN SLAYER

KUMO KAGYU

Translation by Kevin Steinbach ✢ Cover art by Noboru Kannatuki

GOBLIN SLAYER vol. 8
Copyright © 2018 Kumo Kagyu
Illustrations copyright © 2018 Noboru Kannatuki
All rights reserved.
Original Japanese edition published in 2018 by SB Creative Corp.
This English edition is published by arrangement with SB Creative Corp., Tokyo, in care of Tuttle-Mori Agency, Inc., Tokyo.

English translation © 2019 by Yen Press, LLC

Yen On
150 West 30th Street, 19th Floor
New York, NY 10001

Visit us at yenpress.com ✢ facebook.com/yenpress ✢ twitter.com/yenpress
yenpress.tumblr.com ✢ instagram.com/yenpress

First Yen On Edition: October 2019

Yen On is an imprint of Yen Press, LLC.
The Yen On name and logo are trademarks of Yen Press, LLC.

The publisher is not responsible for websites (or their content) that are not owned by the publisher.

Library of Congress Cataloging-in-Publication Data
Names: Kagyū, Kumo, author. | Kannatuki, Noboru, illustrator.
Title: Goblin slayer / Kumo Kagyu ; illustration by Noboru Kannatuki.
Other titles: Goburin sureiyā. English
Description: New York, NY : Yen On, 2016–
Identifiers: LCCN 2016033529 | ISBN 9780316501590 (v. 1 : pbk.) | ISBN 9780316553223 (v. 2 : pbk.) |
    ISBN 9780316553230 (v. 3 : pbk.) | ISBN 9780316411882 (v. 4 : pbk.) | ISBN 9781975326487 (v. 5 : pbk.) |
    ISBN 9781975327842 (v. 6 : pbk.) | ISBN 9781975330781 (v. 7 : pbk.) | ISBN 9781975331788 (v. 8 : pbk.)
Subjects: LCSH: Goblins—Fiction. | GSAFD: Fantasy fiction.
Classification: LCC PL872.5.A367 G6313 2016 | DDC 895.63/6—dc23
LC record available at https://lccn.loc.gov/2016033529

ISBNs: 978-1-9753-3178-8 (paperback)
        978-1-9753-3179-5 (ebook)

10 9 8 7 6 5 4 3 2 1

LSC-C

Printed in the United States of America

GOBLIN SLAYER

❖ VOLUME 8 ❖

GOBLIN SLAYER

✝

Character PROFILES

"I am to goblins what goblins are to us."

GOBLIN SLAYER

A strange adventurer active on the frontier. He is famous for reaching Silver (3rd) rank hunting only goblins.

"Protect, heal, save."
—The Three Holy Tenets of the Earth Mother

PRIESTESS

Works with Goblin Slayer. A sweet young woman who must put up with her partner's antics.

"Ignorance is bliss, for learning is the highest joy." —Elven proverb

HIGH ELF ARCHER

An elf girl who adventures with Goblin Slayer. A ranger and a skilled archer.

The only things that matter to her are the weather, the animals, the crops…and him.

COW GIRL

A girl who works on the farm where Goblin Slayer lives. The two are old friends.

"How can you go adventuring without pen and paper?"

GUILD GIRL

A girl who works at the Adventurers Guild. Goblin Slayer's preference for goblin slaying always helps her out.

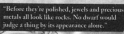

"Before they're polished, jewels and precious metals all look like rocks. No dwarf would judge a thing by its appearance alone."

DWARF SHAMAN

A dwarf spell caster who adventures with Goblin Slayer.

"A naga does not run."

LIZARD PRIEST

A lizardman priest who adventures with Goblin Slayer.

"Train yourself: kill with the blade. If blood flows, let it be the enemy's." — First of the "Secrets of Steel."

HEAVY WARRIOR

A Silver-ranked adventurer associated with the Guild in the frontier town. Along with Female Knight and his other companions, his party is one of the best on the frontier.

"Only a tangled skein awaits those who carelessly spin tales about love or the universe's mysteries...not to mention a woman's beauty."

WITCH

A Silver-ranked adventurer at the frontier town's Adventurers Guild.

"I won't make friends tomorrow with an enemy I respect. I'll do it today."

SPEARMAN

A Silver-ranked adventurer at the frontier town's Adventurers Guild.

"Love does not consist in gazing at each other, but in looking outward in the same direction." —A poet

SWORD MAIDEN

Archbishop of the Supreme God in the water town. Also a Gold-ranked adventurer who once fought with the Demon Lord.

CHAPTER 1

The Prime of Youth, Now Ashes

The female bishop bit her lip, holding back a cry at the cold gust that cut her like a sword.

The chill air, summoned from the ninth level of the world of the demons, instantly turned the dungeon chamber into an icebox.

Greater demons, their skin blue-black, came from the same realm. Two of them appeared, bulging with magical power and so massive they threatened to fill the entire room. It was precisely the bandage covering her eyes and obscuring her vision that allowed her to sense their presence with such terrible clarity.

High Priestess, her teeth chattering with the cold, desperately tried to force strength into legs that threatened to betray her.

"Taa—ahh!!"

"OUURGGGRERRR?!"

A sweet voice rose in a vigorous shout as the sword and scales flashed. The scales, attached to the sword by a chain, hummed.

The night stalker that had been approaching through the blizzard found its skull cleaved in a single blow and met its end. Night stalkers were just a step away from becoming self-aware vampires, but even the highest-level undead couldn't survive the splattering of its brains.

A female warrior turned to where High Priestess was wiping bits of brain and skull fragments off herself.

"Sorry, I let one get through!"

"I'm quite all right!" High Priestess replied as she took stock of her companions. Small fry like this wouldn't trouble them much.

Female Warrior had just pierced the heart of a burglar, a man dressed like a shadow. Confronting the huge, hideous demons was the party's leader, a fighter in plate armor. He would keep them safe on that side. He carried a scimitar, an Eastern weapon, and he looked as much at ease as ever.

Their half-elf scout, standing in a deep stance nearby and watching for an opportunity, looked tense—but was smiling nonetheless.

Beside High Priestess was a bugman monk. Though he was reserved and quiet, he stood calmly at the ready. And on her other side was Female Wizard, searching for the perfect moment to cast her magic…

The whole party was pelted by sleet and hail, dealing them damage as they endured it. Stopping the storm was the priority.

"Sword Prince, to those who see what should be seen and speak what should be spoken, grant your protection!"

She drew a sigil in light, holding the sword and scales in the center. It produced an exceptionally strong Protection but could not entirely stop the cold. The chill—an icy mountaintop in winter must be like this—cut the adventurers deep.

"Hold on, everyone, I'll heal you—!"

"No! It's more important to silence the enemy's magic! If they hit us again, we might not make it!" Female Wizard, holding her short staff and surveying the battlefield, spoke despite her skin turning blue, her body shaking. How many times had they been saved by her careful instructions?

"All right!" Bugman Monk called from beside High Priestess who still held her sword and scales aloft as he began to weave a seal. "I'm on it! Even a demon should be weaker if we can cut them off from magic!"

"We're counting on you!!" High Priestess cried.

The monk was the most advanced member of their party and had been a mentor to her ever since they first met. High Priestess felt the pain of the icy blast and all fear of the enemy melt out of her heart. Her prayer to the gods above rang out, cutting through the blizzard.

"My god the roaming wind, let all we say on the road stay secret among us!"

"You have the light to remain silent!"

Silence.

An invisible power filled the chamber, and the awful demons began to smirk.

Adventurers were always like this. They thought that neutralizing the demons' spells would give them the edge. But demons were creatures most intimate with magic. No half-baked seal would prevent them from using their spells.

Moreover, taking adventurers' thin hopes and trampling them underfoot was a true joy for such a creature. Demons savored above all the despair of those who possessed language.

Come, let's give them another taste of blizzard.

The men might survive, but they would be ravaged if they did—perfect for a good meal either way. The two female spell casters might die, but the warrior, she might make it.

Well, even dead, women's meat could be put to any number of—

"—?!"

When they opened their mouths, though, they realized they couldn't speak.

Our spells have been sealed?! By a little human girl and a literal bug?!

"Fantastic! You're mine!!" As soon as the scout registered the demons' confusion, he dashed between them, dagger in hand. An instant after he passed by, twin geysers of blood erupted, and the massive bodies slumped.

He had cut the tendons in their feet—but by the time the monsters noticed that, it was too late.

"You're one step behind!" Female Warrior's spear came whistling through the air, landing a critical hit. A heart, pierced by it, gushed blackish blood.

"—?! ——?!"

"Ahhh-ha-ha. We can't hear you, remember?" Chuckling, the warrior jumped back, not a trace of gore on her. Just one left.

Without hesitation, their leader, the swordfighter, closed the distance, scimitar in hand.

Shhp. A single, easy cut. One stroke from low to high. Then he grabbed the hilt of his sword, turning it in his hand, and brought it down again for a second blow.

One arm went flying, then another. As he swept back at his target, the blade took flesh and bone with it.

"_____?!"

Blood gushing, the greater demon thrashed and opened its mouth as if howling.

Normally, it was impossible to hear a voice suppressed by Silence. But this cry reached the ears of High Priestess ever so faintly. The slightest sound.

"He's trying to call his allies!" she told her friends, having guessed what the demon was up to. Bugman Monk made a clicking sound with his jaws.

"What to do. We're definitely finishing them off regardless—would you rather do it after there's a few more? I'm happy either way!"

Half-Elf Scout, still using his dagger to keep the enemy at bay, exclaimed, "Any more of them and we're going to have our hands full—I say we finish him off now!"

"Do it." The growled order from their leader settled the question for the party.

"All together, then!"

"Right!"

Female Wizard raised her staff, High Priestess readied her sword and scales, while their leader shouted and began weaving a sigil with his free hand.

"_Ventus!_ Wind!"

"_Lumen!_ Light!"

Libero! Release!

The next moment, a gale of wind, accompanied by a burst of light and heat, streaked through the chamber. Noiselessly, without ceremony, the ice and snow melted away. Nothing, except perhaps for the most exalted of dragons, could maintain its form in the face of this forbidden spell, which drew on the power from which sprung all things.

The demon, slammed by the burning wind, was annihilated before it could even scream, reduced to mere ashes.

Then the wind blew through, leaving only a lingering warmth and nothing living where it had struck.

Now only a treasure chest remained. The adventurers looked at one another and breathed a sigh of relief.

Their leader, the swordfighter, shook the blood from his blade before offering words of thanks to the others.

"Welp, guess that shows you what greater demons are good for," Half-Elf Scout joked.

"Yeah—without their spells, all they've got are their numbers." Female Warrior giggled as she watched the scout make for the treasure chest. She was keeping an eye out; they may have defeated the monsters in the burial chamber, but there could still be enemies elsewhere in the dungeon.

Likewise, their leader naturally remained alert. The battle was over, but that was no excuse for a lapse in vigilance.

"How far have we come? I'd like to see the map, if I may."

"Oh, certainly. I'm still in the middle of mapping... Hold on a second."

High Priestess, startled out of a reverie by Female Wizard's request, quickly dug through her bag.

She produced a notebook made from a sheaf of sheepskin paper with grids scratched on it. She used a writing instrument to connect the little boxes, marking out the new burial chamber. She enjoyed work like this precisely because of her inability to see. Although she couldn't be quite as proud of her skills as she once was.

"Two long, two wide..."

"There may be a hidden door. We'll have to check later."

"Right. I'll prepare Holy Light..." High Priestess nodded at Bugman Monk then passed the map book to Female Wizard. "Here. I think we're just about in the middle of the ninth floor."

"Thanks." Female Wizard smiled and took it then trotted over to their leader.

He scrutinized his blade, inspecting the rivets on the hilt then examined his armor. He sighed as Female Wizard came to show him the map with all the pride of a child displaying her drawing.

High Priestess smiled at the way Female Wizard pouted, as if saying, *I'm the elder here, you know!*

Truly, greater demons were not to be underestimated. But they who had braved their way to the ninth level of this maze were experienced veterans of the hack and slash.

"Even so," High Priestess said, letting out a soft *ah* of relief as she focused her attention on each of the four walls of the burial chamber. She placed a hand on her not-yet-ample chest. "I'm so glad it wasn't goblins…"

Her voice was so soft that no one else heard it, and then it sank into the darkness of the labyrinth.

CHAPTER 2

BEARD-CUTTER GOES TO THE SOUTHERN SEA

"Hrkpf...?!"

A splash of water flew up and drenched Priestess where she stood on the boat. The spray got into her eyes, and it was all she could do to cling to the side, struggling not to get washed away. The water made even the rail slick, though, and the moment she realized this, her hand had already slipped away.

Her feet went out from under her, and she floated in midair for an instant. A second later, she fell.

"Are you all right?"

"Oh yes...!"

A gloved hand reached out casually and grasped her small arm hard enough to hurt.

"You are wearing your mail?"

He had a cheap metal helmet; grimy leather armor; a small, round shield on his arm; and a sword of a strange length at his hip. He stood firmly on the deck in boots he had chosen for this purpose, supporting her sturdily.

"You may drown if you fall overboard. Walk carefully."

"...Right." Priestess nodded several times in acknowledgment of Goblin Slayer's words. She let him pull her back to her feet, then once again, she grasped the rope tied to the side of the ship.

They were in the middle of a storm.

Thunderheads had piled up; rain lashed at her face like a hail of stones; the wind was cutting, the sea violent, and the waves deadly.

Amid the raging storm, a great writhing shadow fixed its gaze on Priestess.

"MMUUUUUANNDDDAAAAA!!"

The creature with its body coiled, baring its fangs, with the dark sea-bottom's gold for scales, was a sea serpent. A follower of Chaos, bent on upsetting the order of the oceans. A Non-Prayer Character!

"Just a second, Orcbolg! What do you think you're doing?!"

For a high elf, the crazily tilting deck of a ship was just like a tree swaying in the breeze. With agility and lightness beyond that of any human, High Elf Archer jumped from one spot to another, loosing arrows. The bud-tipped bolts flew toward the sea serpent as quick as magic.

Every one of them, though, slid on the slime covering the creature's scales, bouncing off in some other direction. High Elf Archer ground her teeth, realizing she'd done no damage.

"That's a bad roll...! Think I should stock up on some iron-tipped ones?"

"What about your pride as an elf?! Just keep shooting and distract it, already!"

"You don't have to tell me! You just do something to help, already!"

"Blast it all! I'm tryin' t'think of something!"

A short distance away from the elf, who was shouting and twitching her long ears, Dwarf Shaman held fast to the side of the ship as well. He was a spell caster and a dwarf, so he was plenty stubborn, and even he was at a loss in this situation. He doubted how much effect either Stone Blast or Fear would have on the massive snake...

It hardly mattered, because it was all he could do to hang on to his bag of catalysts.

"Hrm." Goblin Slayer kicked the harpoon by his foot over to Lizard Priest then picked up another for himself. The projectile hurtled through the air, a brave throw, and lodged in the skin of the sea serpent. The ooze that covered the monster was enough to deflect an arrow, but it wasn't much by way of defense.

A foul yellow liquid went spewing into the sea; Goblin Slayer watched it from inside his helmet.

A sea serpent, though, is a sea serpent. The wound was hardly fatal.

"MUUUUUNNND!!"

The creature gave a great cry and buried its fangs in the prow of the party's vessel. Wood splintered with loud cracks as the ship began to be dragged down into the sea before their very eyes.

If they were pulled into the storm-ravaged waters, they couldn't expect to reach land again. They would simply be added to the number of the dead.

"Oh, e-eeek...!" Priestess was thrown off-balance by a crashing wave and tried desperately to think of anything she could do.

There was always at least one thing. She could pray.

So Priestess bit her lip, standing as firm as she could on the tossing deck. That was not, in fact, very firm; but she quieted her heart and clutched her sounding staff imploringly.

"O Earth Mother, abounding in mercy, by the power of the land grant safety to we who are weak!"

It was a miracle.

A force field of sacred energy appeared without a sound, tearing the sea serpent from the ship. The blessed hand of the compassionate Earth Mother could reach even to the open waters of the sea.

"N-now!"

"Indeed! River-Walker, Mosasaurus, see my deeds!" Lizard Priest was quick to put his power on full display. Supporting himself on his tail, he lunged forward with the claws of his feet outstretched, his shoulder flexing visibly as he flung the harpoon.

His technique was not as refined as Goblin Slayer's, but he threw with immense strength—with all the power of a lizardman, the descendent of the fearsome nagas.

The missile struck home, biting much deeper than the last one.

"MUANNDDAAADA?!?!" the sea serpent howled, wheeling around. Right after one wave subsided, the monster smacked its tail into the ocean, throwing up another massive surge of water toward the party.

"Aww!" High Elf Archer groaned, shaking her soaked head like a dog. Then, though it offered no real rest and didn't provide any extra breathing room, they found themselves the briefest of respites. They couldn't let it go to waste.

Seawater was flowing mercilessly into the ruined prow of their ship. The craft tilted ever more severely; if they couldn't take care of the snake, there would soon be no hope for them.

"Are you all right?" Goblin Slayer asked Priestess and Dwarf Shaman, who were still gripping the side of the ship.

"Somehow or...other. I'm holding on...!"

"We've not got long before we sink straight down!"

Goblin Slayer grunted, ignoring the agitated "What about me?!" from High Elf Archer, who had not been asked about her safety.

"What do you think?"

"Ha-ha-ha, we haven't much time indeed," Lizard Priest answered calmly. In fact, he rolled his eyes as if he were enjoying the moment. "They say even an ant can kill if it bites enough times. I thought perhaps that last hit was critical."

"That—what do you call it...?"

"Sea serpent, I believe."

"Yes," Goblin Slayer said, nodding. "Is it a fish? A snake?"

"Now then, I would hate for anyone to think a relation of mine was causing such trouble, but..." Lizard Priest wrapped his tail around the mast for support then stretched out his neck to peer at the prow. The fangs had been ruthless, and water was rushing in noisily.

"...But the bite has not left any poison I can see. I think that means the resemblance is entirely coincidental. It must be a fish."

"What we cannot do with weapons, let us do with spells." Goblin Slayer performed some quick mental calculations then set off across the slanted deck. He kept one hand on the railing so as not to slip on the slick surface and slid his way over to Priestess and Dwarf Shaman.

Goblin Slayer grabbed hold of the rope with the help of Dwarf Shaman, and Priestess was quick to hold down the hem of her skirt lest anything be too visible.

"Tell me what your remaining spells and miracles are."

"I ain't had my moment to shine yet. I'm full up."

"Me... Another one or two, maybe."

"All right," Goblin Slayer said with a nod. "When the creature appears again, we hit it."

Then he quickly outlined a strategy; Priestess had no objection. "Leave it to me!"

Dwarf Shaman grinned to see her put on such a brave front despite being completely soaked.

"You heard the lady. 'Fraid I'll look bad if I don't keep up with her."

"We will be counting on you," Goblin Slayer said.

That was when High Elf Archer, feeling left out, cried, "What about me—?!"

"Shoot some whistling arrows. Draw him out."

The brusque instructions left High Elf Archer muttering, "Geez," but she complied. She ran up alongside Lizard Priest, slipping easily past the mast, holding on to the rope to maintain her balance. She drew an arrow from her quiver, putting it in her mouth and biting down on the bud tip. She sent the shaft flying from her spider-silk-strung bow, and the shrill sound could be heard even over the storm.

"When he reappears, use the harpoon."

Lizard Priest had been listening to the whistling arrow, but he responded happily to Goblin Slayer's orders. "Very well, very well. I don't believe anyone has tried such a thing in battle yet."

The sea serpent took the bait. It rose up as a dark shadow from directly beneath the ship, perhaps hoping to break the bottom of the craft, and then it thrust its head above the waves.

"Hrr, why...you...!" Priestess clutched her cap and scrabbled along the deck as she was nearly tossed free of the vessel. One hand, though, held as always to her staff. She glared at the golden snake and shouted, *"O Earth Mother, abounding in mercy, grant your sacred light to we who are lost in darkness!"*

Her second miracle.

From the staff Priestess held aloft in the raging storm came a flash of light as bright as the sun. The serpent howled at this luminance, the likes of which it had no doubt never seen in the depths of the sea.

"Eeeeyah! No more than a cousin of the eels, after all...!" Lizard Priest chortled.

There was a rushing hiss, and blood sprayed from the sea serpent's side after his attack.

"Now!"

"On it!"

Goblin Slayer's voice cut through the air, greeted by Dwarf Shaman's answer.

Dwarf Shaman produced a white powder from his catalysts and sprinkled it in the monster's direction. The instant it touched the water, it began to bubble—the powder was soap.

"Nymphs and sylphs, together spin, earth and sea are nearly kin, so dance away—just don't fall in!"

Immediately, something changed. The serpent attempted to dive back onto the water, but its head bounced off the surface as if it were solid land.

What's more, its entire body, so long hidden beneath the waves, was lifted up and exposed.

"MUAAANNADA?!?!" The monster repeatedly opened its mouth as if struggling to breathe and slammed itself against the water again and again.

When the Water Walk spell was cast on a creature with gills, all it could do was suffocate.

"Yikes…" High Elf Archer found herself staring upward, but Goblin Slayer continued to bark out orders.

"It will soon run out of breath. If it looks like it'll come this way, shoot it. In the eye."

"Yeah, sure." High Elf Archer sighed at the serpent, which continued to flail at the water, and readied her bow.

It felt like it would be cruel to leave the snake alive any longer at this point. And elves didn't have it in them to laugh at the suffering of a doomed creature.

The bow creaked, and the arrow flew true, piercing the eye and continuing on into the brain.

That was the end. The sea serpent collapsed into the water, the effect of the spell fading as the monster sank in a great white spray.

There was no one to stop the snake's body from slipping back under, and soon the waves had washed away even the last bubbles it had left behind.

"How was that?" Goblin Slayer asked after a long moment—presumably to make sure the creature was dead. "There was no fire, or water, or an explosion."

"Ahh... Hrm..." High Elf Archer steadied herself with a frown and gave a sort of groan.

Was this a proper adventure? Well, there hadn't been any explosions, or floods, or cave-ins. That much was true. But...

High Elf Archer's ears twitched as she wrung out her sopping hair.

"S—" she said in a strained voice. "Six out of ten."

"I see," he said, nodding. "...I see."

"...What, are you upset?"

"No." Goblin Slayer shook his head slowly from side to side. "I was thinking it would be good if it were so simple to get rid of goblins."

Priestess giggled at this thoroughly in-character answer. She had been worried for a few moments there, but it looked like the worst was over. She pulled up the hem of her dress, revealing her leg, and squeezed out the water.

He's getting to me... I thought this was easier than goblins, too.

In any event, it was always good when an adventure went well. When everyone survived. Especially if they completed the quest, too.

Priestess pushed aside the touch of confusion she felt and gave an affirmative little nod.

"We'd better hurry up and fix this boat," she said. "It's not far to land, but we don't want to have to swim the rest of the way, do we?"

"That's why we brought a dwarf along."

"Y'could stand to help, yourself. Anvils don't float, y'know..."

High Elf Archer's ears flew straight back and she uttered an angry noise, which Dwarf Shaman ignored as he spread out a sail. He licked his finger to check the direction of the wind then grabbed one corner.

"Sylphs, wind-maidens, spare a kiss upon my weathered cheek. And spare my humble sailing ship a fairer wind to seek!"

The Tail Wind spell filled the sail, and Priestess held her hair down against the salty spray.

Before she knew it, the storm was past; the sky was blue and the sea calm.

It was just turning autumn.

Priestess let out a relaxed breath. Yes, several hours before, she had been the one to suggest they go into battle, but for a few minutes, it had seemed like an awfully close call...

§

"Are you a goblin?"

"I am *not*! That's discrimination!" The Innsmouth woman, with the race's distinctive resemblance to a fish, flapped a flipper in annoyance. Her words—mingled with her breath, which sounded like a rush of bubbles—echoed off the walls of the watery cave. "And I hate how you humans insist on calling us 'fish-people'! Like you're confused: *are they fish, or are they people?*"

"We're perfect just the way we are!" one of the women exclaimed, and the man facing her simply nodded.

That man was wearing a cheap steel helmet, grimy leather armor, and a sword of a strange length, along with a small, round shield on his arm.

Goblin Slayer was at a loss as to why the gillmen were sometimes called Innsmouth. Some claimed it was related to the term *Deep Ones*, but no one was sure.

Goblin Slayer, however, had no interest in the matter. These people were not goblins; that was enough.

"...I came because I had heard the fishing grounds were being attacked by sea-goblins."

"That's discrimination!"

"I see."

The Innsmouth looked this way and that around the tide pool deep in the cave. Their bulging eyes showed no emotions; their jaws worked open and shut; they were utterly eerie. He couldn't tell what they were thinking, but the tips of tridents peeked out in places from below the water...

Are...are we in danger...? Priestess asked herself from where she stood listening to the negotiations at a distance. She kept both hands firmly on her staff.

And understandably so. When they had worked their way into the deepest cavern on the understanding that this was a goblin-hunting quest, they had found themselves surrounded by murderous gillmen. Then the very moment had they started to talk, their party had been met with accusations of discrimination and worse—even Priestess found the entire series of events a little hard to follow.

True, she had heard of some human rulers who so despised elves and dwarves that they levied a "pointy-ears tax." Whatever the case, this was certainly outside the experience of a typical cleric.

Then again, I guess most clerics have never been goblin slaying, either...

So what was the best way to interpret this? The other three party members surrounded Priestess protectively.

"H-hold on, Orcbolg. Try not to antagonize them...!"

"Well, look who's a scaredy-cat. I guess elves are lacking in courage... just like they're lacking in another particular department!"

"...! ...!!"

High Elf Archer frowned comically as Dwarf Shaman nudged her with his elbow. She looked like she wanted to shoot something back, but the situation being what it was, she kept her mouth shut. Her twitching ears, though, made her feelings clear.

Any kind of outburst now could be the end of them. Lizard Priest gave a somber sigh.

"Sea-goblins? How rude! You could at least call us *Homo piscine!*"

"Ah, meaning 'fish-person.'" Lizard Priest gestured with his jaws in the direction of the gillmen, very interested. "Then were you once fish, who gained lungs and limbs to climb out of the water...?"

"Ugh, what a barbarian."

Leave it to water-dwellers to offer no safe harbor!

"Our ancestor is the great Octopus Lord who descended from the Sea of Stars!"

"An octopus."

"Well, maybe a squid."

"Perhaps... These before us are certainly intelligent enough not to mistake the corpse of a dried squid for one of their kin..." After muttering to himself for a moment, Lizard Priest appeared to come to some kind of conclusion. "Us, we have come here thinking that fish supplies may have dwindled on account of you here, if you will forgive my saying so. Have you any thoughts on this?"

"Oh, for—! It's not *our* fault there's fewer fish than before, arrgh!"

What would we want with your dumb fishing grounds? The fin smacked some water at him.

Frowning at the splash, Priestess nonetheless tilted her head questioningly. "Do you know what *is* causing the shortage of fish, then?"

"Yes, yes we do. Sheesh, this is why no one likes rustic fishermen!"

Hmm. Priestess put a slim finger to her lips in thought.

They couldn't just ignore this. Unless somebody did something, it would eventually turn into all-out war between the villagers and the gillmen. In fact, things had already gotten quite bad. Their party's presence was the proof.

In which case…

"As long as it's within our power, I think we can try to help you clear your names."

"Hrmph… Well, how about that? Someone decent." One of the gillman females blinked her haws. "I can tell you what's causing it: the sea serpent."

"Sea serpent?" Dwarf Shaman exclaimed. "Didn't think you had those around here.

"No?" High Elf Archer asked, surprised.

"Mm-hmm," Dwarf Shaman replied. "I would have said they were a bit farther offshore. Sometimes a ship traveling the high seas will be attacked by one, sunk, and its crew eaten."

That, he explained, was why there was so little information about the monsters. Clearly, they were formidable foes, and the gillman leaned anxiously against the rock face. "Yeah, it's like it was sent here from somewhere. Gah, it's like nothing is normal on this planet anymore."

"I see," Goblin Slayer said, nodding. "The point is, it is not a goblin."

For him, that meant only one thing.

"…This was not a goblin quest… Shall we go home?"

The rest of the party gave a collective sigh. Priestess and High Elf Archer each raised an eyebrow and looked at the other.

Argh, really. This man.

"We can't just leave them when they're clearly in trouble," Priestess said. "Look, the rest of us will handle this one, okay?"

"Yeah," High Elf Archer piped up. "I mean, even if it *will* be super dangerous without anyone on the front row."

"Hrk..." Goblin Slayer crossed his arms and grunted.

The girls looked at each other and chorused, "Right?" clearly enjoying the moment.

"Forget about 'em, Beard-cutter. That elf may have huge ears, but she won't listen to a word you say."

"Ha-ha, they are already well acquainted with milord Goblin Slayer's disposition."

The other two men in the party piled on, looking equally pleased.

As for the outcome—well, surely there's no need to spell it out.

§

"Ahem, the sea-goblin quest, how did it—?"

"They were not goblins."

"I gather it's just easier to call them that..."

"They were not goblins."

"So, the quest..."

"They were not goblins."

"...was canceled. I understand."

"Because they were not goblins."

The Adventurers Guild was lively and bustling, as always.

Guild Girl found her smile ever so slightly strained in the face of Goblin Slayer's grimy metal helmet. She certainly hadn't intended to mislead him, or to tell any untruth, but these things happened sometimes. Different regions or races had unorthodox names for things that were difficult to parse. It was no one's fault.

She looked to her colleague in the next seat for support, but there was no sign of any help forthcoming. Alone and unaided, Guild Girl fell back on the standard Q and A.

©Noboru Kannatuki

"So, was the issue with the sea-goblins—sorry, I mean the gillmen—resolved?"

Rather than sit there and make excuses, she would do her job. She would do her best to salvage her good name and redeem her honor, as if her fitness as a bride was on the line.

"Yes," Goblin Slayer said with a nod, but then he almost immediately shook his head. "...Actually, wait. We ended up hunting a monster called something or other."

"Then, could you please describe that monster to me in detail?"

"It was long," he said. Then after a moment's thought, he added, "It was a fish."

Guild Girl opened up a worn copy of the Monster Manual and thumbed through the pages. Every time, it was like this; trying to follow his descriptions of monsters was both virtually impossible and part of the fun.

I think that's what she told me once anyway, thought Priestess, sitting and observing from some distance away in the tavern. She held her sleeve up to her nose and gave it a sniff. "I think it still smells like seawater..."

"You're not just thinking that— It *does*," High Elf Archer whined, her ears drooping dejectedly. These things were harder on the elf, cursed with extra-sharp senses.

"Are you okay?" Priestess asked, even as she took a distracted sniff of her own hair. "I took a bath *and* changed my clothes..."

"I don't think it'll come out for a while," High Elf Archer said. "And *this* isn't helping."

She looked at a big bag sitting in the middle of the table. The ocean scent it emitted was almost palpable. Dwarf Shaman, seated before it, grinned broadly. "Those gillmen are downright generous, they are!"

Inside the bag were black and white pearls, flame-red corals, translucent tortoiseshell, rainbow-colored spiral shells, and a glistening white helix.

True, it wasn't money, but it was a heartfelt reward from the fish-people. Even after replacing the ruined boat, which they had originally borrowed from the fishing village, the adventurers still had all this left. It wasn't precisely a fortune, but it was plenty if they wanted to enjoy themselves for a while.

"Ugh, and you wonder why people call dwarves greedy..."

"Bah, that's enough out of you. You wouldn't understand the beauty of this, Long-Ears! You agree, don't you, Scaly?"

"Ha-ha-ha-ha-ha-ha. Well, if amassing a fortune is good enough for the nagas, I can hardly turn up my nose." Lizard Priest raised his tail to call over the waitress and ordered cheese and wine. He was clearly in high spirits, his eyes rolling in his head, as he pulled something largish from the bag. "I myself consider this to be our greatest gain."

"Wow..." Priestess's eyes sparkled with wonder, and who could blame her? A gorgeous striped gemstone carved in the shape of an animal's skull held her attention. She touched it with a trembling finger, but it was indeed rock and not bone...

"This is a gemstone...isn't it?"

"Indeed, even so. It is the jaw of a terrible naga, turned to agate by the passing of countless years." Lizard Priest held up the skull with the pride of a little boy showing off a treasure; it was a side of him Priestess rarely saw.

"Hmph, you're like some child..." High Elf Archer puffed out her cheeks and released a sigh of obvious annoyance. Granted, it didn't spoil the rather friendly atmosphere.

"Heh, heh-heh... Boys, do like, this sort of thing, don't they?"

"Eh, they're lucky enough to be making some money. I wouldn't complain."

There at the table appeared Witch and Spearman—or rather, Heavy Warrior.

"Well, this is unusual," High Elf Archer commented.

"Have you two formed a temporary party?" Priestess asked.

Heavy Warrior gave a little shrug. "Nah. We're just waiting."

Now that he mentioned it, Priestess spotted Female Knight over by the board, muttering to herself as she compared quests: "We could take the minotaur, but the hydra's good, too... Wait, here's a manticore..."

Scout Boy and the others were with her; Priestess could hear him grumble, "Make up your mind already."

"And he, is over there," said Witch, indicating the reception desk with her pipe.

Spearman, completely ignoring all the perfectly good open windows with no waiting adventurers, had lined up for Guild Girl's counter. The look of displeasure on his face came, perhaps, from the conversation he was listening to, which involved Goblin Slayer. Still, when other female staff members or female adventurers called out to him, as they did from time to time, he would answer with a smile…

"He seems popular," Priestess said.

"About, that…" Witch, who had produced her pipe from nowhere, gave Priestess a heavy-lidded look.

Erk…

Priestess felt her heart skip a beat; she put a hand to her chest.

Would she be able to have this effect on people someday? It was going to be a long time coming…

"Beard-cutter could learn a thing or two from him. Make himself more likable."

"What? No way. I can't even picture a cheerful, grinning Orcbolg," High Elf Archer groaned. Dwarf Shaman, apparently satisfied with his count of the treasure, was putting it back in the bag.

Priestess tried to picture Goblin Slayer with an upbeat grin on his face and found herself chuckling. "It *is* a little hard to imagine."

"Yeah. Orcbolg is—"

"What am I?"

"—supposed to be exactly who you are." High Elf Archer fluttered a *don't worry about it* hand in the direction of Goblin Slayer, who had appeared rather suddenly. It seemed he was done talking with Guild Girl.

"I see," he said without a trace of suspicion. Then the metal helmet turned to regard Heavy Warrior and Witch. It was impossible to see his expression behind the visor. "What is your business?"

And that was Goblin Slayer.

Heavy Warrior smiled wryly, while Witch blew sweet-smelling smoke from between her lips, unfazed by the entire exchange. One had to avoid reading anything into whatever the quiet, almost mechanical voice said. No skill would help with that, only cold, hard experience.

"Just killing time and saying hi," Heavy Warrior said.

"I have a…date, after this."

"I see," nodded Goblin Slayer and then added even more softly, "Be careful."

Heavy Warrior smiled a little then gave Goblin Slayer a pat on the shoulder with his big, broad hand before walking away. "If that's the best you can do, I'll take it."

"See, you…" Witch lifted her luscious body from her chair. The aromatic smoke trailed after her, drawing Priestess's eyes in her direction. The girl harbored a secret hope that she might be like Witch one day—both as an adventurer and as a woman.

Goblin Slayer tilted his head slightly, weighing the exact meaning of the words that had been spoken to him. He came to no particular conclusion, though, dismissing the matter with a "Never mind." He had much to do.

"Let us divide the reward," he said, all but throwing himself down in a chair and looking at his party. "Each of us will take what we want, and the rest we will convert into cash and divide equally. Is that all right?"

"I find that entirely satisfactory," Lizard Priest said, nodding somberly and making a peculiar palms-together gesture. "They say even pirates on the sea do not quarrel over the take. Why then should adventurers do so?"

"I'll bet you want that bone thing, right?" High Elf Archer said. "Me, I'll take this." She reached out with her thin, pale fingers and grabbed a translucent golden crystal—the tortoiseshell.

"Watch it, elf—your hands are as fast as your ears are long." Dwarf Shaman found that his stubby fingers were too slow to stop High Elf Archer, who chuckled triumphantly and puffed out her little chest.

"Complain, complain. I won't say we should go first come, first served, but is there anyone else who even wants this thing?"

"Well…" Dwarf Shaman's gaze swept the party. "…Fair enough. But what are you going to do with it?"

"Hmm? Maybe I'll send it to my sister. Stuff from the sea is really rare where I'm from."

"I'm sure she'll love it," Priestess said, eliciting a "Thanks!" and a happy flick of the ears from High Elf Archer.

The elaborate wedding ceremony held deep in the rain forest was still fresh in Priestess's mind. At the same time, she felt a surge of regret. She looked at the ground for just a second then reached out her own hand.

"…I'll take this pearl, then. I want to offer it to the Earth Mother."

She wasn't sure how to make up for it—and although she had received words of forgiveness, she still wanted to do *something*.

Dwarf Shaman, noticing how Priestess looked, gave a snort to indicate his displeasure. "I think you could stand to be a little more selfish… Well, ain't nothing to me either way." Then he took the helix in his calloused hand, cradling it gently. "This will serve as a good catalyst. The helix is mine. Beard-cutter, what about you?"

"…Me?"

He seemed tremendously surprised. The helmet didn't move but remained fixed on the bag of treasure. Priestess watched him with a smile.

To go on an adventure, defeat a monster, receive a reward, and then divide it up. Everyone had different ways of handling the division of loot, and she had heard that some simply converted everything into cash and then shared whatever they got back, but…

There was only one reason her heart danced the way it did then.

This must be the sort of normal adventure he wished for.

§

It was evening on the farm, and the pigs were snorting in irritation as they gorged themselves on acorns. Maybe they were unhappy because they knew they would be turned into meat when they were large enough—or maybe they just wanted more food.

"Fine, fine, eat up."

The farm's owner had evidently concluded it was the latter, because he allowed them a bit more feed. After all, it would soon be the harvest festival once again, and then winter would be upon them. Fortunately, they had both pigs and chickens, the cows' milk was good, and there had been no trouble with the crops. It looked like they would make it safely through another year.

"…Heavens above." He wiped his face with the towel slung over his shoulder and let out a sigh. His body ached all over.

Somehow, he and his niece had managed this farm together for the past ten years, but he was starting to feel his age. And if it was this bad with both of them, how hard would things be for his niece when she was alone?

Maybe it was time to hire some farmhands…

"Ah, then again…"

The would-be farmhands out here on the frontier were all listless vagabonds, and there was no way he was going to let them anywhere near his niece. He would sooner hire a high-ranking adventurer from the Guild; at least they would have proof that *someone* trusted them…

"Sigh…" The owner let out another long breath. His number-one headache had just come striding up. "…So you're back."

"Yes, sir. I just returned."

The man, with his cheap-looking metal helmet and grimy leather armor, stopped just near the road and gave a bow of his head.

Goblin Slayer. That was what people called him—but the farm owner still didn't really know what he looked like.

"Goblins again?"

"Yes, sir… Well, not actually. Although it was supposed to involve goblin slaying."

It was some other monster.

The owner quickly gave up on trying to get any more information out of the laconic young man.

His niece might be the only one who would ever see what was behind that visor.

"Um, is she—?"

"In the house, I think." The older man suppressed the torrent of emotions in his heart. "…Don't make her wait too long."

"Yes, sir… I believe I can help you around here tomorrow."

"…That so?" The owner looked back at the pigs and nodded.

As he heard the footsteps retreating behind him, he let out a third sigh.

Wouldn't matter if I saw his face. He wouldn't make any more sense to me.

§

"Oh, welcome hooome!"

A cheerful voice greeted Goblin Slayer as he opened the door of the house. A moment later, he detected the sweet, spreading scent of boiling milk.

Goblin Slayer entered the kitchen to the sound of rushing footsteps. He found the table already set, just waiting for the food to be ready. And there was his old friend, standing in her apron, welcoming him back.

"I heard you were going south, but you came home pretty quickly this time. Have you eaten lunch?"

"Not yet." Goblin Slayer gave a single shake of his head in response to Cow Girl's question. He pulled out a chair and sat down heavily; the seat creaked at him—was it because of the weight of his armor?

"Okay. I'll finish whipping this up right away. Now we just need bread and…maybe cheese?"

"Yes, please."

The cheese had been selling well recently, Cow Girl informed him happily then turned toward the stew pot.

He turned his helmet to look at the girl, standing with her back to him. The steady sales were largely thanks to his lizardman acquaintance buying so much of their product.

The stew pot burbled as its contents boiled. He watched her stir it. Suddenly, she glanced back at him over her shoulder.

"You…know I wouldn't mind if you ate with your friends once in a while, right?"

"…" Goblin Slayer was silent for a moment then grunted softly.

"Too much trouble?"

"Hmm…"

She had turned back to her cooking, so he couldn't see her face any more than other people could usually see his.

Cow Girl began to work the pot industriously, as if to distract attention from something.

After a long moment, she whispered, "…I really…wouldn't mind, okay?"

"…I see." Goblin Slayer let out part of a breath.

A few minutes later, Cow Girl announced, "It's done," and presented him with a dish of stew.

"I'll help," he said, starting to get up, but she kept him back with an "Oh, don't worry." She seemed in high spirits somehow.

He and the girl sitting across from him offered their prayers to the gods and then chorused, "Bon appétit!"

Cow Girl smiled as she watched him scoop up stew with his spoon and wolf it down. This was how things went whenever he came home to eat. The familiar scene brought a smile to her face; sometimes she made meals just for this moment.

"I brought you a gift."

But *that*...

...that was *not* how this scene usually went, and Cow Girl found herself blinking.

"A gift? What, seriously? No way!"

"I'm serious," Goblin Slayer said then reached casually into his item bag. The way he rooted around in it looked somehow violent; not the way one would normally appear when giving somebody a present. In fact, the whole notion of putting a gift in a bag of miscellaneous items seemed suspect to her.

But completely in character.

She giggled to herself, careful that he wouldn't notice.

"There it is."

He sounded so exasperated that holding back her laughter got even harder.

"What is it?"

"A shell."

He pulled his hand out of the bag, and in his palm rested a shell with a rainbow swirl on it. It glittered in the slanting sunlight like a jewel.

"Oh...!" Cow Girl exclaimed, and understandably so. "Wait, can I really have this? Did you go to the ocean for this job?"

"Yes." His blunt answer raised a fresh question: which of her queries was it in response to?

Cow Girl took the shell from him carefully, as if handling something very delicate, and set it in her palm. She squinted at the way the light glistened off it, and from her half-closed eyes, she could see him sitting silently.

"There was a fish," he said finally, and then after more thought, he added, "A very long one."

Should she try to ask for details, or what? *Argh, no*—she wanted to ask, but this came first.

"Thank you so much! I'll treasure it!" Cow Girl said, clasping the shell to her ample bosom and grinning. He nodded silently, and she stood up, heading straight for the kitchen.

She took down an old box sitting on the highest shelf and opened it to reveal a collection of what might have been junk. But she set the shell inside as if it was a precious treasure and closed the lid again.

"There, it's safe… Yeah, this way I won't lose it."

"I see."

Cow Girl got on her tiptoes to put the box back then wiped the sweat from her forehead as if she had just completed some difficult job. When she pattered back to the dining room, she had brought a cup of grape wine along for him. Normally, she might not have smiled on drinking in the early afternoon, but she figured it was all right for today. Surely.

"What about tomorrow?"

"I don't have work."

She set the cup on the table; he picked it up with a casual motion and downed the entire contents.

Soon the dish of stew was empty, too; when she asked, "Seconds?" he answered only, "Yes, please."

He followed her with his eyes as she bustled around to get him more food, and then he said quietly, "I'll help around the farm."

Such was Goblin Slayer's intention. Most likely, Cow Girl had expected as much. What would he do, then? What to do? He remembered what her uncle had said. This was his answer.

The conversation meandered pleasantly, and then the sun went down, and her uncle came back, and they had dinner, spent an uncommonly easy time together, and then went to bed.

A perfectly normal night. The way it always was after he came home. They were expecting a perfectly normal day off to follow.

But it was to be nothing of the sort.

CHAPTER 3

The Slayer of Goblins Goes to the Capital

"So you've come," she said.

Her voice contained such heat, it seemed it could melt at any moment. The sun shone through the window behind her, and the lips that peeked out from under her hood smiled softly.

The woman sloughed off her robe, and waves of golden hair emerged like the sea. Her sheer, white garments gleefully exposed the voluptuous lines of her body—the Earth Mother herself might look like this.

The skin her vestments revealed was perfectly white, almost translucent, as if untouched by the sun. It meant that the tinge of rose in her cheeks was probably not just from the light. She almost seemed like a harlot—and there *were* temples that kept sacred prostitutes.

She could have wrapped any man who gazed upon her around her little finger, and yet, her eyes were covered with a black sash. In her hand, she held the downward-pointing sword and scales that were the symbol of righteousness and justice. The way she all but leaned on them, the way she whispered, conveyed intense anxiety.

"Have I...disturbed you?"

"No."

Sword Maiden. That was the name of the frontier cleric whom Goblin Slayer answered in his low, flat voice.

"Is it goblins?"

§

It was morning.

Goblin Slayer was out of bed before dawn and checking his equipment.

Helmet, armor, the layers worn under the armor, shield, sword. All in good condition. Everything in working order. Then he took out his item bag to check the contents.

There were the potions, wound with knotted strings to distinguish among them, along with an eggshell full of blinding powder, a scroll, and an assortment of miscellaneous items.

When he had confirmed that everything was as it should be, he started donning his gear. Then he left his room, going down the hallway as delicately as he could so as not to wake the other two people in the house, who he assumed were still asleep.

He made it outside with hardly the sound of a footstep, and when he emerged from the house, he was immediately enveloped by the cold autumn air. There was a fine, milky mist over the farm, perhaps the product of the morning dew. Goblin Slayer felt like he was inside a cloud. He stopped and looked around.

"...Hmph."

Visibility was poor. He snorted, displeased about this, but then began striding into the fog.

He started the day's patrol by following the fence in a circuit around the farm. He was checking to see if it was broken anywhere, of course, but also to see if there were any footprints around and, if so, how many. It would be easy to leave footprints in these slick conditions, but the thick fog made his work difficult. Goblin Slayer, though, attended to it one stretch at a time, silent all the while.

The inside of a cave was darker than this, after all. He needed to make an effort attempting to see that which could not be seen, in order to train his night vision.

Once he had completed his patrol of the farm, he retrieved several knives and targets from his shed. He lined up a row of bottles and other small things along the fence then practiced spinning around, taking aim in an instant, and throwing.

One after another, the daggers whistled through the morning air, sending the bottles flying, or sticking upright in the fence.

"Hrm."

That was all Goblin Slayer said about the matter as he set about cleaning up the weapons and targets. Dawn was pitching its first rays over the horizon.

He had put his training tools away in the shed when, suddenly, he spotted a figure near the entrance to the farm.

A goblin?

His hand grasped the sword at his hip. The figure was too shadowy to make out, but it took one or two steps. When he realized it was too big to be a goblin, he loosened his grip on his sword.

"Who's there?" he asked.

"Eeyikes!" came the startled reply. The panicking stranger was a young man, one who looked vaguely familiar.

Goblin Slayer closed the distance between them at a bold stride, and the boy's face tightened. Then at last, Goblin Slayer realized the visitor was wearing a Guild uniform. An employee, then.

"So you're from the Guild. What is it?"

"Er, I'd—I'd heard the stories, but… Anyway." The young man coughed discreetly. "You have a visitor at the Guild. Your presence has been requested, immediately."

"I see." Goblin Slayer nodded. Then the helmet tilted just slightly. "Is it goblins?"

"I—I'm not…sure…?"

"Wait just a moment." His tone brooked no argument. He spun on his heel and went back to the house.

Behind him, the young man put a hand to his chest, speechless, but Goblin Slayer paid him no mind.

He cut through the hallways, certain of where he was going, until he found the door he was looking for.

"I'm coming in."

"Huh?— Wah?!"

With a most unladylike shout, Cow Girl tried to wrap a sheet around herself—she had been smack in the middle of dressing and was standing there buck naked.

©Noboru Kannatuki

Goblin Slayer fell silent at the sight that greeted him as he opened the door; then he turned his helmet aside and spoke calmly.

"......I won't need breakfast. I'm going out."

Cow Girl flapped her hand at him helplessly. Maybe she didn't mind showing herself to him, but she didn't want him to simply walk in on her like this.

"Kn-knock! You have to knock!"

"...I see," Goblin Slayer said quietly. "I apologize."

"I-it's okay... I mean, it's fine, but..." Cow Girl pressed a hand to her huge chest and breathed deeply. Her face was red—from surprise, or embarrassment? Even she wasn't sure. He *had* apologized right away, and she was tempted to let it go at that...

"So," she said, her voice an octave higher than usual. "...What's going on?"

Goblin Slayer's answer was brusque. "I don't know, but I've been summoned to the Guild."

"Okay," Cow Girl said softly.

I guess this means he won't need dinner tonight, either. She felt a twinge in her chest.

As if in confirmation, he said, coldly and softly, "If there are goblins involved, I will not be able to help around the farm today."

See you later.

She saw him off with those words and a smile, but after that, Cow Girl had to sit down on her bed for a time.

§

"Oh! Goblin Slayer, sir!" He saw Guild Girl's face light up as he entered the Guild.

It was early in the morning.

Adventurers who had rented rooms at the Guild were just filtering down to the tavern from the second floor, blearily shoveling breakfast into their mouths. There weren't too many of them, though, since the quest papers hadn't even been posted yet; the entire place's atmosphere was relaxed and slow.

The one exception was the staff members in the back rooms, who were rushing around, handling administrative work. They were preparing documents, readying posts, checking the safe, confirming salient information, and so on.

In the midst of all this, Guild Girl found a moment to give Goblin Slayer a little wave as he entered the building.

"Your guest is already waiting!"

"I see. On the second floor?"

"That's right! Er, I..." Guild Girl's formerly cheerful face clouded over. Or perhaps it would be more appropriate to say that her prepared smile simply faltered for a moment.

She trailed off like she couldn't quite bring herself to say what came next. Goblin Slayer tilted his head the slightest bit. "What is it?"

Her braids bounced like a puppy's tail: *poing!* Guild Girl bowed her head apologetically.

"I'm really sorry about the quest last time."

"Last time..."

"The—you know, the sea-goblin one." Guild Girl could hardly get the words out. She had just received his report yesterday.

Goblin Slayer had to give this some thought, but eventually, even he seemed to figure out what she was saying. "Ah," he said, nodding. Then he proceeded to shake his head. "It doesn't bother me."

With that phenomenally brief statement, Goblin Slayer headed for the stairs. He didn't even notice Guild Girl putting a hand to her heart in relief as he began to climb them.

He discovered he was going to the same meeting room in which he had first been introduced to the people who were now his party members. How long had it been? With the fleeting realization that more than a year had passed by now, he opened the door.

As he did so, the woman standing by the window on the far side of the room raised her head and looked at him.

"So you've come," she said.

Her voice had such heat in it, it seemed it could melt at any moment. The sun came through the window behind her, and the lips that peeked out from under her hood smiled softly.

The woman sloughed off her robe, and waves of golden hair emerged like the sea. Her sheer, white garments gleefully exposed the voluptuous lines of her body—the Earth Mother herself might look like this.

The skin her vestments revealed was perfectly white, almost translucent, as if untouched by the sun. It meant that the tinge of rose in her cheeks was probably not just from the light. She almost seemed like a harlot—and there *were* temples that kept sacred prostitutes.

She could have wrapped any man who gazed upon her around her little finger, and yet, her eyes were covered with a black sash. In her hand, she held the downward-pointing sword and scales that were the symbol of righteousness and justice. The way she all but leaned on them, the way she whispered, conveyed intense anxiety.

"Have I...disturbed you?"

"No."

Sword Maiden. That was the name of the frontier cleric whom Goblin Slayer answered in his diffident voice.

"Is it goblins?"

"Yes, there are. I beg you, help me... Or should I say..." Her alluring, sultry voice was almost a whisper as she shook her head. *"...kill them?"*

"Of course," he said with the swiftness of a striking sword.

Her lips softened into the slightest of smiles, her breath coming warm. Her hair spilled over her expansive chest, little waves rippling through it.

"Where are they? How big is the nest?"

"There are some...special details you should know."

"Tell me."

Sword Maiden gestured to Goblin Slayer to take a seat, as though he and not she were the guest. The way he sat down was almost violent; by contrast, when she lowered herself, it was with the utmost grace. She shifted a little, getting her ample butt into just the right place, and then she pulled the sword and scales close.

"The location is... Excuse me, could you bring me a map?"

"Sure, sure, I've got it ready," answered an older female cleric. How long had she been there? This woman almost seemed to meld with the shadows in the corner of the meeting room.

The cleric spread the map out on the tabletop with hardly a sound despite her voluminous vestments.

She is some kind of monk, no doubt, Goblin Slayer thought and then immediately shifted his focus. She had nothing to do with goblins.

Sword Maiden must have guessed what he was thinking, for she let out a quiet chuckle. "She's a helper of mine. A bodyguard, too... Though I said I didn't need one."

"Skilled though you may be, milady archbishop, even you might be in danger traveling alone. What else were we to do?"

Boo. Sword Maiden seemed like she was almost pouting—but then she coughed gently, a little embarrassed. "In any event, the goblins are appearing..."

She ran a finger along the map gently, almost a caress. She somehow traced the roads expertly, even though she was effectively blindfolded.

"...here, on the highway that goes from the water town to this one and toward the capital."

"The highway..."

"It's terrifying. The road hasn't become quite impassable just yet, but..."

...it almost is. What would the average person think if they heard Sword Maiden's assessment?

"Hrm," Goblin Slayer grunted as he glanced at Sword Maiden, whose shoulders were shaking. "Do we know the nature of the nest, its size, or any other details?"

"Eyewitness accounts suggest about twenty goblins, all with the same tattoo. We don't know where the nest is, but..." Sword Maiden's voice dropped, like that of a child recounting an especially disturbing dream. "...reports said they were riding on wolves."

"I see," Goblin Slayer said softly then grunted again as he lapsed into thought.

They had encountered riders before, in the rain forest, a battle that had involved the two groups shooting at each other along a cliffside. It had been considerable trouble to finish them off on that occasion...

"Milady archbishop is obliged to participate in a council that will be taking place at the capital soon." *Sigh.* The attendant's words seemed intended to supplement Sword Maiden's explanation and perhaps to clarify as well. Perhaps she couldn't bear the idea that one of the great protectors who had brought peace to the frontier should be perceived as afraid of mere goblins. Or perhaps it was out of genuine compassion for the mistress she served. "The quest, then, isn't technically monster slaying but private bodyguard work."

"Will there be other guards?"

"None. Not least because the urgency of the conference has not permitted time to make such arrangements."

Why not use soldiers, or let the military handle things? Any such needling questions from an adventurer would no doubt have wounded Sword Maiden to the core. Her acolyte, it seemed, protected not only her mistress's physical well-being...but her emotional state as well.

In any event, Goblin Slayer's answer was as clean as split wood: "I don't care. I suspect they're wanderers without a nest. A wandering tribe." He stared fixedly at the map, calculating the distance and direction to the capital in his head.

He had never been to the capital. But then, there was a time in his life when he had never been to this town, either.

The map was unlikely to be exactly like the reality. He would make sure his plans included time to react to the situation on the ground.

"If we encounter them, we'll kill them all, and that will be the end of it."

"I didn't know there were goblins like that."

"There are. They're sometimes called field-goblins." Goblin Slayer nodded firmly, then thought a moment and added an important clarification. "But a sea-goblin is a kind of fish."

"Well." It was hard to believe. Or anyway, Sword Maiden's open mouth suggested a sort of disbelief—she quickly covered it with her hands. If her eyes had been visible, they might well have been wide open and blinking.

"I have to think that almost any adventurer could have helped us deal with a few goblins." Apparently the acolyte was also dubious, although for different reasons. She glanced at Goblin Slayer—or more precisely, at the Silver-ranked tag hanging around his neck.

This adventurer in the grimy suit of armor was the one who had buried the blasphemous creature in the sewers of the water town. She couldn't doubt his abilities. She simply thought perhaps taking someone of his level was a bit excessive.

"Milady archbishop, however, won't even consider hiring anyone but you," she said.

"He's the one I trust most of all," Sword Maiden said, pursing her lips in a pout.

"Hopeless," the acolyte could be heard to remark. She sounded like an older sister going along with some whim of her younger sibling.

Goblin Slayer watched the two of them intently then spoke in a low voice. "I will call my friends," he said, using a word even he hardly believed he was uttering. "It won't take long."

§

"And you took the quest without even hashing out the reward?!"

"...Reward?"

"Don't tell me you forgot, Orcbolg!"

A tree would forget its roots if it were as dumb as you.

From her place beside Lizard Priest on the driver's bench, High Elf Archer flicked her ears in disgust.

Accompanied by the party, a carriage pulled by a pair of horses clattered out the town gate. A breeze cool with the first breath of autumn sent clouds scudding across the sky; the weather was clear, and it was still comfortably warm out.

But it was also her day off. This was supposed to be her break. The day when she could sleep until noon if she wanted.

Instead, she had been shaken out of her sleep with "We have a job" and "It's goblins." Even an elf would be upset, and High Elf Archer was perfectly willing to demonstrate as much with the use of her ears.

"Well, er, come on, now..." Priestess, her face strained, attempted to calm the archer, but it wasn't like she didn't understand the feeling. After all, it had been goblin hunting yesterday and it would be goblin hunting today. She adored adventures proper, so she couldn't have been happy about this.

Not that it will keep me from going with him, of course...

He had come to them as usual with his discussion-that-wasn't-a-discussion; he was truly hopeless.

"Goblin Slayer, sir, you need to make sure you get the details, all right?" She held up her pointer finger the way she had done when scolding the junior clerics at the temple.

"I see," he said and gave an attentive nod—that made him less trouble than most of the young disciples.

"I guess we can just talk about the reward later... Can't we?"

"Certainly. Of course, I'm prepared to compensate you." Inside the carriage the party surrounded sat a woman wearing a hood and a small smile. The attendant seated across from her was quite beautiful, but the sheer glory of her form, and the mysterious and alluring shape of her mouth, were nothing compared with those of her mistress.

Adventurers going this way and that along the road turned disinterested looks on the beauty staring out the window of the carriage.

The scene was, well, unremarkable. This was hardly the first time the man who accepted nothing but goblin quests had done something strange. He was a strange one, and now he had taken on a goblin-related quest and was guarding this woman.

The somewhat indulgent atmosphere, though, was probably lost on the man himself...

"For starters, I'll offer you all a bag of gold coins in advance. Then another when we arrive."

"One bag *each*?" Dwarf Shaman said.

"That's right."

That provoked a "Hmm" and satisfied stroke of the beard from the dwarf. For goblin slaying, even if it was goblin slaying plus some body-guard work, that was a good price. "Not bad, not bad. Might even be a good chance to do a little sightseeing around the capital..."

"Uh-huh... The—the capital. I *have* always wanted to see it once..." High Elf Archer was still annoyed, but she seemed to realize that an outburst here would be less than tactful and contented herself with grumbling a bit.

Well indeed, ha-ha. Lizard Priest cackled from where he sat on the driver's bench, holding the reins.

There was Goblin Slayer, who looked to be guiding the carriage. Lizard Priest and High Elf Archer were sitting on the bench. Dwarf Shaman and Priestess went on either side for support. No one had needed to say anything; they simply fell into this formation.

Ultimately, they had all followed "milord Goblin Slayer" without any of them asking about the reward, and that was that.

Not to say they hadn't put any thought into the trip or adequately prepared. They had given everything due consideration.

Yes, most agreeable. Lizard Priest was pleased to know most people would not be able to read his expression as his smile deepened.

Suddenly, not far outside town, Goblin Slayer spoke up. "…Stop the carriage."

"So I shall." Lizard Priest put a scaled hand to the reins to check the horses.

"Wait a moment," Goblin Slayer said and began walking. They didn't have to ask why. Just a short distance from the road, on the other side of the fence, they could see a young girl with red hair.

"Beard-cutter's nothing if not devoted. Eh, Scaly?"

"They say that to be seen face-to-face is to form a bond. But a bond may loosen without proper attention."

Dwarf Shaman came over to the stationary carriage, popping the cork out of his wine jug and taking a swig.

"Drinking before noon?" High Elf Archer remarked with surprise, but a dwarf who doesn't drink is no dwarf at all.

"Don't be dense. This is fuel; it keeps me going. How'm I supposed to chant my spells if my tongue's not loose enough?"

Priestess found herself smiling at Dwarf Shaman's apparent complete seriousness. "It's easy to get thirsty, isn't it? It may be autumn, but enough walking will still make you sweat." She opened her collar a bit (even though she knew it wasn't at all ladylike) and fanned herself.

It wasn't quite hot enough to qualify as an Indian summer, but the last vestiges of the warm season were still quite noticeable. Adventurers were accustomed to walking everywhere, but even so, sweating could be draining and tiresome.

That makes her even more impressive, Priestess thought as she watched Cow Girl conversing with Goblin Slayer. The farm girl was always upbeat and smiling, despite how demanding her farm work must have been.

At the moment, she was making a *don't worry about it* gesture toward Goblin Slayer. He must have told her that he needed to leave right away.

What if I were in her position...?

"If..."

The word, spoken softly and reluctantly, came from inside the carriage.

Priestess peeked in the window to find Sword Maiden shifting uncomfortably. Her breasts, which invited comparison to some very large fruit, jiggled a little as she pressed herself to the window frame. Priestess found herself quite startled.

"...Ahem, may I inquire who is out there?"

Hmm? Priestess thought but quickly connected the dots.

She was talking about him.

"Er, it's the young woman from the farm where Goblin Slayer lives."

"I see..." A breath, carrying a hint of sadness, slipped from between Sword Maiden's moist, red lips.

"Ma'am, is there a...?"

"No...," Sword Maiden said, shaking her head and tilting it down ever so slightly. "...It's nothing."

"I... I see." Priestess forced herself to look away from Sword Maiden, despite her desire to steal another glance at the woman.

Priestess was well familiar with that feeling of infatuation. It was the same one she felt toward that beautiful witch.

So then, what was this feeling she had toward Sword Maiden, the exalted archbishop?

I don't think it's quite reverence.

When she thought back on her time in the water town, recalling that bath and the ritual of the Resurrection miracle, she could still feel something deep inside her grow hot.

Erk!

She shook her head vigorously to keep her cheeks from flushing at the thought of that moment in bed.

"I'm finished."

"Oh, of course!" Priestess looked up quickly as the striding footsteps approached. She made sure she had a good grip on her sounding staff, checked that the luggage was all in order, and wiped the sweat from her brow with a handkerchief, and then she was ready to go.

"Mm, let us be off, then." Lizard Priest gave a toss of the reins and the carriage started moving again.

Dwarf Shaman rifled through his bag, producing an apple out of which he took a big bite while walking along.

Priestess giggled and could be heard to pointedly mutter, "Really, now," over the tinkling of her staff. "You'll be too full for lunch."

"What, you mean this? The likes of this hardly reaches a dwarf's stomach."

"Oh, give me some!" High Elf Archer said, reaching down from the driver's bench; Dwarf Shaman tossed the apple to her with a "Here y'go."

She caught it in both hands and, grinning, polished it with her sleeve...

"Ahhh..." Without warning, the elf gave a contented yawn, wiping at her eyes as she did so. "Man, I'd be just as happy if we didn't run into any goblins on this trip."

But that seemed very unlikely.

§

Sword Maiden awoke to the rhythmic crackling of the fire's dancing flames.

She hefted herself up from the seat of the dim carriage. She felt for the sword and scales, being careful not to wake her attendant, who slept across from her, as she moved the blanket.

Then she pulled her vestments on and slipped quietly out of the carriage.

They were camped for the night. The sun had sunk, the moons were out, and the stars were shining.

They were in a spot by the road where the grass had been cleared so travelers could rest. The question was, had the weary travelers come first, or the place for a campfire?

Normally, one might have expected an inn at such a place, but with all the monsters about these days, that was too much to hope for.

Sword Maiden headed for the center of the campsite with only a slight rustling of cloth. She'd heard there were no other carriages. That meant whoever was tending the fire had to be a member of her party.

A figure loomed up dimly against the light of the flames, a man she recognized from her very dreams.

"...Good evening?" she said as she approached, seating herself beside him on her plump behind. She left some space between them—because she couldn't bear to get any closer to him.

Goblin Slayer's shadow moved, his helmeted head turning toward Sword Maiden. Her attendant complained that it looked grimy and cheap. And it had felt that way, when she had removed it once.

"You are not asleep?"

"Er..."

His voice was so soft and cold, disinterested, almost mechanical. Sword Maiden put a hand to her mouth to keep her heart from jumping clear out of her bounteous chest.

What to say to him? The words she had imagined speaking vanished in an instant. It was, she thought, like when one was working on a letter but then wrote the wrong thing, balled up the entire piece of paper, and threw it away.

"...After everything you did, I was finally able to sleep well again. I wanted to thank you once more..."

"But you're awake right now."

She had finally managed to speak from the heart, but Goblin Slayer had struck her down with his remark.

"That's..." Sword Maiden puffed out her cheeks, pursing her red lips. "...You, sir, are the worst."

"Is that so?"

"I certainly think so."

He didn't even realize how she felt.

Sword Maiden turned away from Goblin Slayer, but beneath her blindfold, she glanced in his direction. He was a dark presence that stared into the flames, never moving. To her, he looked like a sword waiting for the moment it would be drawn.

I don't suppose he's at all interested in what kind of council they're holding in the capital.

They were surrounded by dozing adventurers in their sleeping bags and blankets.

Sword Maiden let out a soft breath. In the end, she found herself with only one choice of conversation topic.

"So we didn't see any goblins today..."

"They will come," Goblin Slayer said, stirring the fire with a long stick. A piece of firewood splintered, sending up motes of flame.

"We have a carriage surrounded by armed guards. It would be difficult to attack outright."

"..."

"Tonight, or tomorrow."

Sword Maiden could say nothing more. Her womb felt as if it had been stabbed with an icicle, the cold spreading out and causing her to shiver.

She clutched the sword and scales to her chest. Darkness pressed in from every direction.

The wind danced through the leaves and grass with a hushing sound. Sword Maiden felt herself stiffening.

She looked to the right. The sound of branches bobbing. She looked to the left. The breeze blowing across the plain. *Hush, hush.* The cries of birds. The cries of beasts.

A sour smell of earth came drifting. *Crackle, crackle.* The fire jumping. The odor of burning wood.

Hideous laughter echoed in her mind. Pointing and cackling. The fire drew near before her eyes.

She shook her head and shook it again, *no, no.* She felt as if she were begging for she knew not what.

A crimson tongue wiped her vision blank. A half-heard howl. A burning like hot tongs between her legs. Wailing.

A cry like a death rattle, unending, pounding against her eardrums. The voice was her own. She had reached the extremity, her soul and her very dignity shattering—

"Sleep."

The low voice gave the impression of steel. The word came from the black shadow looming in front of her.

"Close your eyes, and when you open them, it will be morning."

"You make it sound..." Sword Maiden spoke in a strained voice, trying to control breathing that had grown harsh without her realizing it. "...so easy."

"I know it's hard," Goblin Slayer said with utmost seriousness. "When I was a child, I would lay in bed trying to find out how long I had to keep my eyes closed before it would be morning."

The simplest of words. And they evoked from Sword Maiden the slightest of smiles. Just as there had been a time when she was a pure, undefiled girl, the man before her had once been an innocent boy.

Sword Maiden said nothing further. She doubted she could give voice to the things she really wanted to talk about anyway.

About herself, about him, about that girl at the farm, and that courageous priestess.

Various thoughts swirled in her mind, and every time she attempted to say something about them, her tongue would shake and no words would come out.

But there was a man like a shadow beside her, and for her sake, he silently tended the fire.

I wish morning would hurry and come.

I wish the night would go on forever.

She felt as if all she had forgotten for the past ten years was about to burst forth... Yes, so she felt.

Sword Maiden drew her knees close and rested her elbows on them, propping her head on her hands. She let out a sigh that mingled sweetness with pity.

"...Mrn, ugh... Ooh."

Sword Maiden had been about to speak when one of the lumps of blankets shifted and turned, and Priestess sat up. She rubbed the sleep from her eyes, yawned, and murmured something indecipherable.

Ahh. Sword Maiden exhaled in disappointment. So much for talking. And dawn was still so far away.

Priestess got unsteadily to her feet; she had removed her mail and was wearing only her vestments. With all the uncertainty of an acolyte walking through the temple halls in the middle of the night, Priestess went over to her cargo. She had opened her bag before she murmured "What?" as if finally waking up. "Milady archbishop...? And...Goblin Slayer?"

She blinked, inclining her head in perplexity. Her gaze wandered back and forth between the two of them where they sat next to each other.

Goblin Slayer she expected; he was on guard. But Sword Maiden next to him—what was she doing there?

"...Um, is something the matter?"

"..." Goblin Slayer grunted quietly and turned that metal helmet toward Sword Maiden. "She woke up."

"Please," Sword Maiden said. "You make me sound like a restless child."

This would be it for tonight, Sword Maiden decided. She puffed out her cheeks, indeed very much like a child.

Then, before the startled Priestess could even make an expression of surprise, the archbishop had composed herself again.

She was no longer a little girl. She wasn't even a young woman of an age to be smitten with boys. She was under no obligation to admire anybody unconditionally.

The only person who could be described in all those ways was in fact the puzzled girl before her. The fact caused a prickle in Sword Maiden's heart, but she smiled wanly all the same.

"I found I couldn't quite sleep," she said. "...And you? Is something wrong?"

"Er, uh, no, ma'am," Priestess said with an emphatic shake of her hand. "I was just a little thirsty. I thought of my water..."

"I see." Goblin Slayer grabbed his own canteen from his bag and tossed it to her casually.

"Eep!" Priestess exclaimed, but she caught it, bowing her head politely and saying, "Thank you."

She unstoppered the canteen and drank audibly, consuming its contents with each gulp. Sword Maiden watched her closely—and then her hidden gaze suddenly turned toward empty space.

"..." Goblin Slayer didn't ask what was wrong. He quickly checked that he had his sword, made sure his armor was fastened.

When Priestess saw that, her face stiffened. "I'll go wake the others...!"

"Don't let them realize you know."

"Right!"

Priestess took her sounding staff in hand and began to circle the camp as nonchalantly as she could. The rings on her staff shook with each step, jingling out with a sound like a bell. In response, the other three blankets started to move.

Lizard Priest was the first to awaken, rising silently. He crawled out from under his pile of blankets, shook his stiff body, and quickly took up his dragon fang.

"They come, then?"

"...Could be. C'mon, wake up."

The response came from Dwarf Shaman. He gave High Elf Archer something of a kick to get her out of bed. With many an "ooh" and "ahh," she got up, rubbing her eyes.

"...It's not even daybreak yet," she said.

"Hurry," Priestess said. "I need to get my mail on..."

"Look who's a big girl," High Elf Archer said, grabbing her bow. Then she picked up a spider crawling nearby and drew out some silk for a bowstring.

When he saw each of his companions preparing for battle, Goblin Slayer got to his feet. "Go back to the carriage."

"But..." Sword Maiden looked up; his rough hand was already grasping her arm.

"It's dangerous."

He pulled her to her feet without giving her time to argue. Then he set off for the carriage, and Sword Maiden had no choice but to follow.

With her skills, she could easily have participated in the battle with minimal danger, but...

——*!!*

But the fingers digging into the soft flesh of her arm would not allow it.

She understood perfectly well that this wasn't her fight. And yet, part of her still wanted to argue.

Sword Maiden was joyful as she let herself be pulled along, but when she was thrust into the carriage, she let out a small "oh" of disappointment.

"Bar the door and wait for us."

The entryway closed with a clatter. Sword Maiden breathed out, sorrowful, then touched her arm, where there were still red marks from his fingers.

"...We will. We'll be waiting for you."

Her voice was so soft, it couldn't possibly have been heard outside the carriage door. It was, instead, a prayer. Whether or not *he* heard her was of scant consequence.

"Mrf... What's happening?" Her sleepy-eyed attendant sat up, still covered in her blanket.

Sword Maiden didn't answer but bit her lip and pulled the sword and scales close to her.

"..." Her sharpened senses could already detect the presences outside. As she pulled the symbol of her deity to her abundant chest, her body began to shake, her lips began to tremble.

"...Goblins. They're here."

Please, please don't let any of them escape alive.

Her strained voice offered up one set of words, her heart another.

If there was another way for her to fight the goblins, she didn't know it.

§

"GOOROBOROGB!!"

The ambush began with an order from a goblin rider.

The wolf burst out of the bushes and closed quickly, covering the last of the distance in a single great leap. Its jaws streamed filthy saliva, and Goblin Slayer met them with a backhanded pound of his shield.

"GYAN?!" The wolf yelped and rolled on its side next to the fire; he crushed its throat underfoot then stabbed the neck of the rider, who had been thrown clear.

The wolf, its spine broken, twitched once, while the goblin drowned choking on his own blood. Goblin Slayer confirmed this then moved on to the next enemy.

A second wolf—there were perhaps four or five in total —was already jumping out of the bushes.

"…Hrm." Goblin Slayer gave a click of his tongue as he went to pull out his sword and discovered it was lodged in the goblin's flesh. Without missing a beat, he let go of it, grabbed the corpse's club instead, and swung it around.

"GGBORORB?!"

There was the sound of a backbone breaking, much like that of a cracking branch, and the wolf went tumbling to one side. Goblin Slayer attacked its rider as the monster tried to get to his feet.

"GORGB?!"

"This makes two."

The goblin took a sharp blow to the head; one eye and all his brains came flying out, and he fell over dead. Goblin Slayer flung the club at the next goblin rider then wrenched out the sword piercing the other corpse.

"Don't let them escape. Kill them all."

"…No matter how you cut it, that just doesn't sound like something the heroes should be saying," High Elf Archer grumbled from her position beside the carriage.

The campsite, bathed in the glow of the fire, already appeared to be surrounded by goblins. In front of her were the wolf mount and the rider Goblin Slayer had knocked from it.

"Heh-heh." High Elf Archer pulled two arrows from her quiver; they left her bow almost the instant she looked at her target. The first bolt hit the wolf in the eye; the next, released in lightning succession, tore through the throat of the advancing goblin.

"GOROR?!"

"One for the road!" She kicked the death-rattling goblin with her long leg then nocked an arrow into her bow and let it loose.

The arrow arced through the night at the strangest of angles, dropping somewhere behind the carriage.

"GROBORB?!"

A scream. A goblin wobbled out and fell over, clutching his chest, from which the arrow protruded. That made two for her.

High Elf Archer gave a flick of her ears. The goblin had had a spear, but he was on foot. "I should have known that five of us couldn't cover this whole area—not with them all around us... Dwarf, lend me a hand!"

"Oh?"

Dwarf Shaman was standing beside the horses, ax in hand. Almost before he had answered, High Elf Archer was already moving with the grace of a little bird dancing along a twig: first her foot was in the palm of his free hand, then she stepped on his shoulder, before finally jumping up.

"I'm taking up a position on top of the carriage. You handle the ground!"

"Blast it, Long-Ears! I'm not a stepping stool!"

Even as he groused, he swung his ax with those strong dwarven arms.

"GBORROB?!"

This goblin found himself split like firewood from the chest down, his internal organs spilling out.

Now the goblins on foot were advancing along with the riders. Ten of them, or maybe twenty.

I see—enough to overwhelm any carriage, Dwarf Shaman thought.

The cackling goblins had already pushed into the campsite. He didn't have time to focus long enough to prepare a spell.

Dwarf Shaman frowned and shook the blood from his ax then raised a ragged shout. "No choice... C'mon, girl, get over here, over here! I'm in trouble!"

"Oh right, sorry...!" Priestess answered. She was having trouble finding a good spot, constantly watching her back as she waved her sounding staff. Come to think of it, there weren't many occasions where she'd had to fight while having to defend a target.

Priestess moved at a mincing run as the goblins pushed closer, leering at her.

"Eeep?!"

Well, now—was it fate or chance that caused her to crouch at the moment she did?

A wolf, snapping for her soft flesh, went flying over her head and was met by Dwarf Shaman's ax.

"GYAN?!"

"Got 'im. You okay?!"

"Y-yes! I'm... I'm fine! Sorry about that."

"Ah, let the wolf apologize!"

The rider had a fumble—when he was thrown from his mount, he broke his neck in the fall—and Dwarf Shaman kicked the corpse aside then steadied his breathing.

Priestess came up, sticking close to Dwarf Shaman. Her eyes wandered the night for a moment, seeking for *him*.

It's okay, he's over there.

A figure in pitiful-looking armor, brandishing his weapon in the firelight. Priestess took a breath in and let it out.

"...It looks like a sling would be more useful than a miracle right now," she said.

"My thoughts exactly. Holy Light would probably just make the buggers run away..."

Priestess nodded at Dwarf Shaman then leaned her staff against the carriage and took out the sling she kept at her hip. She grabbed a stone from the ground and started spinning it, and then with an adorable "Yah!" she sent it flying.

The night didn't help her aim, and she only struck a goblin in the foot, but—

"GROB?!"

"That's an assist!" High Elf Archer sent an arrow into the creature the moment he paused. The goblin gurgled something then fell over backward, the arrow in his chest.

Lizard Priest, needless to say, was in fine form.

"Ha-ha-ha, a little supporting fire makes everything easier. Still—"

He worked his claws, his claws, his fangs, and his tail to keep himself warm in the chill night. Two goblins he tore apart, another he grasped in his great jaws and flung into the sky. By the time the corpse landed on the ground, his trunk-like tail was already sweeping the monster behind him.

That was four goblins dead, and he wasn't even breathing hard. Lizard Priest's eyes rolled in his head. "I'm afraid simple defense is not in my character."

"Eleven... And I agree."

It looked like the adventurers had already buried at least half the goblin number, but they couldn't let down their guard. Goblin Slayer drew his spear from a goblin's windpipe and threw it at a rider attempting to jump the campfire.

"GBORRO?!"

"Meaning...?"

The goblin, knocked sidelong from his mount, fell squarely into the fire. There was a puff of smoke and ash, and the creature could be heard screaming as he roasted alive. He rolled on the ground, trying desperately to beat out the flames, but the goblins around him merely chuckled to themselves.

Goblin Slayer kicked aside the corpse of the monster he had slain with his spear, taking the creature's dagger for his own.

"That makes twelve," he continued. "Can you get around to the outside?"

"The vocabulary of my people does not contain the words *I can't*." Lizard Priest chuckled jovially, touching the tip of his nose with his tongue. His mouth twisted fearsomely, and he rubbed his hands together. "Kindly give me just a moment."

Then he went sprinting off through the smoke without a sound.

Once he had seen the scaled giant safely away, Goblin Slayer took an unlit torch from his item pouch. He touched it to one of the weaker-looking embers nearby. The fire could not be allowed to go out.

"GRRO?!"

Next, he dealt the closest goblin a blow with his shield then buried his dagger in the monster's neck. He started running, straight over the fresh corpse. His objective? His friends (still a strange thought to him) and the carriage they protected.

"Thirteen... Fourteen!"

He sent a rising kick into the face of a goblin trying to block his way, smashing the creature's mouth in. One more step.

He glanced at the others quickly; no one appeared hurt. He let out a breath.

"Goblin Slayer, sir!"

He nodded at Priestess, who greeted him with shining face and said brusquely, "We're making an anvil."

"What?" Priestess asked, her face taut and red.

High Elf Archer exclaimed "*What?!*" from atop the carriage. "Now, you listen to me, Orcbolg—!"

"We have to redouble our defense," he said, summarily ignoring her. "Invoke Protection. Hurry."

"Oh, r-right!" Priestess nearly clung to her sounding staff; Goblin Slayer kept her behind him, to cover her. He caught a blow from an encroaching goblin on his shield then struck back with his dagger, aiming for the solar plexus.

"GOROB?!"

"That makes fifteen. Eight left, three of them riders." He pulled out his dagger as he kicked away the goblin, who was wheezing his last breaths from lungs that could no longer keep air inside.

Goblin Slayer shook the dark blood from his knife and resumed a fighting posture as he said, "Hold the far side. I'll take this one."

"You got it! Though I'm not much of a vanguard fighter m'self..." Dwarf Shaman's immediate response was somewhat undercut by his chagrined addendum, but then he went tromping off.

He was lightly armored, but he was still a dwarf. A full-strength blow from his ax would be more than any goblin could handle.

"...Grr. Okay, but I don't have to like it!" High Elf Archer lamented, her bow still singing even as her ears laid back in annoyance. "You'd better apologize later!"

"I don't understand what you mean," Goblin Slayer said flatly. It wasn't clear if he understood how brusque he sounded.

Though I doubt it, Priestess thought, smiling a little. She slid her hands along her sounding staff, raising it high. The fact that she was being protected by someone—no, by *him*—helped tremendously to set her mind at ease.

"O Earth Mother, abounding in mercy, by the power of the land grant safety to we who are weak!"

As a result, her prayer reached the heavens, and a holy protection manifested itself as an invisible barrier around the carriage and the party.

"GOROROB!"

"GROBG! GROORBBGRB!!"

What, then, did these adventurers look like to the goblins?

They looked very vulnerable, was the answer.

The goblins cackled to themselves that there was one less adventurer on the field, but they didn't notice anything else. The enemy was weakened; that was what mattered to them. It just looked to the goblins like these stupid idiots were doing something foolish. Now they were focused on only one question: what would they do to these adventurers?

How should they kill the men? In front of the women, perhaps? There was a woman inside the carriage, as well! In other words, they could have their fun, and if some of the women died in the process, well, there would be others. Wonderful.

One of the grinning goblins licked his lips, provoking a look of disgust from the little girl with the staff.

Then there was that prideful elf up on top of the carriage—how she would scream when they dragged her down from there.

The goblins were swollen with anticipation and lust. That's what goblins are, after all.

And so they didn't realize what had happened, even after it was too late.

"GOBRRRR...?"

The first to notice was a goblin rider near the rear who was looking for his chance to jump into the fray. He heard rustling footsteps coming through the underbrush. Some of his comrades, late to the fun, he suspected.

The rider pulled on the crude leather straps that served as reins, wheeling around to give them a piece of his mind.

"GOROBBGB?!"

He never got a word out; he died spurting blood on the back of his wolf.

"GYAN?!"

"GOOR! GOBG!"

The wolf's yelp was the goblins' first indication that something was wrong.

One, two, three white shadows came at them through the night—wait, were those bones?!

"O horns and claws of our father, iguanodon, thy four limbs, become two legs to walk upon the earth!"

The Dragontooth Warriors under Lizard Priest's command howled and rattled as they attacked the goblins.

The monsters would never have imagined that one of the adventurers might have escaped the melee using the smoke screen from the campfire for cover, let alone that the adventurer might then pray to his forefathers to raise up soldiers for himself...!

"Ahh—I do believe this should settle matters until we reach the capital, milord Goblin Slayer."

Pressed by the Dragontooth Warriors, the goblins had no choice but to move forward. There, however, they found the sacred barrier of Protection waiting for them. Not to mention a quartet of armed adventurers...

"Are you...just going to let them crush themselves?" Priestess said, clinging to her staff and focusing to maintain her miracle.

"Yes," Goblin Slayer said with complete composure, as he rotated the dagger with a motion of his wrist. "We are going to kill all the goblins."

Before dawn broke, his words had come true.

§

It was a scene of annihilation.

The morning light broke rich and red over a field scattered with the bones and flesh and cruor of goblins and wolves alike.

Priestess knelt, making a holy sign, gripping her staff tightly as she communed with the Earth Mother. It was not a matter of pardoning the goblins: she prayed equally for the peace of all dead.

"Are you done?"

"Oh yes...!" Priestess, caught off guard by the voice, nodded quickly and got to her feet. She looked around and realized Goblin Slayer had already piled up the corpses.

A sour stench prickled her nose. It was an odor she recognized from her very first adventure, and which she still hadn't gotten used to: the filth and sweat of goblins.

"What...are you planning to do?"

"How many?" Goblin Slayer asked, ignoring her question, instead kneeling beside the collection of corpses. "How many did they kill?"

"Umm..." Priestess couldn't quite figure out where to put her eyes.

Watching from the other side of the window, inside the carriage, Sword Maiden supplied the answer in a tight voice. "...A party of five or six, as I recall..."

"I see." Goblin Slayer drew his dagger in a reverse grip. "..."

"Wh-what's going on?" Priestess asked.

"Close the carriage window." The instruction was so short yet brooked no refusal.

"Pardon me," Priestess said as she shuttered the carriage window. As she did so, she saw how pale and sorrowful Sword Maiden's expression was.

Ah...

She understood why then. But it didn't mean she could stop him.

Goblin Slayer raised his dagger then brought it down without hesitation into the belly of one of the goblins.

"Ugh..." Blood came out with a splurting noise, and High Elf Archer, still standing guard atop the carriage, made an involuntary sound of disgust.

Even for a ranger or an experienced hunter, the scene would be disquieting. This wasn't like cleaning and skinning an animal, draining its blood.

"...Hold on, Orcbolg, what do you think you're doing?"

"Making sure."

His answer, given as he continued to dig through the slop of the goblin's body, was no clearer than any of his others.

High Elf Archer waved her hand in exasperation and looked away. Her ears drooped. "Ergh, just…do whatever you want…"

"How can I have meat tomorrow if you keep that up?" Dwarf Shaman joked, rubbing his stomach, but he continued to scan the area vigilantly all the while. With their frontline fighter at work, it was more important than ever to be alert.

However…

"…" Priestess alone bit her lip and stared directly at the goblin corpse.

"Allow me to assist you, milord Goblin Slayer."

"Thanks."

Lizard Priest walked up smoothly, drawing his short fang-sword and setting to work. His cuts were rough but experienced and helped the job tremendously.

"Hmm," Goblin Slayer grunted, pulling out the goblin's stomach as he completed his dissection.

He then proceeded to chop open the wolves as well, emptying the half-digested contents of their gizzards onto the plain.

"Oh… Ergh…" Finally Priestess could take no more; she crouched down, her face pale.

Bits and pieces of hands and feet, a chest, strands of hair, all half-dissolved, now littered the field.

"It doesn't add up."

He told Priestess to rinse the canteen as he held the canteen out to her, and she took it with both hands. She drank noisily, water running from her lips, draining the contents for all she was worth.

Goblin Slayer watched her out of the corner of his eye as he considered the number of limbs. There wasn't quite a full set of pairs.

"…What do you make of it?"

"Well, now…" Lizard Priest joined him crouching by the hunks of meat, all drenched in stomach juices, spearing one with the tip of his sword. "Perhaps some of them went to feed the wolves, and others were kept separately… Or more likely, not."

"I agree. This is a wandering tribe. They should have been traveling with their provisions."

"...They didn't have any cargo with them at all."

"*Good grief. I mean really.*"

This perspective came from High Elf Archer, who was careful not to look down from her perch on the carriage.

The whole disemboweling thing had been a big sticking point for her when they'd all first met, but... The elf sighed and flicked her ears then waved her hand. "I don't see any sign of baggage in the distance, either."

"Which means just one thing," Dwarf Shaman said, looking disturbed himself as he observed the carved bodies.

A six-person party. Plenty of goblins and wolves to eat them all.

"...Does it mean...there's still someone out there?" Priestess asked in a small voice, but nobody answered.

§

"Oh wow..." Priestess let her reaction slip out as she exhaled, her eyes shining.

It had been several days of walking along the highway from the frontier town, but finally, they had arrived.

As they approached the capital, fields began to pepper the roadside, and the wind came gusting off the river. In the distance, they could spot the muddy red roof of someone's house that overlooked the scene.

The castle walls, which were visible in the far distance, seemed even now to tower before her very eyes. Made of massive marble blocks piled one on top of the other, they formed a monumental gate. Peering up at them hurt her neck. Did the shadow they cast cover the entire roadway at sundown?

As the thought occurred to Priestess, she found the walls made a much greater impression on her than simply for their size. The beautiful carven stones had not been made with magic. Human skill, human ingenuity, and human strength had made this possible, and that was astounding.

That architecture had stood for thousands of years, resisting the elements, weathering battle, and overseeing many generations of rulers.

She had heard of the place before, but she had never seen it. Her entire world had consisted of the Temple, the frontier town, the field, and then, very recently, the water town. No more than that.

This, though, was vastly larger, and vastly older, than the gate of either the frontier town or the water town. The great gate of the capital had stood for many ages; it was itself the history of those who had words.

"It's incredible…!" Priestess said, smiling, shaking off the gloom of the previous night.

"That thing's probably older than me," High Elf Archer said from her position atop the carriage, twitching her ears as they came under the shadow of the gate. The sparkle in her grass-green eyes must have been one of curiosity. Why was it so thrilling to see something one had never seen before?

"Hey," she chirped, "what're all those people doing milling around the wall?"

"Let me tell you about walls," Dwarf Shaman answered quietly. "They're the linchpin of a town's defense; places take pride in them." Thus, tasking people with keeping them neat and clean was essential. The dwarf looked up at the carriage with an expression of exasperation. "Long-Ears. You've really gotten attached to your spot up there, haven't you?"

"Well, it pays to have someone keep an eye out in every direction. Doesn't it, Orcbolg?" She looked down from the carriage, pleased to be up above the crowd.

"Yes," said the man in the grimy helmet.

Goblin Slayer was looking this way and that, holding a piece of skin. He had cut it off one of the goblins from the previous night—much to High Elf Archer's and Priestess's disgust, of course.

"…Bleh. Tell me again why you felt compelled to take that?"

"There may be surviving members of the tribe, or they may have a leader."

"You could have just copied the symbol onto something."

"I wanted to ensure accuracy." With one gloved finger, he casually traced the geometric pattern of the tattoo on the skin. At length, he gave a small nod then rolled the skin up and stuffed it back in his item pouch. "It looks almost like a hand, but I can't be sure," he said, and then the helmet shook. "Do you find this place unusual?"

"Yes, I do," Priestess said with an earnest nod. "There are so many people…!" She was looking this way and that, virtually bouncing on her feet.

"Be careful not to get separated."

"I—I know that… I do, okay?" Embarrassed at being treated like a child, Priestess tapped the ground with her staff to emphasize her point. From down by her feet came a hard sound. She had been so focused on the carriage that she hadn't noticed when the earthen highway had turned to flagstones.

The crowd had been growing steadily as they got near the capital, and now it pressed in on every side. Even the vast gates seemed narrow compared with the mass of bodies.

The crowd consisted of young and old, male and female alike, the rich and the poor of every race and tribe, some of them belonging to trades and even countries Priestess couldn't identify, all of them mingling together, shouting to one another.

Several other carriages were visible as well, while merchants carrying baskets waded through the crowd, selling water or fruit. The wild colors of the clothing as people walked past or stood by struck her like a kaleidoscope or mosaic. The mélange of languages that reached her ears sounded pleasant, almost like a song.

"Is it…festival time or something?" she asked.

Incredibly, it was Sword Maiden who opened the window and, giggling, informed the astonished Priestess, "This is how it always is."

"Of course, more people means more trouble, but also more opportunities for adventurers like us," Lizard Priest said, picking up the thread from where he sat holding the reins. He rolled his eyes happily.

The carriage rolled toward the gate at a stately pace, looking positively elegant.

"I'm afraid I am naturally somewhat unsuited for shadow-running, though."

"I should think people would love you for bodyguard work," Dwarf Shaman said, chuckling from his place beside the carriage. He looked like he might be in danger of getting swept away in the crowd, but his pace never slowed. The dwarf looked up at Goblin Slayer, fixing his eyes on the helmet. "You should have plenty of free time, Beard-cutter. Wouldn't expect many goblin hunts in the capital."

"We cannot be sure there are none here."

"Forget it," came the blunt reply.

Dwarf Shaman's annoyed answer was the end of it; Goblin Slayer and the others focused their attention forward.

Unlike the town on the frontier, or even the water town, the gate of the capital didn't have soldiers standing guard, but rather a guardhouse. Whether coming or going, it was necessary to spend some time dealing with red tape, and that was probably the cause of this traffic jam.

Dwarf Shaman sized up the line creeping forward under the early autumn sun. "Doesn't look like we'll be getting in there anytime soon," he said with a shrug. Then he took some coins from his pouch and disappeared into the sea of people.

A few minutes later, he came back with several small bottles, one of which he tossed to High Elf Archer up on the roof of the carriage. "Beats waitin' around with nothing to do. Here."

"Whoop. Thanks... Hey, what is this?" She inspected the glass bottle, which had a violet liquid inside. She gave it a little shake and heard it slosh around then pulled out the cork to find a sweet aroma drifted out.

"'S called *sapa*. They take grapes or the like and mix them with lead in a bronze vat to sweeten it."

"Hmm," the elf said, taking an exploratory sniff and then shaking her head. "...Smells too much like metal. I'll pass."

"It's this limited diet of yours that leaves you with such an anvil."

High Elf Archer growled and pursed her lips but didn't say anything as she pitched the bottle back to Dwarf Shaman. It was still uncorked, so he rushed to catch it as the liquid nearly splashed out. He shot the elf a dirty look and drained the contents in two pointed gulps.

"Hrmph, it's perfectly good."

"Er, uh, um, but isn't lead a poison...?" Priestess said, provoking a guffaw from High Elf Archer, who replied, "Dwarves' bodies are too big to worry about trace poisons."

"The word is *sturdy*!" Dwarf Shaman said, letting out a burp and wiping some droplets from his beard.

Lizard Priest looked down from where he was urging the horses on at a trot and rolled his eyes. "Now then, have you anything else?"

"Ahh..." Dwarf Shaman rummaged through his collection of bottles. "Care for some posca?"

"Posca, you say?"

"Ah yes." Sword Maiden smiled from the carriage window. "It's based on vinegar, isn't it?"

"Heavens, you know it?"

"It is easy to forget, but I was once an adventurer myself."

Posca was made by mixing water into wine that had become unduly acidic—or, to put it less elegantly, had turned to vinegar. Honey was added to create a bittersweet flavor, and it kept well, making it a cherished favorite of adventurers visiting the capital.

"Would you care for some now, then?"

"May I?"

"By all means!"

Sword Maiden smiled ever so slightly. She took the bottle proffered through the window in both hands, removing the cork with what looked almost like a caress. She drank the contents noisily then let out a luscious sigh of contentment.

"Gracious... Most unladylike!"

"It can't matter that much. Surely..." *Mm.* Sword Maiden licked the last of the droplets from her lips as she replied poutingly to her attendant. Then she popped her head out the window, giving Dwarf Shaman a nod and a cherubic smile. "Thank you very much... It was perfectly delicious."

"I'm so glad you enjoyed it," he said with a grin then tossed bottles to his companions with a smug "Here."

Priestess and High Elf Archer responded with "Yikes, it's bitter" and "It's just old grape juice in the end," although they smiled in spite of themselves. No girl can fail to enjoy a sweet flavor…is maybe going a little far, but still.

Goblin Slayer caught the next bottle, opening it silently and drinking it down. That was how he treated whatever went into his mouth, be it food or drink, so nobody paid him much mind. Only Priestess smiled as if to say, *Hopeless!*

Lizard Priest was next, but he shook his great hand and said, "No, thank you. I am sated with drink. My stomach rather than my throat is what I wish to satisfy."

"Food, eh…?" Dwarf Shaman muttered, stroking his beard thoughtfully then looking at the panoply of vendors by the gate.

It was already late afternoon, the sun starting to sink in the sky. There might have been someone there selling lunches, but they were probably out of stock by now. They would be much more likely to find something to eat when they got inside the capital.

"You know, I've heard it said that they sell a lot of cheese in the capital," Dwarf Shaman said.

"Oh-ho," came the response from…Goblin Slayer, who had been listening silently to the party's conversation. He had ably drunk the posca through the visor of his helmet in one or two gulps. "That is very interesting to hear."

His absolute seriousness elicited a laugh from the entire party. Even the attendant in the carriage had a hand to her mouth to cover her smile.

The only one who wasn't laughing was Sword Maiden. She was squeezing the sword and scales on her lap.

"Is something the matter, milady?"

"No…," Sword Maiden said, shaking her head as if startled out of her reverie. "…No, it's nothing."

"If you say so, milady…"

Sword Maiden looked away from the window, staring up at the carriage ceiling and letting out an anxious little sigh.

And here I thought any girlish emotions had dried up long ago.

"…It's quite difficult, isn't it?"

That was when it happened.

In the carriage, Sword Maiden's gaze moved again, while atop the vehicle, High Elf Archer's ears twitched.

Wheels could be heard in the distance. Soldiers' voices. The crowd shifted uneasily, opening a path to the gate.

Scything through the sea of people came a carriage pulled by two horses. The golden engraving on the vehicle and the lion crest flying aloft showed that it belonged to the royal family.

The horses were of course the best available. Gorgeous steeds, rippling with muscles. Then there were the soldiers accompanying the carriage—knights all, every spot of armor sparkling! The fine metal breastplates and helms, the spears and swords, made them look like fairy-tale heroes, and one needn't have been a child to be taken by the sight. The soldiers could not have been further removed from the adventurers who had to come tramping many miles across open country on foot.

"Wow...," Priestess breathed, her jaw hanging open, and who could blame her?

"That's getting to be a familiar look on you." High Elf Archer giggled. "But that would explain why we've been waiting so long!" Her expression was suddenly as dark as it had been amused.

"*One or two good arrows could teach them a lesson*," she muttered under her breath, and Priestess quickly waved her staff at the elf. "N-no, you can't *do* that...!"

"Come on, I know that," High Elf Archer snorted. "They're packing serious magical protection besides."

Does that mean she would take a shot if they didn't...? Priestess thought gloomily.

The crazed elf ignored the frowning cleric. "Anyway," she went on, "it looks like the king's been out and about. I wonder what was going on?"

"Taxes." The reply was brusque and clear. Goblin Slayer gave it in a quiet voice, almost as if he were talking to himself. "It is time for the harvest. The king goes in person to visit areas where he has no local representatives, or where an uprising seems likely."

"Huh. You seem to know a lot about it."

"I come from a farming village."

Wha? Was it Priestess or Sword Maiden who let out the sound of surprise?

They must have been picturing this man with his grimy helmet and cheap-looking leather armor tending to a field someplace.

Oh, but I guess he really does help out on that farm he lives on... Priestess nodded to herself, a thoughtful finger to her lips. "It's all right," she said, "I think that suits you!"

"I see."

Once the king's carriage was through the gate, the soldiers appeared to relax a little. They didn't have to be quite as faultlessly vigilant as before. The line of people waiting for admittance to the city started moving more smoothly.

"Still," High Elf Archer said, squinting her eyes against the wind as their vehicle finally began to move. "That was about as fancy a carriage as I've ever seen. And it looked like he had half the army with him."

"Royalty's hardly going to travel humbly and alone, now, is it?" Dwarf Shaman replied, working his stubby arms and legs as he jogged beside the carriage. As a dwarf, he knew a thing or two about ornamentation. Stroking his long white beard, he smiled knowingly. "For them, though, it's not luxury—it's a necessary expense."

"What, all that?"

"How would you feel if your chief or whoever was living in a dead tree, dressed in rags?"

"..." High Elf Archer's ears drooped as she pictured the scene. "...Guess I wouldn't like that much."

"And then if he went around by himself, begging people to hand over tax money?"

"They'd knock him down flat."

"Now you're getting the idea. It's the job of their type to go big."

Pattering along nearby, Priestess gave a small sigh. "I guess it's not easy being important."

In her own life, she had seen the Mother Superior of the temple hard at work, and she herself had once born the responsibility of performing the offertory dance at a festival. She almost couldn't imagine work more difficult still.

But there are people who do it.

She glanced in the window of the carriage beside which she walked. Sword Maiden was sitting there, her slight smile undisturbed, her voluptuous body still filling the seat. Somehow, Priestess found it difficult to read Sword Maiden's emotions from her face.

She doesn't even have a helmet like Goblin Slayer.

"Man, it must suck to be the king."

"Says the princess!"

High Elf Archer waved a dismissive hand from atop the carriage, her comment provoking a grumble from Dwarf Shaman.

It was all just like normal. Priestess found it helped her relax, to know such things didn't change, even within sight of the capital's walls.

She giggled, and in response, Lizard Priest rolled his eyes in his head. "Our own adventuring collectives are funded by taxes." His tone was lighthearted, but he sounded a bit like he was delivering a sermon. "And without our organization, we adventurers would be nothing but unemployed ruffians."

We should be grateful, seemed to be his message.

It made sense to her: Lizard Priest was a rather intimidating figure, and there were those among the lizardmen who had besmirched themselves with Chaos. The whole race of them were close to being Non-Prayer Characters, a status that must have brought its own burdens.

"Lucky they don't have a tax on ear length," Dwarf Shaman offered.

High Elf Archer snorted in response then muttered jokingly that taxes were all well and good. She flicked her long ears pointedly then grinned and said, "Or…a barrel surcharge, maybe?"

"Ha! They'd invite a rebellion, I'd say!"

"Quiet, both of you," Goblin Slayer said, interrupting them. "We're approaching the gate."

Hmm? Priestess tilted her head in surprise. It was unusual for him to be alert to anything but goblins.

As they approached the walls, she could see they were surrounded by a massive, deep, dry moat. If the forces of Chaos attacked, they would be under assault from the castle's archers the whole time they were climbing into and out of this ditch. A great bridge, attached to the castle gate with chains, currently allowed entry across the moat.

Naturally, an interrogatory voice stopped them. "Halt! Let's see some identification."

Lizard Priest tugged on the reins, pulling the horses to a stop, and slowly let his huge body down from the driver's bench.

A soldier, standing there in armor polished to a shine, clutched a spear in one hand. It took no more than a glance to see that he had better equipment than these adventurers.

I guess he ought to—he's dressed for war, Priestess thought.

Unlike adventurers, who could afford to fight only when the mood or the need took them, soldiers had to be ready for anything at any time, even in moments of peace.

Priestess pulled out the rank tag hanging from a chain around her neck. "Will this do, sir?"

General travelers needed an official travel pass, but presumably proof of membership in a trade guild would do as well.

"Can you write?" the soldier inquired, taking a quick glance at Priestess's tag, to which she nodded. This was the first time she had ever been subject to such an interrogation, and while she was nervous, she was also definitely curious.

The soldier produced a thick book containing line after line of people's names and where they were staying.

"Put your name and destination here, then."

"Yes, sir. Er...may I write that I'm here on bodyguard work?"

"If you're an adventurer."

Priestess, still somewhat ambivalent, took a feather pen and ink and inscribed a series of rough but careful characters.

More people were coming and going in the capital than she could ever have imagined. If they needed manpower to oversee all of it... well, then it was no wonder the army needed taxes to support it.

"I see you've also got a dwarf, an elf, and...a lizardman?"

"Indeed, sir," Lizard Priest said, putting his palms together. "I believe you will find my name difficult to pronounce, but perhaps you do not mind?"

"Yeah, that's fine... Not that unusual with other tribes and races."

"Then, if I may excuse myself." A rough, scaly hand appeared, and Priestess politely offered him the pen and book with a smile.

High Elf Archer, watching Lizard Priest write with unexpected facility, flicked her ears. "Okay, me next! I'll even be nice enough to write for the dwarf!"

"What a child," Dwarf Shaman said in annoyance, but nonetheless, he stood by and watched High Elf Archer write his name in the unique, flowing script of the elves.

So they submitted one by one to the entry inspection. The soldiers didn't seem especially on guard; perhaps they were simply used to demi-humans by now. Or perhaps the unexpected was the most normal thing of all when it came to adventurers.

".........And just what are you?"

"I am an adventurer," Goblin Slayer answered shortly, tossing the soldier his rank tag. Perhaps he had resigned himself to the idea that showing the tag would be quicker than trying to explain himself... Or maybe he thought this way was the least confusing.

The soldier caught the tag as it arced through the air and regarded it skeptically. Priestess recognized it as the look of a man trying to sniff out counterfeit currency and thought, *If it were a coin, he would bite it.*

"...You're not trying to pull one over on me, are you?"

"The Guild has recognized me," Goblin Slayer said bluntly, unfazed by the man's sustained suspicion.

The soldiers looked at one another then held a whispered conference.

"You aren't by any chance a dark elf or something, are you?"

"I'm not," Goblin Slayer said, raising the visor of his helmet. "And I have an elf in my party."

"That 'elf' girl could be wearing makeup and stick-on ears for all we know."

Hopeless, Priestess thought with a sigh. High Elf Archer shrugged, equally fed up. Was it going a little too far to think maybe he could do with being a bit friendlier?

You know what, I think that's exactly what I'll say. With that thought, Priestess took a step forward and opened her mouth, but—

"In the name of the Supreme God," came a sultry voice. It emerged from the carriage window, and not just Priestess, but all the soldiers, turned wide-eyed at the sound of it. "I vouch that he is a Silver-ranked adventurer."

"M-milady archbishop...!"

She was leaning against the window frame, emphasizing the soft curves of her body; the soldiers swallowed and stood up straighter.

Was there any man alive who wouldn't be anxious if he were fixed with that smile and those—unseeing—eyes?

"P-please pardon our indiscretion. You may proceed directly inside!"

Sword Maiden smiled gently and nodded, but she seemed to be privately sighing inside that abundant chest. Priestess, for her part, felt she could sympathize.

They say that privilege is power, but it would be so easy to abuse it...

Sword Maiden, however, let none of this show on her face. She stretched a thin, beautiful arm out of the carriage, reaching out to one of the soldiers.

"Procedure is procedure, isn't it?" she said. "Would you be so kind as to give me the book?"

"Y-yes, ma'am! Immediately! Y-you there, write faster...!"

"All right," Goblin Slayer said, sliding the pen along the page.

Priestess pouted helplessly, but when she glanced over, she saw his scrawl running along the line. In the letters, just discernible one from the other, she suddenly felt an odd sense of closeness to him.

"Will this do?"

"Hrmph, fine...!" The soldier swept up the book and hurriedly offered it through the window of the carriage. Sword Maiden took it and flipped the pages, somehow uncertain; her attendant helped her.

Priestess took all this in then looked aside to where Goblin Slayer was standing. He stared up at the massive gate as if not really thinking about anything in particular.

"...Anything wrong?" Priestess asked, looking up at him.

"No," Goblin Slayer said with a slow shake of his head. "I was thinking *So this is the capital.*"

"Ah…" Priestess followed his gaze upward. The gate was so tall it hurt her neck trying to look all the way up. "…Me, I've never been here before. What about you, Goblin Slayer, sir?"

"It will be my first time as well," he said softly. "I always wanted to bring my older sister here one day."

Priestess felt her heart grow warm. The warmth spread to her cheeks.

"I'm sure you'll get a chance sometime," she said.

Goblin Slayer was silent for a moment. Then the helmet shook slowly again. "It would be nice to get a chance."

Not long after, the paperwork was finally over. Goblin Slayer and the others walked through the gate and entered the capital.

OF THE HOYDEN WHO WANTED TO GO ON AN ADVENTURE

"Argh, my big brother's the worst!" The girl danced on the bed, her hands pounding the blankets. "He gets to go here, there, and everywhere, while I'm not even allowed to go outside!"

"He can't help that, right? It's his job."

"But they say the fiery stone from heaven fell on the mount..."

"Were you not told not to speak of that so carelessly?" Her friend and servant, the person who took care of her affairs, gave her a strained look. It was the same expression the girl got every time she complained about her older brother who hurried from one place to the next.

It only made sense that the woman should find the girl's rants discomfiting, given that the girl's brother *was* her employer. The child knew that perfectly well, but human nature kept her from really accepting it.

"Big Brother, he used to be an adventurer, but when I say *I* want to be an adventurer, he gets all upset."

"That's because he knows the evil and the painful as well as the good."

Bah. He hadn't even taken an arrow to the knee. The girl puffed out her cheeks and gazed out the window.

Even from the earliest hours of the morning, an immense stream of people came and went from the capital. Every kind of person came from everywhere in the world, for every conceivable reason. She would never get to experience it, locked up in this room her whole life.

"Lucky them..."

"Are you truly so eager to go outside?"

"Well, sure I am," the girl replied immediately, rolling over on her bed.

"It's not all good things out there," her friend said diffidently.

One outrageous plan after another went through the girl's head as she glared at the ceiling. She had heard stories of towns where girls were *expected* to leave home at a certain age, almost as a rite of passage. So why shouldn't she—and why shouldn't she become an adventurer?

Maybe one day I'll kick those walls down. As if I could.

Everyone has had similar fantasies. Most, of course, never act on them. They know that so many fail and meet trouble in the process.

But then, no one who doesn't act on those fantasies can ever succeed. Neither Fate nor Chance can tell you how the dice will land; the only thing you can do is roll them.

Only those who had never rolled the dice, the girl thought, *could sit and offer platitudes.* But at the moment, she wasn't even allowed to roll the dice. It rankled her terribly.

I hate it when people just make decisions for me.

Decisions about the future, about what she could do, about the world—about everything.

One day, she would likely be betrothed and then married. It was more or less unavoidable, and she knew that.

But I haven't seen anything yet.

She'd heard the world was overflowing with damage caused by goblins. She had heard songs about a hero who assaulted a fortress atop a mountain of ice to rescue a damsel in distress. The king and his ministers and the court mages and the army, they had all known about the goblins, yet none of them had done anything.

Because they had never seen it, I'm sure.

Even her brother—he said he had once been an adventurer, but he refused to share any stories of his adventures with her. He had probably just let his party members protect him. In all likelihood, he hadn't been all that important.

He probably didn't even know anything about goblins.

"Hmm... That makes sense."

She couldn't decide because she had never seen.

She had to see for herself and then make a choice.

The gods might be the ones who rolled the dice, but it was she who decided what to do.

"...Tell me, you said *your* big brother is a merchant, right?"

"Yes. Though he's my cousin. He leaves the moment they open the gate every morning, makes his sales, and then comes home," her friend explained, apparently under the impression that the mercurial girl's thoughts had already turned to other things.

"Huh," the girl said, crossing her arms where she sat on the bed. Her mind bounced from one thing to the next.

Then suddenly, her friend looked out the window and said, "Oh my."

"What's going on?"

"It seems your honorable brother has returned home."

"Really?!"

"Yes, I see his carriage there." Almost before her friend was finished speaking, the girl had jumped out of bed. She ignored the woman's attempts to make her change and went flying out of the room.

Passing servants looked at her in amazement; then they would realize whom it was and simply sigh in resignation.

"Welcome home, Big Brother!"

She greeted him as warmly as she could, thinking:

Now he'll never suspect I'm going to sneak out tonight.

©Noboru Kannatuki

CHAPTER 4

CITY ADVENTURE

After they had passed through three separate massive portcullises, the party emerged into a dizzying bustle.

The first thing they saw was crop fields, probably dating from before the building of the castle walls. A lengthy aqueduct connected to a large building puffing smoke.

The idyllic scene, though, contrasted sharply with the milling crowds of people.

The path soon changed to flagstone and was swallowed up by the ancient town. People hurried down the path like a flood. Whispering voices and the scuff of sandals on stone combined until they sounded almost musical.

"A-are you sure there isn't a festival…?" Priestess asked, her eyes nearly spinning.

High Elf Archer giggled and flicked her ears. "This is about how it usually is," she said. "Human cities are always so busy, I'm pretty used to it by now." Then she flinched uncomfortably. "I have to admit, though… This place does seem a little more cramped than a lot of other towns."

She was right about that. There were at least as many people inside the gate as outside. People pushed their way along the streets; dressed in the latest fashions, they made each road look like a river of color.

Standing on either side of the flagstone street were buildings, both

those that had been there since antiquity and those recently, or sometimes repeatedly, refurbished. The capital had no ceiling, but the mess
of pathways winding around the castle town made it feel a bit like a
dungeon. Perhaps a city that was thousands of years old wasn't so different from one of those ancient ruins.

"Say, milords an' ladies. How about a little help finding your way
around?" A man, hunched over with age, approached them with an
old lantern in hand.

Many large cities had guides like him. The students learning
magic helped light the city's streetlights, but many smaller pathways
remained pitch black.

"We do not have trouble seeing in the dark," Goblin Slayer replied
before Priestess could say anything.

The man blinked but then took in the elf, dwarf, and lizardman.
"No, I s'pose not," he said with a laugh. "Pardon me very much. If you
should need me, call anytime…"

Then, still smiling pleasantly, the old man shuffled away into the
dark.

"Awful inconvenient being a human, huh? You can't even see in
dark places," High Elf Archer opined as she watched him go. "I wonder what happens when he can't get customers."

"Turns tour guide, I'll bet," Dwarf Shaman said knowingly, looking on with great interest. "Doesn't help to see in the dark if you don't
know where you're going."

Lizard Priest looked around, taking in the millennia-old town as he
ran the carriage along a series of wheel ruts. "Well then, milady archbishop. What do you intend to do now?"

"That's a good question," Sword Maiden said with curiosity from
inside the carriage. "I'd like to ask you to take me to the temple, but
have you been to the capital before?"

"To my grave shame, I must admit this is my first time." Lizard
Priest rolled his eyes in his head and opened his jaws happily. "As it is,
I might suspect, for everyone in our party."

"Then, would you be so kind as to direct the carriage where I tell
you?" She sounded almost happy.

From beside her, her acolyte said reprovingly, "Milady archbishop, you need not lower yourself to personally providing—"

Sword Maiden's luscious lips relaxed into a smile. "Many of the streets around here have names, but so few have signs to tell you what they are." *This place wasn't built with travelers in mind.* She giggled. The sound came from somewhere deep in her throat. "I can at least serve as our guide—so that's something."

The adventurers walked casually alongside the carriage as it rumbled along the rutted streets. It seemed they would never get lost following the instructions of the blind Sword Maiden.

It was twilight, the sky starting to turn purple, and the crowding of the capital was especially intense. Being with the carriage allowed them to walk down the middle of the road, but otherwise, they would have been crushed in the crowd. Residents of the capital walked around like they owned the place—which was fair enough—but travelers showed no special regard for other people, either.

The glut of buildings and surrounding fortified walls made the air turgid, and the sun hardly reached street level. It felt as if, were you to get lost in the dark, you would never find your way again. That much was true.

But...

As they looked around, they saw the smoke of cookfires drifting from houses here and there; they smelled dinner being readied. They saw men leaving work and heading for places of drink and merriment. Women trying to attract the men to their various establishments.

Some old men, who had the time to get into their cups early, were sitting by a building on stools, having a competition of some kind. Metal figures of swordsmen were placed on a board with square spaces, and they then moved them about by playing cards.

Some kids noticed them playing, and set up by the roadside with their own little game that they shouted and cheered over. They drew a small circle with spaces in the dirt for a board, using stones for tanks. They moved the stones based on the numbers on their cards; there were occasional shouts of "Long live the King!" at which everyone was apparently required to cheer.

But time is as time does. Mothers called to their sons and daughters, and children answered with "Aww!" but headed home.

The old men watched the kids go, grinned to themselves, and started another game.

By taking five pawns, they could get someone to treat them to a drink—so each of them was bent on winning.

A hawker, meanwhile, held polished, round farsight crystals, claiming they were from another country.

The onset of twilight brought men out to go drinking, and *his* metal helmet followed them closely.

"..."

Priestess scrunched up her eyes, happy for some reason. She liked the scent of people going about their business. The aroma that permeated the air in these few minutes between when the sun began to sink and when it was gone entirely. Be it in village or town, or even in the capital itself, it was always the same.

In her heart, she recited a scripture passage by way of a prayer to the Earth Mother; her steps were light as they headed toward the temple.

It was the first time in her life she had been to the capital. She wasn't immediately enamored, but she certainly didn't dislike it, either.

And then, as she looked around here and there, she found her attention seized by one thing in particular: the students, holding long staves and dressed in black cloaks as they went about the city lighting the lanterns.

Priestess blinked and bit her lip then rushed after the others.

§

The temple—the worship hall of the Supreme God, who governed Order and Chaos—stood in the same quarter of the city as the rest of the houses of worship. It was certainly more elaborate than the Earth Mother's temple in the frontier town, but it couldn't compare with that of the Supreme God in the water town.

It was certainly big, and there were a great many visitors, a crowd of people going in to seek justice despite the hour. And yet it had almost no decorations. Just white walls, a pointed roof, and the sign of the sword and scales…and that was it. A spirit of simplicity in architecture sounded very good, but in practice it turned out rather plain.

"In the capital, it's just one temple out of many," Sword Maiden informed them.

"Is that the story?" High Elf Archer muttered. "I was sure the Great Hero's god would get an especially nice temple."

"Well, even my own residence is in the water town."

The carriage came to a stop, and Sword Maiden's attendant helped her mistress onto the flagstone street. Even though she used the sword and scales like a staff, it was still impressive that she dismounted without so much as a wobble.

"Milady archbishop!"

"You've done well to come here, milady—welcome to our temple!"

A couple of acolytes, presumably brought out by the sound of the carriage, emerged from the temple. One was a boy and one a girl, but both their eyes were sparkling as if they were meeting their hero.

"Thank you," Sword Maiden said, smiling back at them.

Lizard Priest handed the reins to the acolytes as he clambered down from the driver's bench. "Now, to get the luggage… I wonder what we shall do about lodging."

"If you've nowhere to stay, then by all means, please lodge at the temple."

Sword Maiden's attendant was already pulling the luggage down, huffing under the weight. Lizard Priest took the cargo from her easily and lowered it gently to the ground.

"Well!" she exclaimed, her eyes wide, but then she squinted them again and said, "Thank you very much."

"We have several rooms. Please, I insist."

"Hmm. Far be it for me to turn down hospitality. Yes indeed."

Priestess was exchanging greetings with the acolytes. High Elf Archer hopped gracefully down from the top of the carriage. "I'm in. If we're not getting the royal suite anywhere, then it hardly matters where we stay."

"Call it a type of reward. Fine by me—but what do you think,

Beard-cutter?" Dwarf Shaman stroked his white beard and glanced at the setting sun. "You can see it's getting late. My guess is most of the inns around here are full."

"I don't mind," Goblin Slayer said shortly. Then he added, "I have no reason to object."

Sword Maiden clasped the sword and scales tighter to her chest. Only her attendant noticed, and she sighed with a combination of exasperation and amusement.

"There is, however, something I wish to investigate. Do you have a library or the like?"

"We do," Sword Maiden said, almost in a gasp. She spoke as soon as he said *a library or the like*. "I'll show you there immediately. My own authority should be more than enough to allow you access to—"

"Haven't you ever heard the saying 'pleasure before business'? Let's put our bags down and get something to eat!" Dwarf Shaman waved a stubby hand.

"But you just had a meal!" High Elf Archer put in.

"Well, rheas make *me* look temperate," Dwarf Shaman said with a shrug. "How about you, Scaly?"

"I believe it is just about time for me to get a nice, bloodied hunk of meat," Lizard Priest replied, working his jaws and pointedly rubbing his belly with one scaly hand. "If it were to have cheese on it, so much the more fearsome."

"I don't mind," Goblin Slayer said shortly. Then he added, "I have no reason to object."

Sword Maiden clasped the sword and scales tighter to her chest. Only her attendant noticed, and she sighed with a combination of exasperation and amusement.

"...Let it be after you return, then."

"*That's what we'll do. Yes, let's,*" she said under her breath, as if con-firming it for herself.

Goblin Slayer said only, "Yes please," and then his metal helmet turned toward Priestess. "Is that all right with you?"

"Oh yes, uh…" Finished talking with the acolytes, who were about her age, Priestess held her sounding staff in both hands and looked around uncertainly. "Th-there's somewhere I'd like to go…"

"Well now, that's odd," Dwarf Shaman said, his eyes widening beneath his brows. It was strange for this girl, who often seemed so young, yet was so serious, to say such a thing. "You know the way?"

"I do. The address… Well, the way there…they just told me." Her voice trailed off as she looked in the direction of the acolytes, who had already disappeared. "…If you won't let me, I'll understand."

Goblin Slayer's rough-hewn, grimy helmet was impassive in the face of Priestess's beseeching gaze. There was a grunt from inside his expressionless headwear. "Walking solo is dangerous."

High Elf Archer gave an exasperated shrug; he made it sound like she was walking into a dungeon.

"I'll go with her, then," High Elf Archer said. "We should be fine together, right?"

Lizard Priest nodded at the elf as she raised her hand. "We shall split into groups of three and two, then."

"That settles it. Sound good, Beard-cutter?"

Goblin Slayer took in Priestess, still looking at him, and High Elf Archer, with her small chest puffed out. "I don't mind," he said shortly. Then he added, "I have no reason to object."

"I've heard about enough of that," Dwarf Shaman grumbled, but then he rubbed his hands together and smiled. "So, milady archbishop. Any especially delicious restaurants you can recommend?"

Sword Maiden clasped the sword and scales tighter to her chest.

§

They ended up at The Golden Knight, a tavern that had been around since before the founding of the Adventurers Guild.

In the capital, though, the word *tavern* encompassed a number of different types of establishments. There were tea bars and taverns proper, food courts and cantinas.

The Golden Knight outdid them all for sheer revelry.

Once through the door, the visitors were assaulted by a wave of sound. A ranger girl and a warrior in heavy armor were arguing about something; an Eastern-style fighter and a thief girl were watching them.

In another corner, a boy spell caster—he looked like a rookie—took a swig of wine as his party members gathered around and teased him.

One party centered around a human warrior monk but also included a padfoot warrior, a rhea spell caster, and a beautiful ranger.

A female wizard was enjoying a meal with some adventurers who appeared to be her pupils; they showered her with admiring cries of "Teacher, teacher!"

There was a table with a pudgy mage and a medicine woman. They were joined by a knight in armor and helmet and a female fighter; the two latecomers raised their glasses when they arrived...

No doubt such scenes had repeated themselves endlessly, everywhere in the world, ever since people called adventurers had begun to appear. One would expect no less from an establishment that traced its history with adventurers back to the very moment the first Guild was founded.

The number of people seeking adventure had increased dramatically, but all this time later, this remained a place of meetings and partings.

The walls were covered with posts from people seeking parties, as well as parties looking to fill out members they needed.

Over at a table in the corner was a young man, a rookie most likely, his face a mixture of expectation and excitement and apprehension. He must have been nursing dreams of a fateful encounter or an adventure out of legend.

His dreams, though, would not come true.

His brand-new armor and sword, both sparkling; his helmet-less head: all marked him out as a novice warrior. If he knew some magic, that might be one thing, but otherwise, he was likely to just sit on his hands all day.

He would have to give in and approach someone himself, or decide to go solo...

Whichever he chose, it would be on him to make the first move. And if he didn't have it in him to make that move, well, he wasn't going to survive very long as an adventurer.

In the opposite corner, some tables were set up, and some of the tavern's more shiftless residents were alternately cheering and groaning at a game of dice. This wasn't like the games that the elderly and the children had been playing by the roadside; this was serious: money was at stake.

On the wall nearby, the pieces of a broken die were skewered like a criminal's body; it seemed there had been a lead weight inside, and it was being displayed for all to see.

"Ahh, that's a schoolboy cheat," Dwarf Shaman said as he settled into a comfortable seat near the hearth. "Professionals use quicksilver. Lets them pick which way the dice'll fall." He rubbed his stubby fingers together, luxuriating in the aroma drifting from the food in front of him.

Perhaps it was out of recognition that presentation was everything. Perhaps he simply meant to get the most out of all his senses.

There was a boiled egg that had been cooked by being buried in the ashes of a fire, and a sauce of egg yolk, oil, and lemon. There was a stew cooked in a great pot, cream with plenty of cabbage and bacon. As for the entrée, there was a porridge of red snapper fish sauce mixed with giblets. And finally, cooked goose, in the same sauce of yolk, oil, and lemon.

To cleanse the palate, there were honeyed grapes, plums, and apples…

Dwarf Shaman's eyes wandered happily over the feast. He could hardly decide where to look.

"Point is, it's fixed. Bah, leave it to a rhea to go to all that trouble for some measly dice."

"And then there are followers of the god of trade, who use the Luck spell to change the outcome," Lizard Priest said, licking the tip of his nose. "But a roll is a roll. Neither Fate nor Chance has any more to say once the dice are still." His gaze was fixed on a piece of goat cheese.

Dwarf Shaman watched his scaly friend and laughed. "They say not even the gods can change a roll once made."

Four people cheered: a healer and a spell caster, a paladin and a thief. Apparently celebrating the defeat of a demon and the successful conclusion of an adventure. Dwarf Shaman raised a cup in their direction then drained it in acknowledgment of their achievement.

"Got to say, I'm impressed our lovely archbishop knows about a place like this."

"She was herself an adventurer once, or so I hear," Lizard Priest said somberly, inspecting the cheese as carefully as if he was checking the condition of his equipment. "At the time, it seems the owner had relocated from the capital to the northern reaches."

"Huh," Dwarf Shaman said, stroking his white beard. "I suppose that would have been about ten years ago, then."

"Even so," Lizard Priest replied with a slow nod. His long neck made it seem as if he were almost gazing into the past.

Let's see... How old is Scaly, again?

If it was hard to guess Dwarf Shaman's age from his appearance, it was no easier with Lizard Priest. But if he knew about the battle a decade ago...

At that moment, though, Dwarf Shaman's thoughts were interrupted by a voice.

"Evening, sirs. Where might you be from?"

They looked up to see a man with a stringed instrument in hand—a bard or entertainer of some kind—standing and smiling pleasantly at them. Lizard Priest made a strange hands-together gesture toward the man, who showed no sign of consternation at the sight of the lizardman.

"We are from the western frontier," he said.

"I see—the west. Very good, that, very good."

Then the entertainer, who appeared to have something in mind, disappeared into the hustle and bustle of the tavern...

Forever shall her name endure:

Sword Maiden, whom the gods adore

Six Golds, one holy maiden, she:

Just scales, sharp sword, in her hand be

All word-havers love her so

Her prayers give rise to miracles

Among six Golds, she ranged herself

To fight the Demon Lord himself

And now the beast is on his pyre

Guards she the law with equal fire

Forever shall her name endure:

Sword Maiden, whom the gods adore...

The powerful recitation cut through the chatter of the tavern. It told the story of the many adventurers who had beaten back the storm of Death that had come blowing down from the north ten years before. A great many hardened veterans had gathered at the northern fortress to challenge the dungeon there, but it had swallowed them up; they disappeared forever.

Just six people succeeded in attaining this long-sought goal. Some people even referred to them as the Six Heroes, or simply the All-Stars...

Whatever one called them, they were not legends, but true heroes who had appeared in actual history.

"I see. He hopes travelers will be more likely to pay for ballads from home."

"*Clever,*" Lizard Priest murmured and put some change on the table for the bard to collect the next time he came by.

"...So you're saying that after the fighting calmed down, The Golden Knight came back here to the capital, too."

Meaning the keeper of this place must know our archbishop as well as we do, or better.

Dwarf Shaman spared an interested glance in the direction of the barkeep then burped, his breath smelling of alcohol.

"And you, Beard-cutter—you look worried about something."

"…" Goblin Slayer didn't answer immediately. He took a hearty helping of stew, mixing it around with his spoon before sliding it through his visor.

Cabbage and bacon simmered in cream. Goblin Slayer tilted his head curiously.

It did not taste like the stew he ate at home.

"You can tell?" he asked.

"Or close enough," Dwarf Shaman snorted, pouring himself plenty of wine. "It's been a year since this party formed. If humans live an average of fifty years, we've been working together for one-fiftieth of your life."

"That's nothing to sneeze at." Dwarf Shaman underscored the point by taking a gulp of wine. He wiped some droplets from his mustache then went after the goose's thigh, taking a big bite.

Goblin Slayer watched the dwarf closely as he drank and ate in turn.

"…We have not been focused on goblin slaying lately."

"A seabound adventure, then bodyguard work—although we did have that ambush. You are correct," Lizard Priest said, nodding as he gleefully reached out for the cheese.

Dwarf Shaman laughed and waved a hand; so rather than cut just a single piece of cheese, Lizard Priest simply gathered the entire wheel to himself. "Sweet nectar!" he exclaimed, pounding his tail on the floor.

Dwarf Shaman sucked the bones clean, licked his fingers, wiped his mouth, and went for his next helping of meat.

"It was fun."

Both of them stopped.

Dwarf Shaman and Lizard Priest set down their respective meals and looked at each other.

They shared a glance, nodded, then both shook their heads before they looked back at the cheap metal helmet glimmering in the firelight.

"But in both cases, the shadow of goblins was near at hand," Goblin Slayer said softly, a cupful of wine in his hand. He drained the contents in a single gulp then said with a sort of groan, "And if so, then perhaps *that* is not my duty."

©Noboru Kannatuki

"Duty?"

"Yes," Goblin Slayer nodded at Dwarf Shaman. "I am Goblin Slayer."

There was a noisy crackling of the fire, audible even over the sound of the crowd. A strange silence pervaded, as if they and they alone had been cut out of a picture. In the background, the bard had switched at some point to a ballad about the frontier hero Goblin Slayer assaulting a frozen mountain.

"Hmm." Dwarf Shaman stroked his beard and looked up at the ceiling. He wondered how long, how many centuries, it had been there, to grow so blackened with wine and blood and smoke. Was it the sea he saw there, or the stars? Whichever, it was something much older than any one human life.

After a long moment, Dwarf Shaman smiled as if he were about to reveal the secret to a magic trick. "D'you know how smiths temper a sword?"

"...No," Goblin Slayer said after a moment's thought. "I don't."

"All right, well, let me tell you." Dwarf Shaman began counting off on his rough, small fingers. "They heat it. They pound on it. They chill it. And then they heat it again."

"...Heat, pound, chill, heat," Goblin Slayer parroted quietly.

"S'right." Dwarf Shaman crossed his arms. "The process requires each and every step. Whatever else you do to it, you have to do those four things."

"It seems most labor-intensive," Lizard Priest offered.

"Doesn't it, though?" Dwarf Shaman grinned, as satisfied as if he had done the work himself. "A soft sword is supple but doesn't fight well. A hard one can cut but will break before long. So what's a good sword?" Dwarf Shaman was murmuring almost as if he were reciting a spell, but his voice carried as he took a sip of wine to wet his lips. "Cut with a sword and the blade starts to chip. But polish it up, and you've less steel to wield. And all steel's just a speck of history's dew. So what's a good sword?"

"..." Goblin Slayer listened silently. He looked like a child, sitting by the fire and listening to his grandfather tell tales. So when he finally spoke, the directness of what he said was surprising. "I don't know."

"Of course you don't. And it's fine to live without knowing." Dwarf

Shaman squinted his eyes, running his thick fingers along his belly. "The secrets of steel are many, and complex."

The fire crackled loudly again. A log could be heard to split, and the attentive barkeep came over a moment later. He stirred the flame with a poker; Lizard Priest watched him closely until he left. Then he opened his jaws and let out a laugh that came from deep in his throat.

"Heh-heh, master spell caster, you sound like a monk yourself."

"How about a word of guidance from a professional, then? For poor, lost Beard-cutter here."

"Hmm, yes, well, that will be most difficult." Lizard Priest's eyes rolled in his head, and he held up a metal skewer. He took some cheese he had sliced off with his claws, stuck it on the end of the skewer, and put it in the fire. "Few are the things that are incumbent upon all people to do."

Turn, turn. He twisted the metal skewer. The cheese was still solid enough to retain its shape.

"To live, and to die with all one's attention, that is what one must do. And that is more than difficult enough."

The lump of cheese was beginning to grill up, but it was still hard. It wasn't ready yet.

"Even the beasts of the field cannot live precisely the way they wish. How much less those who have words."

At last the cheese had reached its limit. It threatened to drip off the skewer. It was time.

"To worry and to feel lost are well and good. I believe those very things are life itself."

Lizard Priest whisked the skewer out of the fire and stuffed the food, still hot, into his mouth.

"Ahh, sweet nectar!" It was the same tone he used when praising his ancestors. A full-throated cry of joy.

"Hmph." Dwarf Shaman snorted, and then he reached for the goose again. "Sounds like what I was saying."

"Which means that it may indeed be close to truth."

Goblin Slayer suddenly remembered hearing something of the sort long ago. It was when he had been kicked into an icy river, his hands tied behind him.

"Sink down deep! Then kick!" the rhea yowled, gesturing madly with his dagger. *"Do that, and you'll be able to float! Then do it again and again! Otherwise, all that awaits you is death!"*

He had been right.

If Goblin Slayer hadn't kicked then, he wouldn't be here now.

"...I see."

Then this probably was indeed close to truth.

"I much agree," Lizard Priest said with a nod.

"That's how it is," Dwarf Shaman added.

"You are...right."

Goblin Slayer brought some of the cabbage and bacon to his mouth. It didn't taste bad at all.

§

Stones stood in quiet rows there, like islands floating in a sea of fallen leaves that persisted no matter how carefully they were cleaned. It felt as if there was nothing to do in that place but kick one's way through red and gold waves, relying on the numbers etched upon those markers to guide one.

They were graves.

The markers stood, organized by the careful numerology of the clerics of the God of Knowledge.

Deep in the graveyard, Priestess stood by a new tombstone—well, not *so* new; it had been there for at least a year.

The name carved on the stone was one she held dear, though she had only heard it for a single day in her life.

Even though each of the stones was carved to a specific and identical size, this one seemed so...*like* her. Even if Priestess found her image fuzzy when she closed her eyes and tried to picture her.

"...I'm sorry it took me so long," she whispered in a trembling voice. She sank to her knees, heedless of the dirt, then brushed her palm along the tombstone. "...I'm sorry."

In spite of it all, that young wizard girl had been one of Priestess's first party members.

©Noboru Kannatuki

It was a story of *ifs*.

If they had decided to hunt rats and not goblins for that first quest, what would have happened?

Would everyone have survived? Would she and the young man and the women still be adventuring together?

Would they have grown to care for one another? To know one another's likes, dislikes, and interests?

Perhaps. But now all of that was lost.

All of it had been stolen from her.

All those many days and months that should have been had been wiped away, and now, instead, Priestess was here.

Priestess, who adventured with High Elf Archer, Dwarf Shaman, Lizard Priest, and *him*.

She could hardly think of it as good luck. Yet, at the same time, she couldn't imagine considering it ill fortune, either.

Fortune and misfortune, she realized, were inseparable, like milk mixed into tea.

"I'll keep hunting the goblins. Still." Priestess's lips softened as she spoke. "I'll do it even if I tremble the whole time, the way you scolded me for."

That was right. Priestess must have looked ridiculous to this girl, who had been so ready, so into it. She suddenly found herself remembering the girl's squinted eyes and drawn mouth as she shouted.

No doubt she had had other expressions, but Priestess hadn't gotten to see them.

"I met your younger brother, you know... I actually became the teacher, believe it or not."

"Don't be mad, okay?" Priestess whispered. *I may not know much, but I taught him what I could.*

In the end, Priestess hadn't brought flowers or fruit or anything else as an offering. She realized she didn't know what the young woman liked or didn't like. But she did know she seemed like the type who would be upset if a person picked some random item to leave at her grave.

Thus Priestess simply whispered, "I'll visit again," and stood gingerly.

"...Who's in there?" High Elf Archer asked, her ears twitching. She stood a short distance away in the shade of a tree, her arms crossed.

"An old—" Priestess started, but she had to close her mouth once and open it again before she could come up with "—party member."

"Huh," High Elf Archer said quietly. She came over, her footsteps light, asking, "What was she like?"

"...I've often wondered that myself," Priestess said, sounding a bit detached, an ambiguous expression on her face.

There was a gust of cool night breeze that made the leaves dance in the trees, and she reached up to keep her cap and hair from blowing everywhere.

"I never even had the time to find out."

"That happens sometimes," High Elf Archer said, squinting with pleasure as she felt the cool breeze on her cheek. She lifted her face up as if sniffing the wind, exposing her pale, slim neck. "The ties that bind us can be really strange. Sometimes it's for a long time, others, just a short while."

"...You're right."

"So they're all gone now?"

For a second, Priestess didn't quite understand; she cocked her head in perplexity. Then, however, she grasped what High Elf Archer was asking. "No," she replied with a bitter smile that somehow made her uncomfortable. "One of them is left. But..."

"But what?"

"...I just can't work up the courage to see her."

Priestess's voice grew smaller and smaller as she spoke, until it faded into the rustling of the trees.

There was nothing an elf's ears couldn't hear, though, and now High Elf Archer's wiggled. "I'll bet you don't need to worry about it as much as you think." The elf whispered, *"Not like it's all your fault, I'm sure."*

"...I don't want to blame everyone else for it."

"Always so earnest." High Elf Archer sniffed disinterestedly at Priestess's awkward smile. She was starting to think she had an idea why the girl was so infatuated with "Goblin Slayer, sir."

She didn't know if the reason was good or bad and had no intention of giving it any thought.

"…Okay, well, let's go stop being serious!" She dragged Priestess away by the hand, laughing aloud at the girl's astonished expression.

§

"W-wow…"

Priestess had spent most of her time since arriving in the capital being shocked, but, well, there were a great many things she had never seen before.

Now they were in a spacious, cool lobby, with a ceiling that vaulted high above them. The skylight let in the illumination of the stars and the moons; combined with the candles below, it was perfectly easy to see inside the room.

A stream of people in comfortable clothes came and went, relaxing and enjoying themselves. Some sat on benches, reading books; others were working out, holding heavy stones in their hands; still others were drinking to their hearts' content…

Some people had spread cards on a table in the corner and were fighting the Black Death as it spread across a game board.

Someone else was looking at a fresco of an armored warrior the likes of which Priestess had never seen, accompanied by the letters *SPELLJAMMER*. In a corner of the picture was the name of a theater and a date, and she realized it must be promoting a play.

She didn't see any kind of fireplace, yet the room was surprisingly warm.

"There are pipes in the walls to bring in warm air," a staff member told the goggling Priestess with a chuckle. Priestess quickly bowed her head toward the employee, who was wrapped in pure white cloth.

"S-sorry, it's just very unusual…"

"I'd heard about the baths, but I didn't realize how much else there was here," High Elf Archer said with an intrigued wiggle of her ears. She was the one who had dragged Priestess here.

Looks like she likes it here already, Priestess thought, giggling to herself.

Elves always washed in cold water; they had little experience of deliberately using steam or heating water as part of the bathing process. This friend of Priestess's, despite being so much older than her, always followed that same custom, with the exception of the hot spring the one time.

The building attached to the aqueduct, which had drawn Priestess's attention the moment she reached the capital, turned out to be a huge bathing facility. And it was, she suspected, much better to enjoy oneself at a bath than to sit and mourn in a graveyard.

"There sure is. The workout area is open, and we also offer massage, as well as light refreshments."

"I'm sorry, but how much—?" Priestess was concerned: she mustn't waste her money. But the employee simply smiled.

"It's all included with your entrance fee. Please, relax and enjoy yourself."

Priestess nodded eagerly, reflecting once more that the capital was truly an amazing place. She paid the handful of bronze coins then took a fresh look around to discover that indeed, very few people appeared to be using money.

Well, with one exception.

It appeared to be a massive bottle of water, set as if being offered up by a statue of a deity with the face of both a man and a woman. Carved on the statue was the inscription DONATIONS FOR THE DEITY OF THE BASIN, and there was a wooden box with a slot for offerings.

Children shouted and dropped coins into the box; when they did so, water poured from the bottle all by itself.

"That's *awesome!*"

Naturally, one of the girls went flying over to it—namely, High Elf Archer. Her ears stood straight up, and her eyes sparkled, and she got to the statue as quickly as if she were running through the woods.

"Hey, how's this work?"

"What, you don't know?" A boy hardly ten years of age sassed an elf of more than two thousand. "You put in your money, then something happens inside, and then the lid opens and the water comes out!"

"Cool...!"

The boy was flippant, and his explanation was really no explanation at all, but High Elf Archer was already loosening the strings of her purse.

Priestess let her shoulders relax as she listened to the coin clink into the box. The weight she had felt in her small chest until just earlier seemed almost halfway gone.

I know they say people never feel the same way for an entire hour...

Now she felt like living proof. It made her part lonely and part relieved.

And all of it was because she had a friend to drag her around like this.

"...Hee-hee."

That was what made room in her heart for a chuckle to well up from within.

Priestess looked around, planning to just take everything in until High Elf Archer got bored.

There was a path leading to a changing room, a washroom, the exercise area—she assumed the baths were past the changing room. They couldn't keep the others waiting forever while they played, but maybe they could have a little meal. And after a dip in the baths, she'd at least like a nice cold drink...

Hmm. She tapped a slim, pale finger to her chin in thought, but then suddenly she blinked.

Am I being watched?

She detected an intense, almost piercing gaze on her. It was just a feeling, a sensation she probably wouldn't even have noticed a year earlier.

Priestess kept herself turned in the direction of High Elf Archer, who was standing in front of the water bottle yammering, and carefully moved only her eyes.

...A soldier, maybe?

The owner of the gaze was sitting on a bench; the person looked rather military. The touch of grime on them—maybe they were fresh off duty—suggested why they had come to the baths.

But did I do anything wrong...?

She didn't think she had done anything to warrant the attention of a soldier, not since coming to the capital and certainly not since coming into the bathhouse. Increasingly uncomfortable, though, Priestess slid closer to High Elf Archer and tugged on her elbow.

"Um..."

"Hmm? Hang on a second. Just one more time...!"

"No, I think we should get going, okay?" A thought flashed through Priestess's mind: *She's hopeless.* It was a bit like the thought she often had about *him*, although not quite the same, and it made her smile. "We need time for a bath, and...you'll use up all your money."

The two of them only headed for the changing room, though, after High Elf Archer had offered three more donations.

They followed the path running by the female face of the twin-sexed deity and soon found the women's changing room. They found a small cold bath, the walls to either side of which had stools and several rows of cubbyholes.

It was already evening, and they weren't the first guests; Priestess and High Elf Archer soon undressed. There were plenty of humans in the capital, of course, but there were also dwarves and rheas about, so there was no particular need to be self-conscious. It was also surprisingly warm (the pipes, no doubt, as had been explained to them), so they weren't concerned about catching cold.

"Okay, here..." Priestess, looking at the other cubbies for her cues, folded her vestments and put them in a basket. Her slim frame had become noticeably more muscular over a year of adventuring, but she was still willowy. Beside her, High Elf Archer practically tore off her clothes and flung them in a basket.

"They'll get wrinkled if you don't fold them properly," Priestess chided her.

"Aw, I don't care," High Elf Archer said, seeming genuinely indifferent as she waved a hand and her ears at the same time. "Hey. Come to think of it, did you bring any perfume oil?"

"Uh-huh. I asked our receptionist for advice about it once, and, uh, well, the one I got was slightly expensive, but..."

Her uncertain tone seemed to seek approval for this small luxury, and High Elf Archer giggled. "That's fine. It's not like you're wearing it just to show off. I don't think the gods are going to mind."

"...I think maybe you should pay a little more attention to what the gods will and won't mind."

"Ooh, a scolding! You should learn to have more respect for your elders."

"Huh?! Hey, stop that—Ooh...!"

High Elf Archer had reached out to poke Priestess with a finger, and the girls fell to shouting and giggling.

Then, the elf's sharp eyes settled on Priestess's basket of clothes.

"Are you still using that?"

"Huh?"

Priestess followed High Elf Archer's gaze to the suit of mail. She had repaired it wherever it had been cut or slashed or stabbed, leaving little seams between the old and new chains. She kept it diligently oiled, and anyone could see at a glance how careful she was with it.

"Oh yes, I am. It's...very important to me."

"You make it sound like it's some legendary armor or something." High Elf Archer looked at Priestess from lidded eyes, and the younger girl scratched her cheek shyly.

She's definitely spent too much time around Orcbolg.

That was very bad for this young (certainly young from an elf's perspective) girl's education, wasn't it?

Almost as soon as the thought crossed the elf's mind, though, she dismissed it with a smile and a flick of her ears.

I guess it's a little late for that.

Goblin hunting itself was bound to be bad for one's upbringing.

"What's going on?"

"Oh, nothing. Nothing at all." High Elf Archer waved a hand at Priestess then suddenly smiled as a new thought came to her. "Since we're here, how about we wash each other's backs?"

"Sure!"

§

So the two of them chattered noisily as they washed, perfumed themselves, rinsed off, and set off for the baths.

The bathing area was equally warm, thanks to the pipe system; there was one large hot bath and, across from it, a cold tub. Farther in, there was a sauna where it was even hotter.

"I'll be right back!" High Elf Archer said and jogged away, leaving Priestess by herself.

She slid into the water with a quiet splash, stretched out her arms and legs, and let out a luxurious breath. It mingled with the warm air and drifted up to the domed ceiling.

Gee, I could almost just fall asleep here...

She felt like the heated water might soak through her whole body, and she might just melt away. She stretched out a pale arm, not thinking much of it, and noticed that there was some muscle there, even if not much. And she could see scars, whiter even than her skin, running along a few places.

Experience was not normally so visible to the naked eye, but these scars were certainly part of hers.

When she thought about it, it had been two solid years of running around, the occasional day off notwithstanding.

That first adventure, her first party, the goblin nest, her party members dying, and then him.

Again, she felt a welter of emotions she still didn't fully understand welling up in her chest.

But...

Priestess glanced in the direction of the sauna High Elf Archer had run into and squinted.

I really should be grateful.

"...Hey."

"Huh?!"

The unexpected voice interrupting her reverie nearly sent Priestess jumping clear out of the water. She rushed to cover her chest and turned around, and she found a girl looking at her wide-eyed.

She had golden hair that went down to her shoulders, blue eyes, and she was fifteen—no, maybe sixteen—years old.

Priestess, however, could only blink at her. Something felt...off. The girl in front of her seemed to feel the same way.

"Oh," Priestess said, looking into the girl's startled eyes.

It was a face she rarely saw except perhaps in the Temple's reflecting pool, but there it was. The other girl seemed to have more lustrous hair. Her skin was prettier, though she was puffier. Tall, too. But...

We do look similar.

Yes, the other girl was obviously superior. But there was a similarity.

Priestess, growing embarrassed, slid back down into the bath. The other girl was like an improved version of herself.

"Can I...help you?"

"You're an adventurer, right?" The words came down like a judgment from above—which maybe only made sense, since the girl was standing up.

When Priestess nodded in the affirmative, the girl said, "Thought so," nodded with self-assurance, and sat down. Her breasts made water splash aside as she climbed in; Priestess glanced down at the sight. The gods were so unfair.

"Hey, what's your class?"

"I'm a servant of the Earth Mother."

"A priest, huh?" *Not bad.*

Priestess looked curiously at the mumbling girl. "If you're hoping to find someone to join your group, I'm afraid I've already got a party..."

"Huh?" the other girl said, surprised, but then she said, "Oh, no, no. Not what I was thinking."

Then what, I wonder?

Not being able to guess what the other person wanted left Priestess suspicious and worried. She doubted she was in real physical danger here, but she also didn't have a scrap of clothing to defend her. She stiffened slightly, still keeping her chest hidden. She didn't get any bad vibes from this girl, yet...

"I wanted to ask, just for my reference—what kind of equipment do you use? What's your rank?"

"Uh, I'm Steel-ranked. And...my equipment?"

Priestess focused more closely on the other girl, who had suddenly slid much closer. Priestess was a far cry from a warrior, but she thought the other girl didn't look much more physically hardened herself. A wizard—or cleric, perhaps? An adventurer hopeful? That possibility struck her as the most likely as soon as it crossed her mind.

…I wonder if I should try to stop her.

It was only a possibility. But all her own experiences flashed through her mind.

Then again, though, everything that had happened to her since that time, she had gotten from adventuring. She couldn't deny that—nor should she.

"I wear clerical vestments and carry a sounding staff, and I use mail."

"Hmm," the other girl said. "Do they have, y'know, holy power or a blessing on them or something?"

"No, they're just…a normal staff and mail, really."

Still, she had first bought the armor because of the advice he had given her. Thinking about it, she realized that even in the battle in the sewer, the mail had saved her life.

The other girl watched Priestess brush her own shoulder with her palm and grumbled, "Eh, guess that's the best you can hope for as an eighth-rank."

Priestess pursed her lips at the girl's condescending tone. "You don't like it?"

"Huh? Don't like what?"

She looked so thoroughly perplexed that Priestess spared her any follow-up. A moment later, the girl jumped up out of the bath. "Anyway, thanks. I'll keep it in mind."

"Uh, sure…"

Should I say something to her…?

Was it just a grandmotherly busybody-ness that motivated her—or was it a handout from the gods? The moment of anxiety and indecision set off an alarm in her heart: *Don't let her go like that. You have to offer her something. But what?*

Even the gods couldn't say what the dice would do when they fell.

Priestess swallowed heavily; when she spoke, she found her voice shaking unaccountably.

"…Um, if you're going to become an adventurer, you should prepare… I mean, make sure to do your shopping and such, okay?"

"Wha?" Again, that uncomprehending expression. The girl thought for a moment then nodded. "You're right, shopping is—it's important."

Then the girl set off at a brisk clip, all but kicking up the water from the pool. Priestess trailed her shapely form with her eyes then sank into the bath up to her nose. She blew listless bubbles in the water.

"Phew! Ooh, just got a rush of blood to the head, I think. It's wild in there."

At that moment, High Elf Archer came back, slapping her cherry-red cheeks with her hands. Moving the long ears that were a trademark of her people, she looked after the girl Priestess had just been talking to.

"Who was that just now?"

"Er… No idea." That was all Priestess could say. That was all there was to say.

High Elf Archer looked a bit suspicious but then exclaimed, "Ah well," and plopped into the water. "So, whatcha wanna do? Want to check out the back there? I'm just gonna hang out here for a few minutes."

"No…" Priestess thought for a moment then slowly shook her head. "…Let's head out."

§

When they got back to the changing room, they were surprised to discover how refreshed they felt despite the warm air. They toweled themselves off, perfumed themselves again, and dabbed off the sweat before heading to change.

"I wish I brought a fresh set of clothes to change into," Priestess remarked.

"That's the way it goes," High Elf Archer said. "We weren't planning on this. You can change when we get back, right?"

They walked along, their bare feet pattering on the stones, when…

"Huh?" Priestess piped up suddenly, rubbing her eyes. Her basket was gone. She knew where it should be; it had been right next to the one in which High Elf Archer had casually tossed her hunting garb.

"That's weird," High Elf Archer said. "Wonder if somebody moved it."

"But I'm sure it was right here..."

In place of her vestments, she found what seemed to be a soldier's outfit, dirty and sweaty, stuffed into the basket. Priestess looked around to make sure her possessions hadn't simply been misplaced somewhere. "What...? What?"

She didn't see them anywhere.

Her voice grew more and more plaintive, and tears began to brim at the corners of her eyes. It felt like she was on the edge of a precipice.

"Stay calm. You're sure you put them here?"

"Yes..."

"Those aren't the kind of clothes anyone would just take by mistake..."

A priestess's vestments, a sounding staff, a cap, and mail. Not easy to mistake for something else.

What was she going to do, what was she going to do? Priestess, feeling as if she might burst into tears, conducted a nervous but futile search of the other baskets.

"Is there a problem?" a white-clothed employee asked, coming over. Priestess's distress must have been obvious. She opened her mouth to say something, but somehow she couldn't quite get the words out.

"Ah, um, m-my, my clothes...!"

"Yes?" the employee responded suspiciously.

"We can't find her clothes," High Elf Archer offered. "She's a priestess of the Earth Mother, see? I don't think anyone would grab her stuff by accident..."

"...Just a moment, please. I'll check with the guard," the staff member said briefly and then left even more quickly than she had arrived.

High Elf Archer held Priestess's hand as they waited; the girl was pale and restless.

"It's okay. I'm sure they'll find your stuff soon."

"I know. Erm, but... But what if...?"

The employee did soon return. "I'm very sorry," she said, her face seriousness itself. "...I'm informed that someone wearing vestments of the Earth Mother did indeed leave here earlier. It's possible that—"

"They were stolen?!" High Elf Archer exclaimed in spite of herself. Priestess felt her mind go blank.

"Ex-excuse me…!" She pushed away High Elf Archer's hand, flying over to the soldier's clothes and pawing through them.

The soldier in the changing room. The young woman who had spoken to her. The "shopping."

Soon she saw more or less what she had expected.

There was the leather pouch she always used as her purse. Sparkling on top of it were several brilliantly polished gems. They were unmistakably fine stones, and their meaning was equally clear.

They were payment for her clothes.

"Oh—urk—m-my—my…!"

The hat she could bear to lose, and the vestments, too. Her rank tag could be reissued. Her sounding staff, as much care as she had given it, could be replaced. And her most important possessions were all back at their rooms, as was a change of clothes. All of that was manageable, as far these things went.

But—her mail was gone.

The item she had saved up for, using the rewards from her first few adventures, the very first armor she had bought for herself, was nowhere to be found.

She had worn it during the battle with the ogre. In the sewers, on the snowy mountain, at her promotion test, and in the rain forest, it had been with her.

It had saved her life. She had repaired it, patched it, taken extensive care of it.

And all for just one reason.

"It was the f-first…thing he ever p-praised me for…!"

The loss of it finally broke Priestess completely. The strength to stand abandoned her, and she all but tumbled to the stone floor.

"M— My— Myyy…! She took it…!"

"…Geez, I… I'm sorry. I wish I'd never thought of coming here," High Elf Archer mumbled softly from beside her friend, who was weeping and choking like a little girl.

"Oooh," Priestess said—not words, exactly—and shook her head vigorously from side to side.

©Noboru Kannatuki

High Elf Archer knelt down and gently, oh so gently, rubbed the back of the first friend she had made in two thousand years.

"…We'll get it back. I promise."

§

The candle in the stand was the only source of light in the dim room, through which echoed an intermittent sound of scraping metal.

There was a bed beside the window. Sitting on the bed was a man in pitiful equipment; he was the source of the sound.

Goblin Slayer worked the whetstone along the blade in a way that was less sharpening and more scraping away the metal. Maybe that was because the weapon was simply a generic item—but no, this man would have treated a legendary sword in exactly the same way.

The polishing stopped for a moment, and the sword, with its strange length, was held up to the light.

Those who had learned just a tiny bit of adventuring from tales and songs might smirk and say knowingly that a sword is actually an expensive club, but they would be wrong.

A sword is for tearing skin, cutting flesh, and shattering bone. Otherwise, why make swords at all?

Only the massive two-handed blades of knights could cut, pierce, smash, and club all at once. They were like a sword, spear, hammer, and pickax all in one.

The weapon Goblin Slayer was holding at that moment, though, was nothing of the sort. It was for piercing the throats of goblins, cutting out their hearts, lopping off their heads. Nothing more and nothing less.

"………"

It had been a little less than an hour since Priestess had come home sniffling. High Elf Archer, her ears drooping unhappily, had been desperately trying to comfort her but didn't seem to be getting anywhere.

What's more, Priestess hadn't been wearing her vestments, but a dirty soldier's outfit that didn't quite fit her. When he asked what had happened, High Elf Archer had replied despondently, "Stolen."

This was neither the frontier town nor the water town. It was the biggest city in the nation. It was full of people, not all of them good-hearted.

Lizard Priest had been transparently furious, as if he might start breathing sulfur and flame at any moment; Dwarf Shaman had merely looked sour.

"Perhaps we can try taking our grievance to the castle t'morrow," he'd suggested, but Priestess hadn't answered, just shook her head.

Goblin Slayer had stood up from his seat, gone back to his room, and had been passing the time since then like this.

He didn't say anything at all.

"………"

Goblin Slayer's hand stopped again, and he held the sword against the light. He brushed a finger along the edge and nodded.

He put the sword in its scabbard; next, he took out his southern-style bent-cross throwing knife.

"You aren't going to be with her in this difficult moment?" The unexpected voice was sultry, yet pointed, with something of the sound of a pouting child.

"No." Goblin Slayer didn't even turn his helmet in the direction of the woman who had come in without so much as the sound of the door opening.

"I see," Sword Maiden said, her lips pursed. She slunk toward the bed.

Then she sat down, her soft, fleshy body contorting as if she were about to kneel before the man on the bed.

"A crying girl wants to be comforted, you understand?"

"Is that so?"

"Believe me, I know," Sword Maiden said. She cast her gaze down at her hands, which brushed along her legs. "………Because I'm just the same."

"I see."

There was a noisy scraping as Goblin Slayer began to hone the bent-knife blade. Sword Maiden's sightless eyes drank him in as he worked at the evil-looking blade. Her cheeks slowly went from puffed in annoyance to soft, turning up at the edges.

The shadow of his helmet on her face slid and danced with each flicker of the candle flame.

"You mustn't make a girl cry."

"I know."

Goblin Slayer's words were harsh, almost violent in their brevity; for an instant, Sword Maiden was shocked. If she hadn't had a cover over her eyes, they might have appeared wide—but he ignored her and kept polishing.

"I learned that long ago."

"I... I see." Sword Maiden didn't quite know what to say. "I brought you a book." So instead she fell back on the nominal reason she was there.

She placed on the table the book she had been holding, a volume about belief in the Dark Gods and its associated symbols.

"I was afraid we wouldn't have time for me to show you to the library personally anymore..."

"I see."

The answer was brief—and not elaborated.

Sword Maiden stood there for a long moment, until finally, she gave a little snort. She turned around and was about to leave the room, when—

"All things become lost," Goblin Slayer said with particular softness. This was a man who rarely spoke loudly to begin with.

"You're right," Sword Maiden said just as quietly.

"When I was a boy, my father promised to give me his dagger after I grew up." The hands stopped working, and Goblin Slayer held the blade up to the light, inspecting it, before running a finger along it. "It was a very good dagger, I believe, with a hawk's head carved on the grip."

He tossed the whetstone away. It landed on the floor with a heavy thump.

"I don't know where it is now."

Then he shoved the throwing knife back in his item bag and fell silent again.

Sword Maiden used the shadow of his helmet to hide the slight change in her expression, whispering only, "I didn't know." She brushed Goblin Slayer's knee with her pale, shapely fingers. She let them keep going until she was caressing his leg, as if she was touching something very dear to her. "Tomorrow, I'll be going to the castle. I have a council with His Majesty the king."

Like I told you at the beginning. Sword Maiden giggled like a child.

"His Majesty and I have a long history together... When I see him, I'll try to bring it up with him."

Goblin Slayer's head turned slowly toward her. It was the first time the helmet had faced her.

"..." He appeared to be struggling to find the words, until finally he said, "I see." He was silent for another moment before adding simply, "Please do."

On Sword Maiden's face, a flower blossomed. "I will—just leave it to me." A wide smile appeared on her full lips, and she stood excitedly. She struck the floor once with the sword and scales she used in place of a staff, causing the scales dangling from the hilt to jangle. "I'll put everything I can into it... Tell me, will that be enough for you?"

The sweet, inviting whisper. Goblin Slayer said, "Yes," and nodded. "Pardon the trouble—but please do."

"——!" Sword Maiden didn't answer but walked away almost as if she were floating. She opened the door, again silently, went out—but then looked back in briefly. "Er, ahem..."

"......"

"Good night, and...sweet dreams."

"Yes," Goblin Slayer said with a nod. "You as well."

Her face flushed like an adolescent girl's, and she closed the door.

With the door shut behind her, Sword Maiden put a hand to her face and fell on her bum—not that Goblin Slayer was aware of any of this. He had instead picked up the whetstone he'd cast onto the floor earlier, rolling it around in his hands.

He silently polished the rest of his daggers, checked the state of his equipment, and made sure his item pouch was organized.

Then he opened the book Sword Maiden had brought him, comparing it with the shred of goblin skin, which he had produced from his bag.

It was a very strange symbol. It looked something like a hand drawn in red pigment, but there was no entry for anything like it.

That thief, he thought, *was like a goblin.* Perhaps it had *been* a goblin. *One must be prepared at all times.*

Such was the conclusion he reached, and he spent the rest of the night readying his equipment, until, as the first rays of dawn came through the window, he napped a little.

This was not his farm. There was no need to patrol. But if goblins appeared, he intended to kill them.

There was nowhere in this world without goblins, as he well knew.

That was simply the way things were.

That worked like a charm.

The girl, now wearing vestments of the Earth Mother—*gosh, the chest feels tight*—giggled to herself in the darkness of night. Then a cap and sounding staff, with cheap mail under the vestments. That was all it took to make her look every bit a cleric.

When she spotted someone coming the other way, carrying a lantern, she put on a smile and puffed out her generous chest. The passerby first looked surprised then bowed his head in thanks as he went by. The girl smiled again.

She could definitely get used to this.

She saw that what people respected was the priest's outfit, not the priest. It confirmed to her that she had been right to distract her brother and make off with the uniform of one of his soldiers.

When she looked like a soldier—even a dirty, disheveled one—nobody paid her any mind. Granted, she had tromped through the sewers in it and had to live with the smell of sweat.

And that dip in the baths was so refreshing—this is perfect.

"...This really is tight, though," she muttered, tugging at the outfit's collar.

The vestments themselves weren't the only problem; the mail didn't make it any easier to breathe.

Why would that girl even bother wearing something so cheap…? she found herself wondering. Adventuring must really be tough.

"……I've done a bad thing, I guess."

When she looked closely, she could see the mail had been repaired and restored in places. That other girl must have been using it for a long time. She'd grabbed it up so quickly she hadn't had time to look earlier, but now she realized what an important piece of equipment it must have been.

This girl knew from experience how much it hurt to lose something she had used and loved for a long time. Yes, she had always intended to return the clothes at some point—but now the smile on her face had turned to sorrow.

It wasn't—it wasn't that she had *wanted* to cause trouble for a girl who looked so much like her.

There were plenty of excuses she could make. It had been for adventuring, for the sake of the world, for the sake of humanity, for her own sake. She had wanted to see what adventurers were like with her own eyes, understand it, then tell her brother and surpass his abilities.

But the fact that she had stolen what belonged to that other girl—that one fact was immovable.

"…When this is all over, I'll have to return these and give her a proper apology."

The girl nodded firmly to herself. One more reason why she had to pull this off.

And she had left plenty in trade, too—enough to cover her apology, and the possibility that she might fail.

Naturally, she didn't have the slightest sense or expectation that she might fail (everything in the world was decided by the roll of the dice, after all), but if nothing else, the other girl could at least afford to get herself something that was way better than this.

"Okay… Argh, the gate must be closed by now."

The girl looked around, goggling at everything. It all looked so familiar, but she had only ever seen it through a window. And now she was there among all of it.

The thought made her strangely giddy, and her footsteps grew lighter.

She headed for the shop where she had always heard one went if one wished to become an adventurer.

The Golden Knight.

The name was legendary, among the oldest establishments in the capital, famous all over the city as the tavern of adventurers. She could hardly contain the buzzing of her heart from finding herself in a place even older than the organization known as the Guild.

She pushed the door open with a creak and went in, to discover the establishment still lively despite the late hour. She stiffened as the gazes of people who—she could tell at a glance—were of no account settled on her.

It only lasted an instant, though. A rookie adventurer come to the Knight was in no way unusual. She relaxed as the eyes left her. Then she straightened up and started forward with her best imitation of fearlessness.

A young man staring down at a table in the corner suddenly looked up, but she quietly ignored his uninvited gaze.

"Ahem, do you have any rooms for the night?" She thought she heard her voice scrape.

"Hrm?" The owner eyed her from behind the counter. He looked her up and down then gave a quiet sigh. "The royal suite, the regular suite, economy room, cot, or..."

"The stables!" She was surprised at how loud her voice suddenly was. Attention turned to her again, and the girl looked at the ground.

"...Around back. Hope you get some sleep."

"Th-thank you very much." She nodded in acknowledgment then left the tavern. Her face felt so hot.

Adventurers slept in the stables. That was what they did. So why shouldn't she? She loved adventurers.

Best of all, the stables were free. If she went scattering gemstones all over the capital, it would be too easy for her brother to find her.

"If I can avoid him, just for tonight..."

Then there would be a chance. She could get outside the gates. She could do it. She could do it—she thought.

The girl went around back, glancing about as she undressed in the shadows.

She pulled off the overly tight vestments and mail and threw them aside then buried herself in a bale of hay with the sounding staff and her bag of jewels.

The stables stank something awful, and the straw scratched her all over; there was no chance she would find any sleep.

Then again, that might have been because of the priestess's crying face, which she had never actually seen, but which haunted her mind's eye the whole night through.

"So, do you have anything to report about the flaming stone from the heavens that supposedly fell at the holy mount?"

The throne was a tiring place to be. Then again, it was a symbol of the king's power, not a place to relax.

Still, the next chair I get is going to have a softer seat.

The young ruler, however, let no trace of this thought show in his expression; his royal bearing was unmoved.

His traveling court had only just returned the night before, and now he had this council first thing in the morning.

The huge stone hall was decorated with tapestries, each with an august history, and shafts of autumn light came in through the windows. They brought with them the colors of the stained glass down upon the gorgeous, round stone table where his most important advisers were now gathered.

An elderly minister, a red-haired cardinal, a tan-skinned court mage, a royal guardsman in silver armor, and a Gold-ranked adventurer.

In addition to these, there were notable nobles, wizards, scholars, religionists, and merchants—people of every stripe.

If one was to be king of this nation, one had to *know* from the moment one became king.

From the founding of the nation—from the founding of history—disaster and chaos had come again and again: the Demon Lord.

And each time, the kings of the dwarves and the elves, and the chieftains of the rheas and the beast people had gathered for a council of war around this table.

There were adventurers and knights-errant present as well, along with mages and sages whose origins he didn't really know.

The table had been carved centuries ago by the king of the dwarves, who had found it quite amusing that with the table round, there would be no distinction of status among those who sat at it.

And anyone who had ever been on an adventure understood immediately that no one type of person could dictate what his group did.

Well, some don't. But they die off pretty fast.

He saw his royal guard grin slightly—perhaps his old friend had picked up on the hint of a smirk on the king's face.

"Very well, each of you, please speak in turn," the king said soberly, suppressing his smile. First, a towering royal mage got to his feet.

"The stargazers have seen an ill star fall unexpectedly upon the board."

"Well, now—unexpectedly?"

"Yes, sire. The school is poring through the ancient texts, but they have yet to find any prophecies resembling what has happened."

The king nodded deeply at the tan-skinned man's words then made a broad gesture for him to be seated. "You think, then, that it might be the work of Chance and not Fate...?" He rested his elbows on the arms of his throne and put his chin in his hands, thinking carefully. It would be best to handle one thing at a time. "And what about the holy mount? I want to know what this flaming rock from heaven has done."

"As ever, one does not climb the holy mount, Your Majesty."

This answer came from a man who stood out even among the members of this council. He carried no weapon, but a horned helmet sat on the table in front of him, and he was wearing a well-used set of mail. He had bushy black hair in abundance, and from his neck hung a Gold-ranked tag; he was the only padfoot present.

His doglike face was contorted in displeasure, and he ate the snacks sitting on the round table with abandon.

"A cave or the like, maybe. But climbing the outer walls? A bit difficult."

The man of the royal guard raised his hand in a smooth motion. His muscled body was protected on the battlefield by a suit of platinum armor. When the king nodded, the man—the captain charged with protection of the royal person—ran a hand through his hair and said, "Majesty, it would be a challenge to get the army onto the mount."

"I might have guessed."

"Indeed, sire. It doesn't have room for much of a crowd. I'm not sure how many of you blue bloods could even make the trip."

The captain, of common stock himself, spoke as if this were the most natural thing in the world. He viewed the physical strength of the royal family and the nobility rather lightly.

And he's right to do so.

The king took strength from this old friend, who was now a staff officer at his side.

The holy mount was the tallest, most dangerous mountain to tower over his kingdom. No mountain really *belonged* to those who had words, but the holy mount even less than most. If he sent in the army, there was no telling how many casualties there might be.

"However, sire, it would be possible to surround the mount in case anything should come down from it," the captain went on. The words were proud, with tested military experience behind them. "Not a freak or foe would get past us into the known world."

That, he submitted, was the army's duty.

If adventurers were arrows that could be loosed directly at a target, the army was a shield protecting the realm. The army would not get him to the Demon Lord's stronghold, nor, being there, would it triumph against the enemy. Soldiers used only mass-produced weapons and armor that smiths turned out as quickly as they could. Their only experience was endless discipline, day by day. It gave them no hope of victory.

But meet the oncoming forces of the Demon Lord? That they could do. They could stand in the way of the encroaching enemy, forming a wall of spears to prevent their advance. And that—that was something adventurers certainly could not do.

"A small number of people acting alone might have a better chance." The Gold-ranked adventurer, well aware of all this, crossed his arms and leaned his small frame back in his chair. "But it pays to be careful. I've been up to the foot of the mountain, just to check things out, but I sensed something there. Something I didn't recognize."

"What do you mean by that?" the red-haired cardinal asked with interest.

The Gold-ranked adventurer pulled an especially uncomfortable face. "I'm thinking, something that's not even in the Monster Manual."

"I see…" The king let out a breath. It had been nothing but trouble since the battle with the greater demons the year before.

Greater demons, heretic cults, giants, and so on and so forth. He couldn't believe how far peace seemed from his world.

"Meaning, it looks like it's going to be *her* turn now."

No one objected to the whisper. They all looked at one another and nodded. They should play their wild card while the playing was good. If she accepted, at least.

I'm glad that girl was born with a good heart, the king thought gratefully.

He didn't want to further burden the girl, who wasn't so different in age from his own younger sister. But each thing and each person was given their own role to play. All one could do was go along with it. Just as he accepted his place as king. The only thing he really wanted was not to be one of those weaklings who threw a fit and rejected the place in life they'd been given.

"All right," he said. "Make preparations so you can provide the best support possible if called upon."

"Indeed, sire, as you wish," said the minister, an old man, working hard to bow respectfully.

The king could leave the details to him. Yes, that would do nicely. What was needed from the king was decisiveness and direction; precise understanding and careful consideration could be provided by his ministers.

But I guess too much of that kind of thinking is what gets you turned into a puppet ruler.

"How has the city been during my absence?"

"The cults continue to run rampant, though that's nothing new…" The answer came from the red-haired cardinal. He had been seconded to the city as an adviser, and his eloquence was unimpeachable. "While you were on the circuit, Majesty, a strange sect devoted to the God of Wisdom began to take hold to the south of the capital."

"And I suppose those who don't believe are visited by a terrible curse?"

"We know not what the truth of the matter is."

"We'll have to strike at them." The young king's eyes lit up, and his mouth curled into a smile.

The cardinal could see what was happening. "Majesty...," he said tiredly.

The king answered only, "Yes, I know," and looked at the papers he had in hand.

"Is this God of Wisdom different from the God who gives knowledge?" asked the court mage.

The cardinal nodded solemnly. "The God of Knowledge walks himself in the darkness, offering up the light of learning."

"But this God of Wisdom doesn't?"

"He does not lead and reveals no path. He simply, suddenly, flings the flame of insight into the dark."

"...It seems a subtle distinction." The mage let out a sigh. This description seemed not so different from that of the one called the Dark God.

The king considered this exchange carefully then asked a question of his own. "What, then, of what is beyond our sight...?"

"At the moment, the Order of the world shows no sign of being upset."

The response to his question came from a woman so inordinately beautiful she hardly seemed to belong there. Her luscious body and soft chest were ensconced in white clothing; in her hand, she held the sword and scales, and her eyes were covered by a sash.

"The battle has resulted in more refugees, orphans, and homeless people, but they don't want for employment in these days." The woman was the archbishop serving the Supreme God, Sword Maiden. Her words sounded like music, and she smiled. "We never have enough hands, after all, no matter how many there are.

She seems very different these days.

The thought came to the king suddenly. He had known her for close to ten years now. Today as ever, she was so full of beautiful curves that any man would have gone flying to her. Before, though, her beauty had been like a peony that might fall from the branch at any moment. Now—now it was different. Her form and expression were as luminous as a flower holding itself forth in bloom. Her friend the king thought surely this was good.

"Oh, but..." The lovely expression clouded over slightly. The eyebrows drooped under the weight of trouble, and her body slouched just a bit.

"What is it? Speak."

With much trembling, then. Sword Maiden's smile was like a secret.

"A precious friend of mine was a victim of a theft at the bathhouse, of her priestess's garments and a set of mail she cherished. Just yesterday."

"I'm sorry...?"

"The thief, it seems, was dressed as a soldier..."

The king raised a dubious eyebrow. It seemed a minor matter, but perhaps it warranted his attention after all. A thief in the guise of a soldier could not be overlooked.

Sword Maiden, however, changed the subject before he could voice any other questions. "Furthermore," she continued, "I consider that the goblins must be destroyed."

Her declaration was bracing, her smile gentle, and both seemed to declare this the end of the matter.

"Again with the goblins," the other councilmembers murmured, looking at one another. She always said that.

The king forced his face into a neutral expression and coughed.

Damn it all, I guess I can't let it go.

"Very well, I'll have the matter investigated... Next, what's the status of the adventurer training centers?"

"......"

A female merchant, the person charged with overseeing matters related to the training centers, blinked. She was the youngest of those gathered there, and now she found every eye in the chamber focused on her. She glanced quickly at Sword Maiden then gave a deep bow and began to speak. "…A report has been prepared, sire. May it please you to look at it."

This woman was young, but she comported herself with an unusual composure and little of the idealism that so often accompanied youth. Neither was she a benighted pessimist, though; she took a realistic, pragmatic view of things.

Maybe it was the toneless quality of her voice, the way her expression rarely changed, that made her seem so adult. Her punctilious personality was reflected in the careful, precise characters on the sheet before him.

She was the daughter of a certain noble household; it was said that after a period of convalescence from illness, she had entered into business on the strength of her family's assets… But what, he wondered, had been her experiences, the life that had led her to walk onto the political stage in these past months?

Where indeed do such talented women come from?

The king rested against the arms of his throne, a small smile coming over his mouth, hidden by the paper in front of him. Rulers and nobles were not supposed to show their feelings to others so easily. He would have to work on that.

"…The facilities as such are approaching completion at the Guilds in several towns. However…" The woman trailed off, searching the thin air in front of her for the rest of the words. "…as we expected, the notion that one might become an adventurer and then immediately have to embark upon a course of study has had some trouble gaining acceptance."

"I'm hardly surprised," the king said, nodding seriously. "Back when I was an adventurer, many of us considered it a nuisance that we even had to write our names to register."

Then again, most of those people made a beeline for the tavern, got drunk, ran their mouths, and were shortly adventurers no longer. Then they would complain: if only they had skill; if only they'd had the luck to be born into some better situation…and on and on.

The ironic thing was that other novice adventurers were all around them, people who might not be experienced but who were going through the evaluation process, earning their daily bread by carrying bags, and working themselves to the bone finding ways to become more skilled. Yet, the drunkards (the king remembered with disgust) derided them as doing all that work for nothing.

"People don't change their minds overnight," he said. "We must take the long view when it comes to education."

"...Yes, Majesty. For that reason, I suggest we provide meals to those in training, so that we might attract hungry adventurers."

"Provide meals? You're suggesting the state offer catering?"

The ranks of adventurers were frequently filled with the young, disenfranchised sons of farmers with nowhere else to go, or runaway tenant farmers. Even those who came with nothing but their dreams of glory could not escape the need for food, clothing, and shelter. If it was possible to address even one of those needs... Well, it could only encourage the acceptance of their educational system.

"I like the idea, but do we have the budget for it?"

The real problem wasn't the methodology. It was the money it would take to bring it to life.

The woman's eyebrows drooped unhappily at the king's pointed question "...That, sire, is the crux of the matter." She summarized things briefly. "...As a matter of fact, I expect it to put us in the red. We can't expect to charge class fees, after all."

"You understand the national treasury does not exist simply to pour out money like water to put food in the mouths of vagrant good-for-nothings?" the king said then shrugged. Maybe they would discover a land where grain and gold welled up from the ground—then it would be a different story.

Maybe if I went and slayed just one little dragon.

"Majesty," a voice intoned sharply. The red-haired cardinal was giving him a grim look. *Bah.*

The female merchant went on in complete seriousness, seemingly oblivious to the exchange. "...I do, sire. I thought perhaps the training centers could be entrusted with clearing rats or roaches out of the sewers."

Such quests would technically be issued to the adventurers by the cities or by the nation itself—in other words, they would fall under activities funded by taxes. The money would only nominally be going to the training centers, but would in practice be used to pay the adventurers.

"...It would be an introduction to actual combat, Majesty. What you might call a tutorial."

The king's eyes widened slightly: On the merchant's lips was something resembling a triumphant smile. Like ripples on a pond caused by a passing breeze, it would be easy to miss if one were not paying attention. The expression made her look younger than her age; it struck him as quite cute.

"Do you think we should have them slay goblins as well?" At the minister's heedless words, the smile disappeared as abruptly as if a stone had been cast into a pond. Doubtless he had no ill intent. The smiling minister was nodding to himself, as if to congratulate himself on what a good idea this was. "That would address the archbishop's concern as well—"

He interrupted himself at a glare from Sword Maiden's unseeing eyes. He looked to the merchant for help, but she gave him an equally icy stare.

"...Er, well, it was...merely a suggestion," he finished lamely, thoroughly cowed.

The king bit back a smile as he said, "Very well," and waved his hand. "That's not bad, but it would be best if we could limit the work to the sewers. Proceed with your plan."

"...Thank you very much, Your Majesty," the woman said, bowing deeply.

That was when footsteps could be heard pounding from outside the council chamber, along with shouts of *Halt!* The door came bursting open.

"What is the meaning of this? We are in council!"

"Terrible, t-terrible news, Your Majesty! I apologize with all my heart, I truly—!"

The king recognized the person his security forces were currently tackling. An attendant to his younger sister, he thought. His sister seemed to truly like the woman; they were like siblings themselves.

Now, though, the attendant's face was completely pale—and she had a man with her. He looked ghastly, as battered as if he had just come from the field of combat.

"Majesty, your— Your honored younger sister—!"

The news that the first princess had been kidnapped by goblins was enough to make the king stand up from his throne.

§

It was dawn when the girl had appeared before him; he had been loading cargo onto his cart.

"Um, excuuuse me…," she had called in a sweet, nasal voice.

He turned to see what she needed, and there she was: A priestess of the Earth Mother in ill-fitting vestments with a sounding staff in her hand. Her eyes were bloodshot—whether because she had just woken up or because she hadn't slept at all, he couldn't tell—and she blinked at him as he stared at her. He could see bits of straw stuck in the hair that peeked out from under her cap. It brought a smile to the merchant's face.

A novice adventurer, maybe?

"Yes? What can I do for you, my little adventurer?"

"I'd like to get just out of town. Could I ask you for a ride?" Then she mentioned the name of a younger female cousin of the merchant. A fine young woman who served in the palace. If she was a friend of his cousin's, very well then. The merchant nodded.

"Okay. But I'm going to the North. You don't think you'll be a little cold?"

"I'll be all right, *thank* you. North is just the direction I wanted to go."

The girl laughed out loud and helped herself to a seat among the cargo. She was energetic, but her movements seemed somehow ambivalent, in a way that made him worry for her.

She squeezed in between some bags then appeared to remember something. "Oh, this is to thank you."

She offered the merchant a small ruby. His eyes nearly bulged out of his head. Counterfeit currency was rife these days; there were many who shaved down the edges of their coins to "economize." Gemstones were certainly more trustworthy, but...

Is she really a novice?

That was the moment he had his first doubt.

It certainly didn't seem like a form of payment one would expect from a disciple of the Earth Mother, all of whom vowed to be moderate, frugal, and poor.

But he could stand there wondering all day, or he could get going. The merchant finished loading his cargo then set his wagon rumbling off along the wheel ruts.

Needles of dawn pierced the milky mists of early morning, but the capital never slept.

There were some tavern dwellers who had been out drinking until first light, stumbling along the street, and a slave carrying a water bucket at a quick pace.

Servants, awake before their masters, were opening windows, letting in the morning air. Cookfires accounted for some of the smoke rising from the many houses. But offerings to this god and that explained others.

They passed a shop just getting ready to open for the day, and soon they had arrived at the north gate.

Outside town were a number of fields for competition and combat, and banners had been put up indicating what the day's events would be. A line of people stood looking at them, possibly waiting to be permitted past the guardhouse. There was quite a crowd; it must have been gathering since well before the hour at which the gate would be opened.

"Well, well, it's busy today," the merchant said, putting a hand above his eyes and looking out at the line as he slowed his horse's pace. "We're in for a bit of a wait, my friendly adventurer."

"Really?" The girl sounded dejected, and when he looked back, he saw she had her cheeks puffed out. "Hmm... I guess we have no choice, sigh."

He smiled wanly at the pouting girl then waited for the line to start moving.

The area around the gate was full of adventurers and merchants, patrols and travelers, coming and going; it was, in fact, a bustling scene. Behind them was the skyline of the capital with its pips of chimney smoke and people starting their days.

The city was waking up. The merchant took a loving look at it, and then his turn came and he moved his cart up to the gate.

"Hullo, soldier. Good morning!"

"Mmf. We've got a lively one. Cargo and destination?"

"Woolen textiles, don't you know. I'm heading over in the direction of the holy mount."

"Huh," said the soldier, whom the merchant seemed to know; he handed the man a passport even as he spoke.

It looked like the merchant went through this gate every day. Both of them knew how this went.

"Listen," the soldier said. "Rumor has it a fiery rock came falling from the sky in that area. You be careful."

"Thank you, I certainly will! Oh, that's right," the merchant said, pulling up the reins just before he drove away. "I've got myself a passenger today."

"Oh?" the soldier remarked with a nasty smile. "Not getting into the slaving business, are you?" He sounded as if it was a joke.

The merchant shrugged, and the soldier peered at the girl riding among the cargo.

"Let me see your identification."

"Yessir." The girl fumbled at her collar until she produced the rank tag hanging around her neck.

"Steel rank, golden hair, blue eyes, fifteen... No, sixteen, I see. Priestess of the Earth Mother, this says. You an adventurer?"

"Yes, I am," the girl said, puffing out her chest especially boldly. "I'm investigating the disturbance at the holy mount."

The merchant couldn't see the soldier's expression under his helmet. The man simply said, "Yeah? Good luck with that" in a tired voice and gave the horse a gentle pat. "All right, you can go."

"Thank you very much, sir."

The merchant urged the horse out onto the highway, following signs that led in the direction of the mountain. Maybe the rumors about the holy mount were true, for few travelers seemed to be going that way. For company on the road, they had only the blowing of the breeze, the clopping of the horse's hooves, the clatter of the wheels, and the songs of the birds.

The sun was glittering just over the horizon in the east; the autumn air was cool and refreshing.

It would all be for naught if there had been a throng of travelers. The merchant took a deep breath, filling his lungs with that sweet air.

"Ahh, what a lovely day!"

"It certainly is. Being outside is wonderful." The girl in back stretched like a cat and squinted her eyes. She appeared to be enjoying the feeling of the breeze herself, and the merchant smiled pleasantly.

"You sound less like an adventurer than a prisoner," he said.

"There are many places where one can be a prisoner," she whispered. "The jail, the temple…the castle."

Very much so. The merchant nodded. His cousin had mentioned to him that the princess led a most constricted life.

"Well, nowhere is completely free of trials," the merchant said.

"You think so?" the girl answered. "Myself, I don't—"

That was when it happened.

The merchant thought he spotted movement from a nearby bush. "—agree," the girl finished.

Just my imagination?

He reached instinctively for the hilt of the sword he kept far down by his hip as he took a quick look around. He had no intention of confronting any adversaries, of course. But even to run away, one needed a weapon.

"…? What's wrong?"

"I thought something—"

—moved, he was about to say, but he was interrupted by the howl of a wolf. The merchant jerked on the reins.

"GORRBG!!"

"GRROB! GRROOBOR!!"

"—?! Goblins?!"

Wild dogs, or a pack of wolves alone, would have been better. But this was worse. Goblins, mounted on wolves and waving crude spears.

A horde of goblins—he was amazed to see them. Weren't they supposed to be in the west?!

"Hrk! Get your head down!"

"Ee-eek?!"

Ignoring the girl's cry, the merchant wheeled the horse about and whipped it on. The faithful animal whinnied once then took off running for the capital. They had no time to lose.

The goblins' faces twisted into vicious smiles; they must have noticed the woman aboard.

"GGBBGRBBG!!"

"GBOOR! GBBGROB!"

They cackled, moving to surround the merchant and cut off his escape. A few clumsily thrown spears came past, flying over his head or lodging in the roadway. It would not matter to them, he was sure, if they hit the girl with an errant toss.

If they crit on us, we're finished…!

The merchant drew his sword. The blade glittered in the morning sun. He had never used it in his life; now he grabbed it in an ice-pick grip.

"S-so you're going to fight? Good, I'll help!" The girl raised her sounding staff unsteadily.

Absolutely not. "Fight?" the merchant shouted. "We're going to run!"

Holding fast to the reins, he climbed from the driver's bench onto the horse's back. The horse didn't slow for an instant. A good animal.

"I'm going to cut the cargo loose! Come over here!"

"Abandon your cargo?! You can't! We'll fight!!"

"They're just goblins!" she shouted, but the merchant was hardly listening.

The girl stood, trying to find her footing on the careering cart. One of the goblins took the moment to launch a spear at her, which lodged in the cargo. "Eep!" she exclaimed.

"We have to give up the wagon! This way!"

"…! All right… I understand!"

It was a pathetic sight: The girl turned tail and scrambled along the wagon, puffing and shouting. Her tail, as it were, was not lost on the goblins, who cackled and grinned, adding insult to injury.

The merchant looked back and saw the girl with tears in her eyes, her face red as she bit her lip.

But she came this far.

He stuck his sword in the buckles, held the reins in his mouth, and reached back to her with his left hand.

"Quickly, girl, to me!"

"R-right. I'm com— Ahh?!"

Then the wagon hit a rock.

It wasn't a fumble, a matter of bad luck. It was just a highly difficult maneuver for a girl without much in the way of physical training.

She didn't immediately understand what had happened; her hand was still outstretched, her mouth still open. It was almost funny how easily her small body was thrown off the unstable cart and into the air.

I'm falling.

She slammed into the earth butt-first with a heavy thump then rolled along the ground.

"Ahh, ugh, oww...!"

The merchant, looking back, hesitated for an instant, biting down on the reins in his mouth. He raised the sword then brought it down on the buckles.

One strike didn't do it. Two blows, then three finally sliced through the leather fasteners, setting the horse free.

"GOOBRR!!"

"GROBOG!"

"Hyaaaahhh?!"

He could hear her scream.

The fact that the merchant looked back at all as the horse pounded onward was only because of his good heart. He saw the girl fallen in the mud, surrounded by dozens of goblin riders.

At length, one of the monsters jumped down, spear in hand, and advanced menacingly toward her. The girl swung the sounding staff in a wide circle, like a child with a stick.

"Wha?! Now you st— Wh— Who do you think I— Hrgh?!"

He saw the girl take a terrible blow to her face. He heard the dull sound, saw something red go flying. He knew her uncommon beauty was marred forever.

The goblin grabbed the girl's hair when it burst out from under her hat and tried to press something to her cheek.

A hand…?

"GOOBOBOB!"

"GROB! GGBORBG!"

It was some kind of dried branch that looked like a hand.

The girl shook her head weakly, *no, no,* but they forced the thing against her face.

There was what seemed to be a flash of light from the claws of the hand, but the merchant had no time to watch further. He sent his horse dashing toward the capital at a full gallop.

How else could he possibly help her?

Was he to fight the goblins himself? Cut them down with his sword? And if he was dead, nobody would know the girl had been taken.

The merchant was not a brave man, and he was afraid of dying. But that was not the reason he'd run away. Still, when he reached the capital, he felt a twinge of regret that he had fled.

In fact, he regretted ever having let that girl onto his cart.

Because waiting for him there at the gate when he arrived was his cousin, her face completely drained of blood.

§

When he had heard all this, the king slumped onto his throne. He seemed to have aged many years in an instant.

One of his administrators spoke up urgently. "Your Majesty, help must be dispatched immed—"

"The king's younger sister flees the castle, commits an act of thievery on a priestess, and is captured by goblins—and *then* the army is sent in?" The king's response was practically derisive.

The administrator swallowed his words, comprehension of the situation dawning on him.

The king pressed his hand hard to his forehead, trying to hold back the headache and the fatigue. "Don't tempt me into being the fool who levels the state military against goblins only when those he cares about are involved."

Yes: they were just goblins.

This much would never change: Goblin slaying was and would always be a minor matter.

It was obvious enough, from the broad perspective. This might be important to him personally. But that was all.

Across the northern passes were hordes of beasts and barbarians, and the south was in chaos as well. Every nation around him was training a hawk's eye on him, waiting for a chance to invade, a steady stream of spies coming and going across his borders; he couldn't afford to let his guard down for an instant. Evil cults were on the rise, the most powerful merchants left no means fair or foul untried in the pursuit of profit, and the denizens of the capital's shadows were many.

And in the midst of all this, mere goblins.

They were a small matter and always would be.

"...But, Your Majesty," the cardinal said hesitantly.

"I know," the king said with a wave of his hand. "But if even a word of such an ugly matter got out to the soldiery, the rumor would be in other lands in the blink of an eye. This is a matter of life and death for our nation."

Reputation and renown did more to protect the country than half-baked walls ever would. The stronger people thought you were, the less likely you were to be attacked. And if you were not strong, then why, the people would ask, should they bother to pay their taxes?

"Not to mention, no noble house would want to take some goblin's mistress for their bride, eh?" the captain of the royal guard said in a loud whisper. The archbishop—Sword Maiden—and the female merchant both gave him reproving glares. He didn't seem to notice, though, a big grin spreading across his rugged face. "Me, though, I'm different. I wouldn't mind."

The king heaved a sigh. "...A trustworthy adventurer. That's our only hope now."

"Agreed," said the dog-faced Gold-rank with a deep nod.

These were the moments he was here for. Moments of national

import, when the military couldn't be brought to bear, but a diligent operator was needed nonetheless.

After he returned the king's nod, the Gold-ranked adventurer reached out his short arms to spread a map open on the table. "The problem is the enemy's location," he said, tapping the map with stubby fingers. "Where did you say you were attacked?"

"In the North. En route to the holy mount..." The merchant leaned on his hazy memories as he pointed at the map. "...Right around here, I think."

The cardinal, the court mage, and the assembled researchers of the school looked at one another.

"...Could it have something to do with the fiery stone from heaven?"

"I can't say. However... Well, but..."

Whispered conferences broke out in ripples around the room.

It was impossible to say when or from where a danger to the world might arise. Was the world to be thrust into calamity once more by this rock that was said to have fallen from the skies onto the mount? Could the princess's actions, and her fate, be the seed of Chaos...?

The Gold-ranked adventurer, however, ignored the rest of the onlookers and conferred with the captain of the guard.

"You remember anywhere around there that seemed like a likely goblin nest?"

"Not entirely sure... Those bastards can live just about anywhere, after all."

Both of them studied the map grimly, thinking as fast and as hard as they could.

"A-and wolves! They were riding on wolves..."

"Yes, yes, I heard you. Goblins riders are nothing remarkable. The real issue is their nest. We have to—"

—*find their nest*, the adventurer was about to say to the merchant.

"The Dungeon of the Dead."

The words were like a stone thrown into a pond; silence spread like a ripple through the room. The people seated around the round table looked at one another, and then they all looked at one person.

That person sat back in her chair, smiling, not intimidated in the least. She had the air of a woman relaxing in bed as she waited for her husband, and surely more than one man among the assembly entertained less than reverent thoughts about her.

"...Are you claiming a handout?" the king asked.

"Call it inspiration, I suppose," Sword Maiden said quietly.

"That's a name I've not heard in a long time."

A dungeon at the farthest edge of the North, near the holy mount—the deepest of all dungeons, the Dungeon of the Dead.

Ten years before, it had also been the place of the battle between a great crowd of adventurers and the greater demons.

A city had been built like a lid atop the labyrinth, and excavation had proceeded for a very long time. Many people, seeking the head of the greater demon that waited in the innermost chamber of the tenth level underground, had never returned.

The cardinal and the captain frowned, and the Gold-ranked adventurer swallowed heavily. That was a magical pit in which it was said one could easily lose one's soul, and none of them were eager to test themselves against it. A nimbus of fear hung about it now, an impregnable dungeon from which none returned.

"That labyrinth is the only place in the North where I would expect goblins to live..." Did anyone hear the tremble in Sword Maiden's voice as she whispered the words? Did anyone see the slight shaking of the sash over her eyes?

A dungeon, goblins, a kidnapped woman and the fate that awaited her.

Did anyone know she was biting her lip to keep her teeth from chattering...?

"A distinguished adventurer of wisdom, discretion, and trustworthiness, fit to delve that deepest dungeon," the old counselor said with something akin to levity. He shook his staff—perhaps not quite seeking revenge for earlier but certainly taken with his own idea. "Would this not be the moment to call upon the services of that great hero, the honored Sword Maiden?"

Sword Maiden squeezed the sword and scales tight in her hands.

There was a shout of approbation from someone in the crowd.

"Excellent idea," someone else agreed.

Even among Gold-ranked adventurers, Sword Maiden was something special. She was one of the questers who had reached that deepest point of the deepest dungeon, defeated the greater demon, and come home to tell the tale.

With one of the "All-Stars" fighting for them, there was nothing more to worry about.

After all, they would be pitting this great hero against *simple goblins*!

"Oh..."

Sword Maiden opened her mouth to say something, but no words came. She could suck air in, but she couldn't let it back out.

What might she have been trying to say? She hugged her own quaking shoulders, embracing her generous chest.

I won't go. I'm afraid. I'm sorry. Such things she certainly could not say. *Help me, please.* Impossible words to speak.

She was the most distinguished priestess in this entire nation. How could she be afraid of goblins?

"And I can't ask *her* to go..."

The king appeared absorbed in thought. Sword Maiden could tell she had no time. A matter of seconds, maybe. Then the mouth of her ruler would open again.

The first words would be these: "What do you say, archbishop?" He understood nothing.

Then he would go on: "Will you do this for me, please?" It would be a death sentence for her.

Sword Maiden, terrified, scooted back like an overawed little girl.

But then she ran up against the back of her chair. She ran up against her position and the stares of those around her, and there was nowhere for her to go.

"What do you say, archbishop?"

The executioner's sword was raised high...

"...Ahem."

The sword was met by one small but clear word.

"Wha...?"

She couldn't believe it. Sword Maiden, her whole body stiff, turned her hidden eyes toward the voice.

Someone had her hand up, fearlessly: the female merchant, who had slipped out somewhere during the discussion and had just come back.

"Impudent!" the elderly counselor exclaimed, but the king silenced him with a hand and the words "It's fine."

The king seemed to have taken an interest in this girl—or, at the very least, in what she would say next. "What is it?" he asked.

"...The honored archbishop's escort is demanding to be admitted to the chamber."

"We're in council."

"...He is a Silver-ranked adventurer."

The merchant took a step before the old counselor could object further. Without waiting for the king's response, she opened the door to the next room. By the door, a diminutive silver-haired attendant shook her head in exasperation.

"I have heard the situation."

The voice was indifferent, cold, like a breeze blowing underground.

He approached unhesitatingly, at a bold stride.

Beside the speaker came a girl who appeared to be an elven archer, her ears flicking proudly.

On the speaker's other side was a girl, still young, and smiling helplessly as if she had given up hope of holding the man back.

Behind him came a dwarven shaman, shrugging in resignation, and a towering lizardman who seemed thoroughly amused by all this.

They were a motley fellowship. They wore mismatched equipment, like a gang of toughs that might be found anywhere in the world.

Everyone in the room, though, did a double take at the sight of this adventurer.

He wore grimy leather armor and a cheap-looking metal helmet. At his hip was a sword of a strange length, and a round shield was tied to his arm.

Even a pure beginner would have had better equipment.

But the rank tag dangling from his neck left no room for doubt: he was Silver, the third rank, the highest rank for those who worked independently.

"I knew it was goblins."

Without thinking about it, Sword Maiden stood up from her chair. The sword and scales dropped from her hand, but she didn't even notice.

"Yes, it is," came the soft answer from the female merchant—Noble Fencer, who had once been an adventurer herself. Her short hair came down to her shoulders; she brushed it away and looked at Sword Maiden.

"I shall go. Where are they? How many?"

Sword Maiden nodded, feeling as if she might collapse at any moment.

Again and again she nodded, over and over.

©Noboru Kannatuki

"Majestyyy! I'm heeere!!"

The door flew open with a bang, and a whirlwind entered the room in the form of a young woman whose long black hair was flying everywhere.

She was somewhere in her teens, right about the age when she might be taken for a novice adventurer—but it was also obvious at a glance that was not what she was. The armor that covered her body had been crafted to prioritize ease of movement, but it was also studded with magical protections. The massive sword that hung at her hip was equally clearly of extraordinary workmanship.

"...Huh?"

The girl reached the middle of the room then looked around in surprise.

Almost none of the VIPs were left. Was the council over already?

The Gold-ranked adventurer was standing there scowling, which made no sense to her.

The next instant, she saw the cardinal stand up from his chair and bow his head, a tense smile on his face.

"Eeyowch!"

Someone bopped her on the head with a staff, provoking a scream from the girl as if she had been singed by the flames of hell.

"Disrespectful." Sage, wearing a flowing robe, sighed, holding her staff, which was imbued with who knew how many spells. Kneeling before the king and his advisers, she ignored the girl's tearful glare.

Look at her, acting all courtly. The girl stuck out her lip and grumbled, "Hmph. Who even cares? His Majesty and I are like best budd—erk!"

This time, the smack came on her behind, but with utmost effort, the girl managed to restrain another shout.

"His Majesty has his station to think of—as do we, and as do you. See that you observe it."

The person who had made the girl jump this time was a female fighter who spoke in measured tones. A woman unparalleled in renown in all the land, she waved a slim but fearsomely muscled hand at the girl. "One would expect the hero to be embarrassed at such conduct, hmm?"

"...I think 'one' would expect to be even more embarrassed by not being able to find a boyfriend."

"It's the men's fault that none of them are stronger than me."

The girl gave the unfazed fighter a resentful look but saw a wave of Sage's staff out of the corner of her eye. "Anyway, Your Majesty, you called us, so we're here!"

"...Mm, I can see that." The king, squinting as if amused, gave a broad, magnanimous wave of his hand. He didn't seek the manners of one born and raised in the nobility from this girl who had fled an orphanage at fifteen years old and become a hero. As long as she could be respectful toward those she met, that was enough.

"Thank you," she said and plopped herself down at the round table. Sword Saint and Sage followed her, each with a polite bow.

Hero looked to her friends on either side as if afraid someone might get angry at her but then opened her mouth. "So what all happened? I'd been told I didn't have to come to the council, but..."

"You're fine," the king said, shaking his head with a smile. "We simply gave a quest to a most unusual Silver-ranked adventurer."

Ah, so that was it. Sword Saint felt the expression on the Gold-ranked adventurer's face said it all. Every adventurer had their strengths and weaknesses, so it wasn't unusual to be passed over for a particular job, but maybe it rankled that this one was at the royal command.

"...And need we not get involved?" Sage asked. Her voice sounded the same as ever, yet her comrades could tell how serious she was.

"I don't know if it's connected or not," the king said. "So I want to ask you to handle something different."

"Sure thing, Your Majesty! Just say the word!"

"Heh," the advisers whispered, smiling at one another over Hero's undue eagerness. They did not, of course, see fit to openly rebuke her. A hero she might have been, but she was also as young as their grandchildren.

"A stone of fire has fallen from the sky on the holy mountain to the north. It seems to be giving off a rather unsettling aura..."

"So you want us to check it out and whoop any bad guys we find! You got it!" Hero smacked her small chest, brimming with confidence.

The king let out a breath, his expression relaxing ever so slightly toward a smile. Things should be all right now. When she said she would take care of something, her word was absolute.

"Good. I've set aside some money for you to make your preparations. I can't promise you fifty gold coins and a sword or anything, though."

"Aw, that's fine. I don't need that stuff. All I need is— Hrk?!"

"We receive it gratefully, Your Majesty."

Whatever Hero had been about to say, she gave it up and rubbed her behind instead. Sword Saint bowed her head deeply.

Hero, her butt still sore from the pinch, pulled a face and leaned back in her chair. "Pbbt. Whatever. We'd be fine without that stuff..."

"It is only polite to accept what is offered to you," Sage said in her quiet, calm tone. She, too, bowed to the king and then said, "And if we should happen to need anything else?"

"Talk to the cardinal and the captain. I've told them to take care of you."

"Thank you, sire."

"Heh, don't thank us." The captain of the royal guard, quiet until that moment, grinned widely. "I could have gone with you, if I were still an adventurer myself. But *someone* is very insistent that the king's own captain not get involved."

"I've been hearing much of the same. People keep saying that it won't do for us to constantly run up the banners and charge into battle. Am I right?" The king looked to the cardinal for support.

"'Am I right' indeed!" the clergyman sniffed. "You have to stop suggesting that the best way to help the state of the national treasury would be for you to go slay a dragon or two."

"You think he'll stop just because you say so?" The quiet interjection came from the silver-haired attendant, who hadn't spoken until that moment. It was impossible to guess how she was feeling from her voice, but the shrug she displayed had a hint of warmth in it. "He's the most important person in the country now, though for the life of me, I can't imagine why."

"That's right, I *am* important."

It was the uninhibited banter of a group completely at ease with one another.

"..." Sage felt the smallest ghost of an understanding smile pass over her face. The connection among them was like that between herself and her own two precious companions—not the same, though; each was something unique in this world. To be able to observe such a thing firsthand was both entertaining and joyous.

Sage offered another bow then engaged the cardinal about the finer details. Sword Saint put in her opinion on the points that involved battle, while Hero, for her part, hardly seemed to be listening at all.

Instead, her face lit up like she had just thought of something, and she rushed over to the Gold-ranked dog-man.

"Hey, mister, mister! Tell me the rest of that story you started last time!"

"L-last time when?" the man said, blinking under bushy eyebrows. "You mean the time I one-hitted the huge bird-monster?"

"Yeah, yeah! Last time you stopped right when the horde of greater demons had you surrounded. I wanna hear how it ends!"

More than happy to oblige, the dog-man took a long swig from the flask at his hip and then began his story of the old days. Sage and Sword Saint glanced over at them, but with warmth in their looks, a friendly resignation.

This is good, the king thought, taking it all in.

The hero was more than her strength alone. Indeed, her strength was more than her fighting prowess alone.

Everyone adored the girl for her ability to break the fangs of disharmony almost as if she didn't know what she was doing.

And that, I think is what will save the world.

He had been an adventurer himself, once, but now, sadly, there was a crown on his head.

How fervently he wished he could gather his old party, stand around a map plotting out an adventure together.

Had that been possible, he would already be on the way to save his sister himself.

The goblin menace, the resurrected demons, the undead necromancer, the flaming stone from the heavens—with his own hands, he would do it all…

But I never shall.

Suddenly, the king realized he was clutching the arms of his throne, and he relaxed his fingers.

He was the king now. It was different from when he had been just a lawful-good lord. He was no longer overseeing a simple party of six people, but the entire human nation. He was no longer confronting gloomy dungeons, but the whole game board of the known world.

I never had to think about any of this before, but I do now.

His eyes went to the door to the hallway. Somewhere beyond it were the adventurers who had gone off with Sword Maiden and Female Merchant.

He and she together would worry about the country, the capital, the world.

So please, adventurers, take care of my sister.

CHAPTER 6

The Princess's Ordeal

"...It's been a while." Noble Fencer flashed a reserved smile as they hurried out into the hallway.

Having accepted the quest from the king, the party was rushing to get underway, begrudging even time for discussion. Goblin Slayer's steps remained bold even as he moved along quickly, while Lizard Priest took long strides. High Elf Archer might be able to keep up, but Priestess and Dwarf Shaman had to work their legs just to stay close behind.

"I'm glad...," Priestess said, smiling as they went swiftly along. She had felt stiff ever since the incident the night before, but now she thought she could feel herself relaxing the tiniest bit. "I'm glad you seem to be doing well. What happened after last time...?"

"...I've been like this ever since," Noble Fencer replied, without a single unnecessary word.

She was not dressed like the adventurer she had been once but was in a starched, proper outfit. Her hair, which she had cut off, had grown slightly, her eyes had a shimmer in them, and her cheeks a hint of rose.

She looks fulfilled.

The thought made Priestess's eyes feel full, and she blinked quickly. "How did you know we were here...?" she asked.

"...Who do you think it was who first put out the quest for my rescue?" The slightest hint of mischief appeared on Noble Fencer's mostly expressionless face.

"Oh," Priestess said; she had a guess.

Sword Maiden, some adventurers she knew, a priestess who had been wearing mail—it all made sense. Noble Fencer had drawn the obvious inference and had come to get them.

"...Are you all right?"

Priestess had to think a moment about this further question. What was she talking about? Was she worried about the nearly a year of goblin hunting Priestess had done since they had met? Asking about the time she had spent working—adventuring—with him? Or was this about the cherished mail that had been stolen from her? Or even the fact that the theft left her without armor?

She had been able to borrow new vestments, but the absence of that familiar weight left her deeply unsettled.

Finally she answered, "I think..." An ambiguous smile. "...I'm fine."

"How are we going to handle this, though?" High Elf Archer asked, turning to speak even as she jogged along balletically. "If the enemy's been moving since first thing in the morning, it'll be too late to chase them down now."

"...I've had horses prepared. Fast ones."

"I don't think that's going to be enough." The elf drew a circle in the air with her pointer finger. "We're dealing with goblin—what is it? Riders. Dogs can move quicker than you think."

"I can make up for that with a spell," Dwarf Shaman said as he came huffing up, already digging in his bag of catalysts. "It's always best to save magic when you can, but when you need it, you need it."

"Take care of it." Goblin Slayer's words were brief and direct, provoking a nod and a "Mm-hmm" from Dwarf Shaman.

Magic spells were an invaluable strategic asset in battle, but if you couldn't catch the foe, then there would be no battle. And if they were going to challenge the deepest dungeon, they would certainly rest for at least a night in any event. If they rushed into the labyrinth half-prepared, all that waited for them was a fate worse than death.

"Ahh, but what fortune that I should be of the bloodline of the nagas!" Lizard Priest, in high spirits, rolled his eyes in his head. "That I should get to slay goblins with milord Goblin Slayer and even attempt that deepest dungeon." His tail slapped the floor as they went, as if to communicate how happy he was. "And speaking of milord Goblin Slayer, you seem rather energized somehow."

"Is that so?"

He was striding boldly straight ahead, not a sign of hesitation in his steps. From behind, Priestess exchanged a look with High Elf Archer and Noble Fencer and grinned.

I guess it would be untrue to say I wasn't afraid.

The deepest dungeon. The place that had served as the redoubt of the Lord of the Demons ten years before. It used to be a training ground of some description, hence why it had ten sublevels. The layout, however, had been drastically rearranged, and a seemingly endless stream of monsters now emerged from it.

The monsters, for whatever reason, had nothing; they targeted adventurers specifically so they could gain something...

I'm sure the world was on the cusp of destruction.

It was ironic, Priestess thought. What had ultimately saved the world was not truth or justice but greed.

Rank, renown, riches, glory, fortune: there was nothing inherently wrong with any of these things. That was something the Mother Superior had taught her when she had left the temple to become an adventurer more than a year ago. To feel desire was a form of wanting and hoping. It indicated the will to live. As such, it was a good thing.

However. At the same time, the Mother Superior had taught her something else.

There were those adventurers who equipped themselves by robbing other adventurers, like common highwaymen.

There were those adventurers who sought holy armor and enchanted blades, not by subduing evil spirits but by prowling the depths of the earth.

Of such people, she must be careful. Such a person, she must not become.

Now that something precious of hers had been stolen, replaced with some hastily tossed gems, Priestess agreed.

That girl in the guise of a soldier, the princess—she hadn't been thinking about Priestess at all. Only herself.

The thought that this made her akin to a goblin—well, maybe that showed *he* was rubbing off on her a bit too much.

"…I hate to ask, but are you okay with this?" High Elf Archer whispered to her.

It was a reasonable thing to ask. Something terrible had been done to her. Why should she care what happened to the thief?

Did such brutal thoughts ever cross her mind? Priestess could hardly claim they didn't.

But…

Priestess clasped her hands together tightly, calling on the name of the Earth Mother to drown out those thoughts.

"I know what she did, but that doesn't mean she deserves *anything* that might happen to her."

That's how I feel. To hope that something terrible happens to someone—to wish for it, to take joy in it? That's not right.

That, she thought, was very goblin-like. And that was the last thing she wanted to be.

So she would help the girl.

Get back what was hers.

Shout and scold and make the princess think about what she had done.

How wonderful it would be if it could all end so simply.

"…Mm." High Elf Archer gave a flick of her ears and nodded. "That's good, then. Let's go!"

"Right!"

As she picked up her pace to catch up with Goblin Slayer, Priestess closed her eyes and offered up a prayer to the Earth Mother.

May it be so.

§

"Please, attend a moment."

The voice came just as the party was settling the matter of their horses at the stable.

Female Merchant had said the horses would be fast—but they were war animals, so they lacked the stick-thin legs of racing horses that looked like they might break at any moment.

There were three robust steeds in all. Lizard Priest chose the most giant of them for himself alone; High Elf Archer took the reins of another, while Dwarf Shaman climbed up behind her.

Goblin Slayer had been just about to mount the final animal, but now he turned with his hand still on the saddle.

"What is it?"

"I thought perhaps you had gone already..." A hand was placed against a generous bosom to keep it from heaving: Sword Maiden stood there breathing hard, having run up to them. She stood in the doorway for a few seconds until her breathing was more even.

She let out a breath, her cheeks flushed, then dipped her head gracefully. "First, I wish...to say thank you, for this."

"You do not need to thank me," Goblin Slayer said brusquely, shaking his helmet from side to side. "It is my job."

"...I know." Sword Maiden nodded, a gesture that almost made it look like she was about to melt.

"I summarized what I researched. There were many things I did not understand." He gave her a violently scribbled text, which she clasped to herself as if it were precious. Then she reached a hand under her garments, which stuck to her skin and had turned slightly translucent with her sweat.

Reverently, she produced several sheets of sheepskin paper, bound together.

"This is everything I remember... The dungeon, down to the fourth floor."

"The fourth floor?" Goblin Slayer took the map and passed it to Lizard Priest without so much as opening it.

From his horse, the cleric took the object with nimble clawed fingers and slid it open, glancing over it. The paper had a grid etched in it, the squares filled in a quick but controlled hand.

"Ho," Lizard Priest breathed in admiration. "This is very well drawn."

"I used to be my party's cartographer..."

"But the map does not go down to the lowest level?"

"On the fourth floor is a whirlpool of magical energy and miasma, the heart of that dungeon." Sword Maiden half smiled, almost embarrassed, but the expression quickly vanished. "And if you intend to go below that level..." Her unseeing eyes gazed at the party. "...none of you will return."

Priestess involuntarily glanced at High Elf Archer. Her shoulders were slumped and her face was drawn—much the same as Priestess, most likely—and her ears drooped.

"That's real comforting," High Elf Archer said.

"...Well, I guess that's what you say when hundreds or thousands have tried and only a few have come back," Dwarf Shaman said. He stood in front of High Elf Archer, his arms crossed, stroking his beard. "I heard some nasty stories about it from m'uncle once, myself."

"Regardless, you will be unable to descend lower than the fourth floor," Sword Maiden said, running her hand along the neckline she had just been pressing it to. "If you don't have this..."

In one smooth motion, she produced a colorful rope decoration.

Priestess's eyes widened at the sight of a brief flash of magical power from the ornament. Then too, it was mingled with amazement, and the things she had heard about it.

Could this be the Wellspring of Power, once said to have been possessed by the Demon Lord...?

"...Is that an amulet?!"

"Nothing so amazing," Sword Maiden said, reassuring the excitable but innocent girl as she worked at the blue rope with her hands. "Just a Blue Ribbon. A key that will permit you deeper into the dungeon." She pressed the Ribbon into Goblin Slayer's hand. "Please, come home safely."

Goblin Slayer didn't answer immediately. The hand sitting atop his glove trembled.

"Understood," he said a second later then closed his hand over the Ribbon. "That is my intention."

He put the Ribbon in his item pouch then grabbed the saddle again and lifted himself onto his horse. Then he reached out a hand to Priestess. "Get on."

"R-right away!" She grabbed his hand, and he pulled her up with surprising strength. She felt like she was floating for an instant, and then she was settled in front of him. "Yikes, oh…"

With no other way to steady herself, not having stirrups, she took the horse's mane in one hand. Then she felt something supporting her back.

The rough gloved hand seemed so firm, perhaps because she didn't have her mail.

"Be careful not to get thrown off."

"R-right. I'll watch out…!"

She shifted her little behind to a more comfortable position, embarrassed to hear her voice scrape. She cast her eyes down, but Goblin Slayer paid her no heed, his helmet turning one way and then the other.

"Let's go."

Lizard Priest barked his agreement then dug his claws into his horse's flanks. The war animal whinnied lustily and started off with a clattering of hooves on the flagstones.

"All riiight!" High Elf Archer said a moment later and gave her own mount a kick, causing the animal to rear up.

"W-watch it, y'anvil! What do y'think you're doing…?!"

"Y-yikes?! Whoa there, calm down… Now, let's go!"

While Dwarf Shaman was panicking after nearly falling off the back, High Elf Archer patted her horse's neck.

Elves had a unique connection to animal life. The horse calmed immediately and, at a snap of the reins, went dashing off.

Last was Goblin Slayer, whose helmet turned to take in Sword Maiden and Noble Fencer standing nearby. He nodded, just once, then tossed the reins himself.

"Eep!" Priestess exclaimed, pressing down on her cap to keep it from flying off as the horse went running.

The sound was only audible for an instant before it was swallowed up in the thundering of hooves, and moments later, the adventurers were on their way. The king must have sent word ahead to the gate, for the party was not stopped as it went charging through.

"…Do you ever wish…?" Noble Fencer uttered softly as she watched the dust settle from the departing horses. "…Do you ever wish you could go adventuring again?"

"That's a good question," Sword Maiden said evasively. Leaning on the sword and scales, she let out a breath as if to say it was complicated. "The reason I was able to recover was because I kept attempting adventures with my friends. And yet…"

Her covered eyes looked far into the distance. To the North. To the place she had once adventured. To the dungeon. To where *he* was going.

But what she was truly seeing, no doubt, were her memories of the past.

Of being attacked by goblins on her first adventure.

She had met her party sometime after that. Thus, the awful experience must have been burned into her eyes, never to fade.

Burned, although it had taken place as she walked through a gloomy dungeon, trying desperately to remain on her feet.

"…I think I no longer have the courage to face terrible things."

Her hands shook suddenly. No, they had been shaking all along. From the moment goblins had been mentioned in the council.

No, even further back than that.

Her hands had been shaking from the time she'd had to come to the capital, traversing a road where she would be attacked by goblins. She was sure the trembling had stopped only in the moment when he had protected her.

"I am a weak woman."

Noble Fencer took the quiet words to be an answer to her question. She glanced up at the sky. Blue, with white clouds scudding through it, the sun shining over all.

Yet, beneath this sky, there were goblins. Always—and everywhere.

"…What is frightening, is frightening."

That was why she spoke so plainly.

Sword Maiden tilted her head like a small child. "You don't feel we have to overcome our fears?"

"Sometimes, I admit." A partial smile came over Noble Fencer's face. "…But other times, it's all I can do just to face them."

"Now let's go." Noble Fencer delivered these words to Sword Maiden then turned on her heel.

Back at the castle, they were surely discussing the stone that had fallen on the mountain and planning what to do about the evil cult. There was much that should be done, much that had to be done, and they didn't have time to stand around.

Sword Maiden knew that as well as Noble Fencer and she followed at a walk. Just as they were about to pass through the door into the castle, though, she stopped and turned.

Her covered—her protected—eyes could not see through the world. The hazy shadow of his presence was already gone somewhere beyond the warm sunlight.

Sword Maiden looked down and placed her hand on the scribbles he had left her, like the last vestiges of a silhouette. If she touched them gently, her fingertips could feel the ink he had left on the page. She could read the words.

She clung to that sensation, let out a breath.

"I wish all the goblins would just disappear."

§

Of all the creatures on the face of the world, the one that can keep walking the longest is the human. But when it comes to speed and (literal) horsepower, nothing beats the horse.

The three horses carrying five adventurers passed through the gate, ran down the highway, and headed northward, ever northward, as fast as the wind.

Yes, the wind. And more than a wind. For horses they may have been, but no animal could travel so preternaturally fast.

"Sylphs, wind-maidens, spare a kiss upon my weathered cheek. And spare our onward-rushing steeds a fairer wind to seek!"

The reason for this was Dwarf Shaman's spell, Tail Wind. The sylphs embraced the horses, pushing them on faster and faster.

"Now I see what you meant. We'll catch up with those goblins in no time." High Elf Archer's expression was seriousness itself. Her ears twitched this way and that, taking in the sounds all around, but finally, she smiled. "I didn't think about it back on the ship, but I'm kind of surprised to discover dwarves have wind magic."

"Eh, can't say it's a specialty."

Should he be happy that an elf had praised him, or sad that he had to ride with an elf?

Dwarf Shaman considered the question briefly and settled on a sullen silence. At length, however, he said, "Then again, we use fire, water, and wind to turn the things of the earth into iron. We need an acquaintance with all four of the great spirits."

"Whatsoever the case, we could hardly hope for a better outcome than if we should apprehend the fiends before they enter the dungeon." Lizard Priest had his horse's reins in his hands, seeming unfazed by the ride as he gazed into the distance. His great tail stuck out behind him to help him keep his balance; he cut a rather impressive figure. "But of course, one does wish for one's chance to challenge the labyrinth. Ahh, we must choose a pinch or a tickle."

Priestess, glancing at him out of the corner of her eye, was privately somewhat surprised. Was horseback riding to be considered an achievement of the warlike types among them?

"Hrm..." A quiet voice came from behind her—or more correctly, above her head. Goblin Slayer seemed to have noticed something.

Priestess quickly looked forward, to discover the broken remains of a wagon sitting in the road. Following Goblin Slayer's lead, the party brought their horses to a halt.

From horseback, at least, it appeared to be a fairly typical case of goblin theft. The cargo had been rifled through, smashed to pieces, with torn scraps of clothing everywhere around. Priestess felt herself go stiff as she realized it was *her* clothing.

Erg...

Something like vertigo assaulted her.

What if, that time...

What if, back in that first cave, he hadn't come...?

"It seems they chose not to simply violate her here in the open field."

But that is all we can say. As Lizard Priest implied, there appeared to be only the aftermath of a typical fight.

Priestess—somewhat disturbed that she could tell the difference herself—looked around the area.

I don't see the mail, she thought. And although she was a bit disappointed, she also noticed something and blinked.

"Oh!"

She hadn't meant to cry out, but there was no blaming her. She squeezed out from in front of Goblin Slayer and off the horse, running over.

"What is it?" he asked, and in answer, she held up a sounding staff that had been thrown to the ground.

The staff of one who served the Earth Mother—her staff.

"So that proves it," High Elf Archer said, sounding moderately pleased.

"Yes," Priestess answered, nodding. "But...I don't see a lot of blood." *Hmm.* Priestess tapped her lip with her pointer finger and thought. No corpses, either. That led to just one conclusion. "I think they took her away immediately..."

"...Yeah, I think he said something about a cursed object or something, right?" High Elf Archer's ears were drooping. She was probably thinking about the dried-out arm the dark elf had wielded with such glee. "So maybe they wanted her for a sacrifice?"

"Sounds like a good guess," Dwarf Shaman concurred, stroking his beard. "There are only a few reasons you kidnap a princess: to marry her, ransom her, or sacrifice her."

"The question is whether they knew she was a princess, or if this was simple coincidence," Goblin Slayer said, surveying the scene. Then he turned to Lizard Priest. "What do you think?"

"By chance, a princess runs away from home, by chance, she travels north on the main highway, and by chance wanders right to her would-be captors." Lizard Priest counted off the circumstances on his fingers, his head shaking back and forth on his long neck. "It needs a great deal of chance."

"I thought so," Goblin Slayer said. "If they were targeting the princess, they did a very sloppy job."

"No need to waste any more time here, then, right?" High Elf Archer said. She was already tugging on the reins and urging her horse on down the road. "Let's go! If we don't keep up the pace, we'll lose them!"

Priestess scrambled to get back on Goblin Slayer's horse; he pulled her up.

Thus, the pursuit began again.

Tail Wind, though, while it might protect the horses from fatigue, did no such thing for their riders. They had been in the saddle since morning, and the strain was tormenting them.

Dwarf Shaman and Lizard Priest, both of whom boasted considerable stamina, were doing all right. And the warrior Goblin Slayer wasn't having problems, either. But the faces of High Elf Archer and Priestess, small women both, were growing increasingly taut.

The sun—hadn't it only just risen?—was already high in the sky, and the creeping heat of early autumn set upon them. Priestess sighed, supporting herself in the saddle, swaying side to side as she took a drink of water.

As she swallowed, she noticed *him* out of the corner of her eye. "Would you like a drink…?"

"No." The helmet remained fixed straight ahead. "I don't need it."

"Um, okay," Priestess said in a small voice. She wet her lips with another mouthful then put the stopper back in the canteen.

"Milord Goblin Slayer," Lizard Priest said, espying the situation out of the corner of his eye. "I don't believe we can maintain this pace for much longer."

"A short rest, then?"

"If I may suggest it."

Goblin Slayer didn't answer, but he also ignored Priestess when she murmured, "I'm okay for now."

He stared straight ahead then turned to High Elf Archer. "What about it? You still can't hear anything?"

"Not yet…" She frowned and strained her ears. "…Hang on." She looked up, narrowing her eyes. Her long ears moved almost imperceptibly. "Wind… The growling of wolves…"

"The goblins?"

High Elf Archer's nose twitched as she took a big sniff. "It smells like rotten meat!"

"The goblins," Goblin Slayer said confidently, and as he spoke, he dug his heels into his horse's sides. His mount neighed loudly and set off at a gallop, leaving only Priestess's little yelp behind them.

Dwarf Shaman, watching him go, smacked his forehead and looked up at the sky. "Gods, nothing gets him fired up like goblins! Gimme the reins, Long-Ears!"

"Take 'em!" High Elf Archer shouted, passing them to the dwarf without a moment's hesitation and drawing the great bow off her back.

The weapon seemed a bit big for horseback—riding double, no less—but she stood straight up as if she were on solid ground and pulled a handful of arrows from her quiver.

In the blink of an eye, three of them were in her bow, and she was drawing the string; she looked fit to be a statue. Twitching her ears this way and that, aiming by feel, she let loose the bolts in eyeblink succession.

The arrows whistled as they arced through the air.

"GOROBGR?!"

"GBB?!"

A wolf cried out, followed by the muffled screams of two goblins.

The enemy was just beginning to come into sight for Goblin Slayer up at the front.

For goblins, noon was effectively the middle of the night. They were in the shade of a tree where they had presumably been taking a little nap, safely shielded from the sun's rays.

Now he counted roughly five remaining riders jumping up in shock at the sudden sniping of their comrades. They had the usual motley assortment of armor and weapons, but they also bore those same strange tattoos all over their bodies.

"GOROBG! GOORO!!!"

"GROBOGORO!!"

They kicked sleeping fellows, stamped on limbs in their rush to be the first to the wolves. They left their half-drunk wine and partially consumed meat in the furor.

"No way that's the main force," Dwarf Shaman said in annoyance with just one look at the scattering goblins. "I'm guessing they got so caught up in looting they got separated from the ones up ahead."

"Aw, come on," High Elf Archer groaned. "What are they, stupid?" "The end result is that it buys the goblins time." *I don't like it.* Goblin Slayer growled quietly.

No goblin would sacrifice himself to help his comrades. But the goblins up ahead might be hoping that the idiots they left behind would have the same effect. Each of them, after all, was convinced that they themselves would never do something so stupid. Even if there had been a goblin who could sympathize with his fellows, he would still certainly have seen himself as exceptional.

That was simply how goblins were.

"Nonetheless, we will kill them all," Goblin Slayer declared dispassionately. This did not change what had to be done. "It will be a running battle. Our enemies are fleeing. Five in number. No evidence of traps. Let's go."

"In very deed!" Lizard Priest grinned the fearsome grin he had inherited from his forefathers. "The heads of our enemies shall speak for our virtue in combat!" He wrapped the reins around his arms and clapped his hands together. *"O sickle wings of velociraptor, rip and tear, fly and hunt!"* The fang he held in his hand boiled and expanded into a Swordclaw. "Milord Goblin Slayer, mistress archer, your support, please!"

"Yes." The middle helmet nodded ever so slightly, then Goblin Slayer casually let go of his horse's reins as well. "Take these."

"Yipes!" Priestess exclaimed, grabbing the reins, but once she had them, she didn't know what to do with them.

I've never ridden a horse before!

This was her very first time on horseback, in fact. Why did her first time doing things always turn out to be so hard?

"G-Goblin Slayer, sir! Er, um, wh-what do I—?!"

The answer that came was brutally simple: "Hold tight to the reins and keep your eyes forward." Goblin Slayer grabbed a sling and a stone from his item pouch. "This won't take long."

He was right.

While High Elf Archer loosed her next arrow, Goblin Slayer began twirling his sling. It spun horizontally beside him then sent the rock whistling through the air. Priestess, clinging desperately to the reins, was wide-eyed at his throwing technique.

He doesn't even let the horse's neck get in his way.

Now was hardly the time to try to learn the technique, but she would have to ask him about it later. She stored the thought deep within herself.

"GBBBOROGB?!" One of the goblins took the rock to the skull and went tumbling, his neck twisting at an unnatural angle.

Four left. No...

"Hi—yah...!" High Elf Archer took aim and loosed.

The shot appeared to miss, but then it bounced up at the wolf's feet, spearing its throat.

"GOORBGRGOB?!"

The wolf cried out and threw the goblin from its back. Goblin Slayer's horse went trampling over the creature's skull, scattering his brains everywhere. Three left.

"Heh-heh!" High Elf Archer puffed out her little chest, presumably showing off for Goblin Slayer.

"What're you so proud of?" Dwarf Shaman grumbled, but the elf's long ears conveniently didn't hear him.

With the goblin numbers thus reduced, the rest of the problem effectively solved itself.

"Eeeeeyaaaaaahhhh!!" Lizard Priest howled and flew into the fray. He had the reins in his jaws, a Swordclaw in each hand.

Before the might of the warrior people, the lizardmen—literally before it, because they were running desperately away—the number of goblins hardly mattered. Lizard Priest struck out right and left, cutting and slicing, and in the space of an instant, two heads and then three went rolling. Geysers of blood came whistling from the headless necks, and Lizard Priest let out a breath.

When the gaze of a descendent of the fearsome nagas fell upon you, you were finished.

The surviving wolves yelped and ran like rabbits into the wilderness, their tails between their legs.

"Would you have us pursue the animals?" The question was full of battle and blood.

"They are not goblins," Goblin Slayer said shortly. "Did you see the tattoos?"

"Surely," Lizard Priest said with a nod of his head. "The same pattern as the little devils before."

"Mm," Goblin Slayer replied with a nod. Then he said softly to Priestess, "That's enough."

"Oh, right..."

He reached toward her and took the reins from her in a firm hand.

Tail Wind or no, they had pushed their horses harder than ever during this battle. Flecks of foam were beginning to appear at the edges of the animals' mouths, and Priestess patted her horse's neck worriedly. "Goblin Slayer, sir, I think..."

"...I understand," Goblin Slayer said grimly as he slowed the pace.

Priestess knew she hadn't done anything wrong, yet still, she stiffened. With no prospect of an opportunity to change horses along the way, they would have no choice but to continue the chase at a reduced speed.

If she looked to the north, she could see the holy mount in the distance, looming dark despite the sunshine. The summit was capped with snow; it didn't strike her as a place people should be going.

The abyss seemed to yawn before them, waiting for the adventurers.

Waiting, like the kidnapped princess. Like the goblins.

"...I guess all that's for tomorrow."

The deepest of all dungeons was still far away.

CHAPTER 7

THE PULSE OF DEMONBIRTH

It looks like a pool of blood.

That was Priestess's first impression.

The top of the mountain stabbed up into the sky, the dawn light running like blood along the ridge.

And there, below, dark as a patch of dried gore, loomed the fortress, spreading through the shadows.

It was a fortress city where adventurers had gathered, built by some former king as a training ground for his royal guard.

But all that was now long in the past.

With the Lord of the Demons quelled, adventurers had left that dungeon behind.

Mantled by the morning light, the city appeared nothing more than a ghost town, a skeleton, deserted and barren.

That's...what it should be anyway.

Priestess shivered at the faint sense of dread that emanated from the place. She glanced at High Elf Archer, usually so stalwart and reassuring, but even her face was drawn, her long ears back.

The deepest dungeon, the endless abyss, the Dungeon of the Dead.

Once home to the Lord of the Demons, a great pit that spat forth death and pestilence.

The very remains even now bared their fangs, eager to consume adventurers.

No fortress, however strong, could defend against them.

"I see footprints," Goblin Slayer said calmly, bringing Priestess back to herself. He was crouched down, looking like always as he felt along the ground. "Wolves and goblins. No question."

"Not going to be so easy to track, though," Dwarf Shaman said, squinting under his eyebrows and shielding his eyes with a hand as he stared at the fortress. Suddenly, feeling a burp coming on, he grabbed the flask of wine from his hip and took a gulp.

To make a long story short, the adventurers had chosen a forced march. They had kept running through the night, not even sparing time to rest. Mounts and riders all were exhausted.

Now they were off their horses for the first time in hours, the animals tied to a tree in the nearby field. Priestess watched them graze, the expressions on their faces conveying a certain annoyance with their masters.

I'm starting to see why most adventurers don't have horses.

They needed food and water, and a place to stay while their owners were delving a dungeon. She knew that most of those who called themselves knights-errant also went on foot.

What about paladins, I wonder?

The thoughts drifted around her tired head.

This wouldn't do. Priestess smacked her cheeks gently and said, "That's right. Even if we only have to get through four levels of the dungeon, we have to face that fortress, too…"

"It won't be so bad," Goblin Slayer said, brushing the earth off his hands as he stood. "They're goblins. They have full faith that they are the smartest creatures around."

"And so?" Lizard Priest asked. He was bathing in the glowing light, warming his whole body. The first hints of winter that came in the night were more than enough to make the lizardman stiff.

"The one who is at the highest place, or the deepest, will think he is the most important." Goblin Slayer reached into his bag and produced a piece of leather, along with two disc-shaped crystals.

He rolled the leather into a cylinder shape, put one of the crystals at either end, and tied them in place with rope.

"Whazzat?" High Elf Archer was, naturally, very interested.

"It is a telescope."

He put the device to his visor and looked down at the city with it; a hand reached out to him as if to say, *Gimme, gimme.*

Goblin Slayer silently handed it over, and High Elf Archer put it to her eye.

"...I see," she breathed. It was no wonder her ears drooped.

OWR TOMN

The sign set above the entrance to the city was scrawled with letters in blood. A child could have written more legibly.

One assumed that one or two of the heads of the soldiers, the former guards of this town, had helped produce the declaration.

Goblins were not strong. But if one was attacked by several dozen of them in the confines of a fortress, it would be no different than being ambushed in a cave.

"They mean *our town,* I guess," High Elf Archer observed. "So what do you plan to do?"

She made a face and tossed the telescope back to Goblin Slayer, who grunted. He undid the rope and unrolled the leather, putting them and the crystals back in his bag. "I'm thinking about it."

"Fire? Water, maybe? Smoke? Or another bomb?"

"No," Goblin Slayer said, shaking his head. "I'm not thinking about those things."

Whatever. High Elf Archer put her hands on her hips and snorted while Dwarf Shaman looked disappointed.

"Thoughts?"

"A fine question..." Though he had just finished sunbathing, Lizard Priest trembled. He stretched out his long neck to get a good view of the fortress then slowly shook his head from side to side. "Myself, I would commit to a siege only if I had reinforcements, or didn't."

"Er, umm...," Priestess said, furrowing her brow in confusion. "Wouldn't that work out to...anytime...?"

Lizard Priest rolled his eyes in his head. "The one is when you know reinforcements are coming and need to wait. The other is when you have no other options." His tail slithering on the ground, Lizard Priest muttered to himself, "Then too, it could be worth attempting to cut off the enemy's supply lines in a surprise attack." He concluded with, "In any case, I should not expect the goblins to understand…"

"Agreed." High Elf Archer nodded. Not that the enemy should be underestimated, but still. "They're goblins, after all."

"…However," Lizard Priest added.

Priestess looked up at him. This gigantic lizardman's expression was difficult to discern, although not as difficult as Goblin Slayer's. "Is something wrong?"

"Speaking of reinforcements, we cannot assume that some might not come welling up out of the depths."

The same chill from earlier struck Priestess again. She gripped her sounding staff tightly.

Was this some kind of mistake? The thought occurred to her fleetingly, although she was Steel-ranked.

"…Guess it really does come down to fire this time, huh?" High Elf Archer said, recognizing there seemed no other choice.

Goblin Slayer, however, responded, "No." The place before them was deserted, no inhabitants left, rotting away. But still… "That is a town."

It was different from ruins or a dungeon, or a cave.

High Elf Archer's expression when Goblin Slayer presented his conclusion was difficult to describe.

"Have a look—it may be quick work, but it's still stone." With a hint of exasperation, Dwarf Shaman said, "Your lot don't know anything about masonry, Long-Ears." He had made a little window with his thumbs and pointer fingers and was looking intently at the distant fortress. "True, ideally we might take out any goblins down there, but not with the few drops of oil we've got with us."

"How about magic?" High Elf Archer asked in spite of herself. "Don't get me wrong, though," she added with a flick of her ears. "I know you dwarves don't usually learn offensive spells."

"Even if I knew any, I wouldn't want to be flat out of 'em when we went in the dungeon."

"We sneak in, then."

There was nothing for it but a full-out assault. At Goblin Slayer's words, everyone else nodded.

"So we duck in the dungeon, rescue the princess, and beat up the goblins," High Elf Archer said, drawing a circle in the air with her finger. "Easy enough. I'm in."

Lizard Priest made his strange palms-together gesture then hissed. "It is like buying a lantern at the store and going to kill the Great Serpent."

"What are you talking about?" High Elf Archer said.

"It is a proverb. It means...roughly, that any adventure is simple if it be finished quickly."

Huh. It wasn't clear if High Elf Archer quite understood or not. She was already restringing her bow with spider's silk, drawing it a few times to test it out. Elves preferred to avoid releasing the string with no arrow, which was bad for the bow.

Dwarf Shaman checked his catalysts—his weapons, in their own way—and said, "This sounds like it's going to be a heap of trouble. But what else is new?"

"I do not agree," Goblin Slayer said as he looked over his gloves, armor, and sword. "We know what we must do. It is simple."

"...I guess you wouldn't be you if you didn't think so, Beard-cutter." Dwarf Shaman gave Goblin Slayer a slap on the back; he tilted his head in perplexity.

"...Heh-heh." Priestess smiled the slightest bit at the sight. She didn't have much in the way of equipment to check over; she only clung to her sounding staff and prayed to the Earth Mother.

May their adventure end safely. May the kidnapped princess be unharmed. May they all emerge uninjured, saved.

If I could have but one miracle from the Trade God and the God of Good Fortune...

Then perhaps she could obtain a blessing that would turn ill luck to good fortune, just once—but she didn't wish to pine for what she couldn't attain. More than anything, it was disloyal to the Earth Mother, her goddess. Priestess shook her head.

She couldn't seem to focus on her prayers. It must have been from going the night without sleep.

"Then there's the question of whether any of the goblins might run away..." Priestess put a finger to her lips and made a thoughtful *Mm* sound. She thought she could feel her dull brain sparking to life in the morning light.

She was thinking about the possibility that some goblin would detect the adventurers who had snuck into the dungeon. Or if the goblins had routine communications with the surface, they might send word of what was happening underground...

"...I've never known a goblin to be that diligent," High Elf Archer said.

"She is right."

When Priestess saw Goblin Slayer digging through his bag, she moved faster than he did. She pulled out something she had placed at the top of her bag for just this moment. "Here! A grappling hook!"

The Adventurer's Toolkit again—never leave home without it.

§

Lizard Priest twirled the rope a few times, hooked it over the wall of the fortress, then grabbed hold of the dangling rope and began to climb, bracing himself with his claws.

As he ascended with hardly a sound, Dwarf Shaman gave a sigh from his back. "Gracious me, Scaly. You've practically got me wanting claws here."

"It would not do for you to remain like unto your ancestors, the monkeys."

When they reached the top of the fortification, they lay on their bellies, looking left and right. All clear. Lizard Priest swung his tail, which hung down the exterior side of the wall, as a signal, and Goblin Slayer nodded.

"We climb."

"Great, me first!" No sooner had she spoken than High Elf Archer practically jumped onto the rope. She shimmied up it, just as silent as Lizard Priest but without putting a foot on the wall. She twisted left and right, her little butt wiggling, and soon she was atop the fortress. That was elves for you; they learned a lot, spending their lives in the trees...

"Scaly might have been right after all."

"I get the feeling you're making fun of me," High Elf Archer said, pursing her lips, and then drew the great bow from her back. She held it loosely as she looked back over the wall—down toward Goblin Slayer and Priestess—and waved.

Goblin Slayer drew his sword, raised his shield and dropped his hips, then turned his back to the wall.

"Go."

"Okay…!"

Priestess, looking nervous, grabbed the rope. It would be unthinkable to leave her until last, as the rear guard.

Instead, with High Elf Archer watching out for her from above and Goblin Slayer from below, she climbed.

It made good sense for Goblin Slayer, who so often engaged in hand-to-hand combat, to take the ground in this case. But even if she knew he wasn't *that* kind of person, well…she couldn't quite put it out of her mind.

"…You won't look, will you?"

"I cannot pay much attention to you until we are up top," came the brusque reply.

"I thought not," Priestess said enigmatically and held tight to the rope. Then she exclaimed, "Hup!" and, with her staff at her back, braced her feet against the wall and began to climb as diligently as she could. Once she got going, she found she had no concern to spare for what was going on below her.

The sun beat down on her, making her sweat, and her hands shook. Her face was bright red and her breath came hard.

"C'mon, almost there!"

"Ri…ght…!"

Forcing her quaking body to stay in place, she somehow managed to reach up and grab High Elf Archer's outstretched hand. The elf's delicate hand didn't have much strength in it, but it felt good just to have someone holding on to her.

Priestess pulled herself up the last small stretch then flopped down on top of the wall.

"There you go. Good girl. Want a drink?"

"Oh, th-thank you…" She took a swallow from the proffered canteen to bring her breathing back under control. One gulp, then two. Priestess let out a deep breath and gave the water back.

"And where's Goblin Slayer...?"

"Ahh, our dear Goblin Slayer? You needn't worry about him, I should think." Lizard Priest was keeping watch with his unique reptilian vision; his tongue flicked out and touched his nose.

Priestess looked down from the fortress wall, and indeed, there he was: a lone figure climbing silently toward them. He moved without High Elf Archer's practiced grace, finding his footing solidly on the wall. Nonetheless, he joined them shortly. He freed the grappling hook, coiled it up, and gave it back to Priestess.

"Th-thank you." As she was putting the grappling hook away, she remembered the question she had wanted to ask. "Goblin Slayer, sir. Where did you learn to climb?"

It didn't seem like an especially useful skill in goblin hunting.

"My master trained me on a snowy mountain," he said in response. "I have sometimes climbed without a rope as well." His voice was even. "I mean a tower."

"Just to be completely clear," High Elf Archer said, eyeballing him, "you mean the inside, right?"

"The outside."

High Elf Archer looked up at the sky helplessly. The sun gave her no answer.

"...How much of a muscle brain do you have to be to do that?"

"At least I and the other one are different." *Though I cannot speak for him.* He conducted a very quick inspection of his equipment. "What do you think?"

"That depends on whether we go down the other side or not," Lizard Priest said.

"Mm," Goblin Slayer grunted. "I don't think there's any need to go all the way down."

"Are goblin sentries apt to be diligent about their work?"

"What do you think?"

"Then, presuming we encounter none such upon the wall..."

Just so. Lizard Priest nodded, taking out the map—the one they had received from Sword Maiden. He traced the flowing brushstrokes with one sharp claw.

"I suggest we travel around the town atop the wall, drop down beyond the city, and enter the dungeon from there."

"Eh, guess we don't have time t'kill slashing our way through town." Dwarf Shaman took a swig of wine, perhaps to focus himself or stave off the fatigue, and wiped the droplets from his beard. "...We made it this far with nothing but Tail Wind. That's pretty good economy, I'd say."

"This time, we shall not be able to come back until the work is done. Even if we were to rest inside the labyrinth..."

...there would surely be no guarantees they would recover enough of their mental energy to restore their miracles and spells.

"Hard limits on what we've got, then. Makes sense," High Elf Archer said.

"Still, attempt not to use magic. As little as possible," Goblin Slayer added.

"I'll save my miracles," Priestess responded, clutching her sounding staff to her chest and nodding seriously.

He was saying that he would trust her to know when to use her miracles. Just the thought that she was being entrusted with that choice made her heart jump.

I don't think there should be any need for miracles until we reach the dungeon anyway, though.

§

"GOROBG?!"

The goblin, drowsy in the middle of the "night," didn't know what had happened. He felt something cold slide into his neck; then an instant later, it felt like burning, and finally, he gasped for breath as if he were drowning.

The goblin, hacking and wheezing, died before he realized his throat had been pierced.

Goblin Slayer approached the corpse of the goblin, who had

literally had his life's breath taken away, and kicked it to the far side of the wall.

"That makes five."

"Not as many as I expected, honestly," said High Elf Archer, who had put an end to all three of the waking sentries they had found.

They had to conserve arrows as well as spells. She started working the bolt free of the goblin's flesh. Then, learning from the master, she gave the body a kick over to the exterior side of the wall.

"...Guess I'm getting used to this."

Or maybe you've been spending too much time around Orcbolg?

Back when they had first met, she would have given a disgusted groan at behavior like this. Well, the refusal to grumble and complain was one of the elves' virtues, or so she claimed.

High Elf Archer brushed her hands together, cleaned the residual blood off the arrowhead, and put it back in her quiver.

"So they really must be inside," she said.

"Looks like it...," Priestess agreed.

A mass of goblins down there. Wasn't it supposed to be dragons that one found in dungeons?

Priestess, feeling her emotions threatening to get out of control, shook her head. "Is it about time?"

"Mm," Lizard Priest nodded, looking at the map. "Perhaps we should descend." His hands were clean; he hadn't taken part in the skirmish just now. But—

"I never knew dwarves could run so fast! I guess they just need the right motivation!"

"Watch yer fool mouth. If the enemy got ahold of your spell caster, what would you do then, eh?"

Lizard Priest said, "I myself would perhaps not be so bothered."

Priestess, afraid lest the shaman should look to her for agreement, said evasively, "Safety first, remember!"

She had been in close quarters combat with goblins more than once now, but it was something she would avoid if at all possible.

Now more than ever.

She had never worn mail before becoming an adventurer, yet suddenly, she felt so alone without it.

Alone?

Not anxious? Priestess blinked at the realization.

She had been praised for it, saved by it; it had been with her every moment. She had repaired it so often, it would probably have been cheaper simply to buy a new set.

"…I see." Somehow, it started to make sense to her why *he* had stuck to that one helmet for so long.

"What's wrong?"

"Nothing. It's nothing," she told Goblin Slayer, and then she took a deep breath.

Then Priestess closed her eyes, clutched her sounding staff, and said a short prayer to the Earth Mother for the repose of the souls of the dead. She hadn't had time on the road, so now she included the riders of those wolves in her heartfelt hope for a blessed afterlife.

The question of life in this world is one thing, but in death, all are equal.

She prayed, too, for the safety of the princess who had made off with her mail. She believed—or wanted to—that the mail would keep that girl safe.

"Are you finished?"

"Yes… I'm ready anytime."

"All right."

Priestess produced the grappling hook again, and Goblin Slayer lodged it in the wall, letting the rope dangle down.

As if on cue, Lizard Priest picked up Dwarf Shaman on his back, and High Elf Archer put a fresh arrow in her bow.

All that was left, with some variation in order, was a repeat of earlier.

Once he was confident the first two were down safely, Goblin Slayer came next. He descended, controlling his speed by planting his feet on the wall. Once on the ground, he looked up and beckoned.

"You going to be okay? Can you make it?"

"…I'll do my best," Priestess said, trying to take High Elf Archer's encouragement to heart. She grabbed the rope uncertainly. If she fell, Dwarf Shaman would catch her with a spell, so there was no danger— but still…

"Errgh…"

Priestess's trip down the rope was so pathetically hesitant that she cringed to think about it.

Hesitant or no, she did reach the ground, and then High Elf Archer slid easily down the rope to the bottom.

"...It's just like you said, Scaly."

"What *have* you guys been talking about?"

How I wish...

Priestess was so taken with so many things. Guild Girl's refined manners. Witch's womanliness. Sword Maiden's maturity.

How I wish I was like them.

As much experience as she had gained, she was still unrefined, still young, still weak. These past few days had truly opened her eyes to that fact.

If she'd had her act more together—yes, yes. If only she hadn't let her mail get stolen, none of this would've happened, right...?

Maybe that's giving myself too much credit.

Neither gods nor people could influence the roll of the dice, much less go back in time to change a roll once made. The very thought was absurd.

"..."

But then, maybe it was the absence of the mail that made her feel so naked.

And that feeling of nakedness, that terror as if everything had been stripped away, was just like that very first cave.

Priestess took a deep breath and let it out again.

The only response to thoughts like those was action.

"I'm ready."

"Is that so?"

Yes.

Goblin Slayer nodded, and Priestess confronted the yawning pit before her.

It had been a massive iron door—once.

Soldiers must have guarded it at one time. They were no longer anywhere to be seen. The door was besmirched with blood and filth, the formerly impregnable portal now standing slightly ajar.

The air coming from inside was chilly, carrying a nose-prickling stench of rot.

"Let us adopt our usual formation, then," Lizard Priest said, giving a wave of his fangs, claws, and tail.

"Looks like it's time for the dwarf to wield his ax," Dwarf Shaman said, pulling out his own weapon and stashing it in his belt.

High Elf Archer nocked her arrow a little tighter, and Priestess likewise strengthened her grip on her staff.

And at their head went Goblin Slayer.

The cheap-looking helmet; the grimy leather armor; the small, round shield tied to one arm; and in his right hand a sword of a strange length.

"Let's go."

On his order, the adventurers set out.

§

"Come to think of it, is this your very first dungeon crawl?"

"Yes, and it's the Dungeon of the Dead…"

I really have the worst luck with firsts.

Priestess could have wept.

Goblin Slayer held a torch in his left hand to beat back the darkness, moving forward into the blank, unfathomable space.

They were in a stone hallway. The architecture was precise and measured, as if constructed with malice aforethought.

Priestess had been in any number of caves, some ruins, the sewers, and a fortress, but a dungeon was different from all of them. The faint illumination from the torch could show them only a short distance ahead, after which was darkness.

This was no place to live, or even to conduct battle. It existed only to entrap and kill those who entered.

"Well, I s'pose if you make it out of here, y'won't find another dungeon that'll cause you any…trouble."

"This is our first experience of such a thing, as well. We are in the same, *ahem*, boat, as you say…"

©Noboru Kannatuki

Bantering but never letting down their guard, the party continued quietly through the halls.

Yes, quiet.

Although goblins were certainly hiding there somewhere, there was none of the raucousness of a cave full of them. And yet, there was no mistaking the sense that if the adventurers let their attention lapse for an instant, a goblin might suddenly appear in front of them. They absolutely couldn't relax, and that made it clear why a rest in a dungeon would do little to restore their energy.

No wonder dungeon-delving competitions had faded away among adventurers who wanted to compete with one another. Even with the Lord of the Demons gone from here, it didn't seem like a place people should be visiting, let alone spending much time in.

"How shall we proceed?" Goblin Slayer asked, to which Lizard Priest responded by taking out the map.

"My personal preference would be to investigate and clear each floor individually, but..."

No way. High Elf Archer was giving Lizard Priest the evil eye; he ignored her.

"...there is an elevator here that will permit us direct access to the fourth floor, and I think that may be the wiser decision."

"I'll let you tell us where to go, then."

"Well and very well. First, to the north."

The party began the "hack," moving forward carefully but with assurance. This was a dungeon—a dungeon from which the monsters had already been cleared. Despite the indelible, lingering smell of death from those adventurers and demons that had been here once, nothing remained on these early floors.

Or at least...nothing's supposed to.

"...Hmm."

"..."

At a movement from High Elf Archer's ears, Goblin Slayer stopped.

That was all it took. Tension ran among the adventurers; they all looked at one another and nodded.

The dungeon's walls were solid stone. Gloomy though it was,

potential hiding places were limited to secret rooms, or the corners of the maze.

It was a simple matter, then, to predict what the goblins would think of.

"GROBGB!!"

"GBB! GBBOROGGBGR!!"

An assault from the front.

It was the best way for the goblins to use their greatest strength, their numbers. Now they came pouring around the corner ahead.

The goblins had a wide variety of weapons in their hands, and their skin was scored with the strange crest.

They came in waves with no evident formation, relying only on the selfish conviction that it was their fellows and not they who would be attacked.

"Ha-ha-ha, come, come! I shall give you each your eternal reward."

"Eh, I think we're gonna be wishin' for spells before this is over."

"...Hrmph, I think a dagger would actually be more useful than arrows right now."

Three people, three opinions. The brave one, the analytical one, and the slightly exasperated one.

Lizard Priest and Dwarf Shaman came out in front, shielding High Elf Archer and Priestess behind them. The dungeon hallway was exactly wide enough for three adventurers moving abreast. Three in front, then, and two behind.

Goblin Slayer looked at his friends—it still took him a moment to think of them that way—and said, "Let's go."

"Right!" Priestess, paying close attention to the footsteps closing in on them, frowned but nonetheless nodded firmly. The adventurers became like a ship cutting through the sea of greenskins that assailed them.

"GBBRB?!"

"GOORBGB!!"

"Incoming!"

"On it!"

Stones and arrows, improvised ammunition of all sorts, came raining down, but Goblin Slayer blocked them with his shield.

Lizard Priest, protected by his scales, howled and deflected everything that made it past Goblin Slayer.

"Ergh! Knew I shoulda taken my uncle up on that helmet...!" Dwarf Shaman exclaimed, working his ax this way and that. "Distance five tiles—four—three—Scaly!"

"Hrah, behold the blade of the lizardmen!!" Lizard Priest howled and jumped at the attackers. His claws and claws and fangs and tail, the traditional weapons of his people, lashed at the goblins.

"GOBORG?!"

"GOORB?!"

Geysers of blood, innards, chunks of flesh, and death cries were suddenly everywhere. Two goblins were torn apart like old rags. Lizard Priest's power seemed beyond what should have been possible in unarmed combat, but regardless, this was by no means the end.

"GOROBG?!"

"Three—four!" Goblin Slayer swung his weapon with absolute precision, fending off attacks from the right and the left. He caught a blow with his shield, stabbed with his sword. He slashed a throat then kicked the body into the enemies behind it to block their movement.

He carried the momentum of the move directly into a throat with his sword then shattered a skull, and that was two more dead goblins.

Goblin Slayer moved forward, grabbing a club dropped by one of the dead monsters.

"I hate! To shoot! In such! Close! Quarters...!!"

A monster that had gotten past Goblin Slayer was closing in on High Elf Archer, where he was met with a rain of arrows. The elf and the human girl in the back had looked like easy pickings to him, and he had advanced with a grin on his face. Now that grin was run through with an arrow; the goblin fell backward with the bolt lodged in his brainpan.

High Elf Archer kicked the body away with her long, slim legs; drew another arrow; and loosed at the next enemy.

He took an elven shot at close range. The impact alone was enough to blow the goblin backward.

"I'm not gonna have enough arrows...! Where are we going?!"

"We push past this corner, then through a door. The other passages lead to burial chambers, which we can ignore. Once we're through the door, take a left!" No sooner had he shouted the instructions than Lizard Priest drove his fangs into a goblin's shoulder and shook him about. "Eeeeeyaaaaaaahhhhh!!"

"GOOROGBG?!"

The monster found himself slammed against the walls, used to push back his companions, and finally flung bodily against the floor. Blood spewed from the shattered goblin's body; Priestess involuntarily looked away.

This was not the first time, however, that she had experienced the carnage of battle. She held her sounding staff tightly in both hands, staring intently at the passageway as she said in a tight voice, "We'll keep an eye behind! Goblins might come out of the burial chambers…!"

"Sounds good! But don't go nuts back there!" Dwarf Shaman called, adjusting his grip on his weapon.

Exactly like we expected.

Room guards in this dungeon had never come out before. In the Demon Lord's army, those who guarded the important places and those who patrolled the halls were separate. Now, though, the only ones who remained here were foolish goblins.

"GGOROGOB!"

"GOB! GOBOGORROBG!!"

They came pouncing out of the side rooms, smashing through the doors with hideous cries.

This, though, was something *she* had known about since her very first adventure.

"Ehh—yah!"

Priestess swung her staff as hard as she could, stopping the oncoming goblins. Priestess was not strong enough to do more than stymie them for a moment, something she well understood. Defeating goblins wasn't her role. She just had to do what she could to support the strategy.

"Take this!!"

"GORRO?!"

One goblin paused when he received a bop on the nose from

Priestess's staff—then died when he received a bash of the skull from Dwarf Shaman's ax. His brains spilled on the floor, his head split open like an overripe fruit.

"No need for ya to take any more risks than y'have to!"

"Right! Thank you…!" Priestess struggled to do all she could, sweat pouring down her face.

Goblin Slayer would send the goblins in one direction, and Lizard Priest would tear them apart, or High Elf Archer would shoot them. Those that came from the sides or behind found themselves corralled by Priestess and then finished off by Dwarf Shaman.

The party flew through the doorway and found themselves at a crossroads. They formed a circle and charged through.

Now in formation though refusing to use spells, the adventurers' attacks became even more overwhelming. But did the goblins feel threatened? Heavens no.

They were simple creatures. They were winning by strength of numbers. They (each individual goblin thought) would not die. And so they would win. They may have looked askance at the deaths of their fellows, but they trod over the bodies just the same to continue the attack.

They attacked with all the force of their lust, their desire to tear the adventurers limb from limb and have their way with the girls.

"GOBOG!!"

The goblin focus shifted from the front row to the back, perhaps seeing that it was more vulnerable. The blades of spears and daggers glinted in the dungeon's phosphorescence, lashing out at every opening. The tips were daubed with black liquid; Priestess went stiff when she saw it.

"Eek?!"

"Look out!"

Dwarf Shaman grabbed her shoulder and dragged her back just in time then came forward to trade blows himself.

He launched a body blow into the goblin with all the strength in his dense little frame. The monster yelped and stumbled back, and then came the ax.

Dwarf Shaman fought like he was cutting down trees; he lacked the refinement of a specialized warrior but had all the power of a dwarf.

"I-I'm sorry...!" Priestess shook her head and shouted, "They're using poison!"

"Won't matter if they don't scratch me!" Dwarf Shaman called back. "But gods, Beard-cutter! There's no end to 'em!"

"Yes." Goblin Slayer smashed a goblin's head with a club then jumped over the dead monster and jammed his torch into the face of another one.

"GGOROGB?!"

A muffled scream and a twitch. But the creature wasn't dead. Goblin Slayer brought the club down.

Goblin Slayer beat his way through the horde with his club and his torch, rhythmically, as if pounding a drum. When the club finally broke after crushing the skulls of who knew how many goblins, he tossed it aside and said shortly, "Eleven. You said left, correct?"

"Indeed!" Lizard Priest howled. "Head for the inner door!"

"...Take the lead."

"What are you planning to do this time?!" High Elf Archer called, clicking her tongue when she saw how few arrows she had left. Goblin Slayer pulled a small bottle from his item pouch.

"It won't be water, or poison, or an explosion."

No sooner had he spoken than he pitched the torch and the bottle at a goblin in front of them.

"GGBOROOGOBOG?!?!"

Doused with gasoline, immediately followed by a source of fire, the creature burst into flame; Goblin Slayer mercilessly kicked him down. "Twelve... Now go!"

"As you say!"

The adventurers moved quickly. Lizard Priest vaulted over the flames, through the opening Goblin Slayer had made, and pressed forward.

With the goblins behind them safely at a distance, Dwarf Shaman came pelting up. "Fire?! We need to *go* that way!" He turned to Priestess. "Can you make the jump?!"

"I'll do it...right...now!"

Priestess hugged her staff and closed her eyes then flung herself over the flames.

High Elf Archer secured her bow on her back and hopped over with a nimble leap, kicking off the wall and settling to the ground.

The door is right in front of us.

"We're all here, Orcbolg!!"

"Okay."

High Elf Archer provided covering fire while Goblin Slayer dug in his bag again. This time he came up with a scroll.

"GBOR!!"

"GOBOGGOBOG!!"

"Goblin Slayer, sir! Quickly…!" Behind Goblin Slayer, who faced an oncoming tide of goblins, Priestess was hardly able to speak.

Goblin Slayer nodded in acknowledgment, thrusting at the monsters with the scroll as he backed up. "Break through the door!"

"You got it!" Dwarf Shaman called, followed by a crash as he rammed the door with his shoulder.

Goblin Slayer hopped backward over the flaming goblin corpses; as he did so, he noticed an old sign hanging to one side. There appeared to be some kind of warning written on it. Now it was hardly legible, but…

Ignoring the "Oh!" from High Elf Archer behind him, Goblin Slayer untied the scroll.

"GGBGROB?"

"GOR! GOOGB!!"

It scarcely made sense to the goblins at first.

A wind began to blow through the dungeon.

Just wind? What is he, trying to scare us?

The goblins were quite amused—until they found themselves floating in midair.

"Eek…?!"

"Get through the door, quickly, or you'll get sucked in!" Goblin Slayer said sharply to Priestess, who was trying to hold her hat on her head.

An instant later, a huge wind billowed up.

The scroll he had thrown at them produced a void scorched by supernatural flames.

"GOOROGGB?!"

"GOBG!! GOOROGOBG?!"

The whirlwind, blowing away the fetid subterranean air, howled like a beast.

One goblin, two. They tried desperately to hold their ground, digging toes and fingers into the walls and floor, but it was no use. The goblins ahead tried to retreat, but they ran into their comrades pushing up from behind.

"GOBG?!"

"GBBOOROGOBG?!"

At last, the goblins were overwhelmed by the crazily dancing wind sprites and dragged into the void.

The adventurers forged ahead to the accompaniment of goblin screams, until Goblin Slayer shut the door.

Only the sound of the closing door seemed louder than the roar of the wind.

§

"Wh-what was *that*...?!" High Elf Archer demanded, panting as they rushed through the darkness.

"It was a Gate," Goblin Slayer answered, equally from the dark. "Connected to a high place."

"A high place?" High Elf Archer asked darkly. *Not that him using scrolls almost at random is anything new.*

"The sky," he said. "I have heard that wind sprites fly toward the place where there are the fewest dance partners." He hadn't wanted to use an item like that at that moment, but there had been no choice. "I had wanted to try it on goblins at some point. It was the perfect opportunity."

"...So what you're saying is, somewhere in the world, at this moment, it's *raining goblins*." High Elf Archer heaved a sigh. If there had been a sky, she might have looked up at it. "Oh, for... Fine. I guess it's better than a flood of water."

"I see."

"And it's not like I can really complain right now." She seemed to mean that she was less exasperated with him than simply resigned.

The small flap of her ears must surely have been because of a last gust of passing wind. "Man, sure is dark in here, though. Even I can't see, and I'm an elf."

The adventurers had fled the whirlwind through the door, and now they were in pitch blackness. They could guess that the width of the corridor and the height of the ceiling had probably not changed very much, but still, there was no hint of light. Priestess struck a flint, trying impatiently to light a torch or a lantern, but all she could get was a few sparks. When she finally gave up, the sigh she let out sounded inordinately loud. "...Guess we can't use fire."

"It seems this place is what is called a territory of darkness, or restraint," Lizard Priest said quietly. With his heat vision, he guided them along. As long as they could hear the scraping beside them, they knew his scaly hand was feeling its way along the wall. "From what I saw of the map just before all the fun started, I am almost certain the elevator is ahead."

"Well, I hope you're more *certain* than *almost*," Dwarf Shaman said. "I guess even the goblins wouldn't follow us in here." He gave a muttered expression of annoyance and could be heard to sit down heavily. Next came the noise of a stopper popping out of a bottle, and then a *glug glug*.

Yes, there were goblins just one little door away from them, but the entire party tacitly agreed to a short break.

"...I'm sorry. I guess I wasn't of much help." Priestess sounded dejected as she sat down (*bumpf*) on her small bottom. She had thrown herself completely into the fight, but all she had really done was swing her staff around. She couldn't use her miracles, because she was saving them; Dwarf Shaman had had to rescue her from being stabbed with a poisoned knife; and now she couldn't even strike up a flame. Those things weren't her fault—but that didn't keep her from feeling depressed about them.

She felt a rough hand pat her shoulder. "Ah, don't worry about it, lass. When the back row has to resort to their weapons, that's a clear sign we're in dire straits." The dwarf laughed. "It's Beard-cutter who should be feeling bad about that!"

"Indeed. It is by no means the role of a monk to wield his weapon in the service of his enemies' destruction." Lizard Priest took up the thread, sounding so serious that Priestess couldn't help but giggle.

That seemed to be enough to cut through the tension. "Right," she said, sounding ever so slightly more cheerful. "Can just holding on be considered a role?"

"Yes," Goblin Slayer replied. "There will always be something for you to do."

They all felt confident that he must be giving his usual deliberate nod, despite being rendered invisible by the darkness.

And I guess it doesn't change the fact that I can't see his expression.

So Priestess nodded back, feeling herself relax a bit. "...Okay. When the time comes, I'll do my part."

And then she smiled from ear to ear, even though nobody could see it.

Goblin Slayer waited for a few moments, letting everyone catch their breath, and when he judged they were ready, he said, "Let's go."

The adventurers looked at one another in the dark, nodded, and then formed up and moved out.

They worked their way along by feel, ignoring other doors they found, ever deeper into the dungeon. At last, on the far side of all the darkness, they saw a dim light. It illuminated a column of letters, *A* to *D*, visible through two open doors.

It was the elevator.

"Hup! Ahhh!"

The cute but powerful shout accompanied an explosion of light that sliced through the darkness surrounding the holy mount.

The darkness was something grotesque, like a great swollen lump of flesh. It was full of pulsing viscera, like a living creature turned inside out.

It had arrived along with the flaming stone from heaven, this thing, truly unknowable, even indescribable.

It had come clinging to the meteorite, which was still warm in its crater on the mountaintop, and then the thing had become a shade, stretching its flesh out toward the four corners of the world.

It was probably, from the perspective of one who could see only three dimensions, not from this plane of existence.

"...I feel like just looking at it chips away at my sanity," Sage said, her face uncharacteristically pale and sweaty. She was not yet a planeswalker. It would be such a shame to go to other worlds when she had yet to see and understand the whole of this one.

Now she gritted her teeth, her fingers on her staff, her very fingernails, the way every part of her body and hands moved, carving out precise words of true power. Sage alone had the ability to seal away this shade, this horrifying thing, this pulsating collection of guts.

Every minute, every second, she felt like her soul was being scraped away by a rasp, but...

"That right?" Sword Saint slid her feet back and forth, exquisitely minute moves that maintained the distance to the enemy. She judged her opportunities, striking out at the stretching, probing feelers whenever she had a chance, forcing them back or slicing them off. Each time, a spray of blackish blood would burst outward, like a crimson flag flying from her sword, painting the sky. Even an observer with no martial ability would have understood that she was the keystone of the party's defense.

"If it bleeds, that means we can kill it," she said. "Somehow."

Not every problem could be solved with a sword. But every problem that could be solved with a sword, she would solve.

To Sword Saint, this monster was nothing more than a lump of flesh that had come to her world from the stars. It came cursing her land, and now that she was within sword's reach, she would destroy it. It was as simple as that.

Yes, simple... That's her.

Sage breathed out, *heh*, and smiled, resigned to her companion's ways. Her shoulders slumped almost imperceptibly.

When they thought you were crude, be technical. And when they thought you were going to be technical, be absolutely crude.

That was best. *So it was in everything,* Sage thought, and then she said lightly, "Maybe I should just use Fusion to blow it away once and for all?"

"Aw, if this mountain ends up shorter than it started, they're gonna blame me!" Hero said, slicing away some tentacles that were making for Sword Saint. Despite her evident fatigue, though, she smiled.

It was Sage who prevented the thing from spreading, Sword Saint who handled defense, and all the attacking fell to Hero. Her small body was already weighed down by a gigantic sword, and now she had the peace of the entire world riding on her shoulders, too.

"At least its movement pattern is easy; that helps." Hero sounded as mellow as if she didn't even feel any of this burden; she readied her sacred sword in her two hands. "It just comes charging at you... Maybe this thing's really dumb?"

"It knows only expansion and attack. That's why we have to stop it now."

"I think His Majesty would really enjoy this, though."

"...I would rather not envision what would happen if we failed here and got absorbed by this thing." Sage gave up her former professed admiration for her bantering comrades. "However, you two are right about one thing. I don't believe its intelligence is highly developed..."

She strengthened her barriers as an attack came from a strange angle; Sage was thinking fast. It seemed likely that this thing, this shade—if it could be called that—learned by absorbing other living things. They were simply lucky that the creature it was trying to parasitize at the moment was so incredibly stupid.

But... Sage gave voice to the obvious question.

"How did the corpse of a goblin *drop onto a mountaintop...?* "

"Some guy on a goblin hunt somewhere must have—done it!" Hero sliced at the monster with all the strength in her slim arms, unconcerned about proper swordsmanship, lopping off a piece of the creature.

All just as usual. The black-haired girl smiled. It would be a big mistake to think she alone could take care of the whole world.

"He's doing his part—so we'd better do ours and not lose this fight!"

She smiled again, looking like a girl who could have come from any village in the world. Then she swung her sacred sword like a club.

"XEEEEEEEENOOOOOOOOOOOOOOOOONNN!!!!"

"As if we ever lose!"

An explosion of sun.

CHAPTER 8

The Heart of the Maelstrom

"GGRROROB!"

"GRBBR! GOORGGBG!"

Grumbled, filthy curses echoed through the burial chamber. The princess heard all of it from where she lay on the floor, bound with torn shreds from her own vestments. She tried to see, but the dark, the gloom, and the clinging miasma made it difficult.

Her face was swollen, her tilted vision blurred with tears, and her nose and mouth were so dry they burned.

Only natural, after the beating she'd received, she thought distantly. She must have looked terrible.

The thought made her nose prickle, and tears threatened to gather in her eyes again. Then they spilled out, along with a stream of sniffles; the resolution to restrain them had been pummeled out of her.

Whatever was waiting for her next, it wouldn't be better than what had already happened. The thought terrified her. When she thought of the awful, blasphemous possibilities, even the chill of the dirty stones she lay on faded to insignificance.

"GOROGGBGO! GROG!"

"GGGOROGB!"

At the altar, the one goblin wearing elaborate clothing was shouting something.

His outfit was that of a magic user, one turned comically, hideously theatrical. His whole body was covered in geometric tattoos—they were "hands"—and he was the goblins' leader.

The princess found herself shaking at the idea that she would soon be beaten, raped, violated to the very brink of death. "Heek... Eek...!"

"GGBGOROGOBOG!"

"GOR! GBOGOGB!"

The goblins had started laughing at the pitiful child again. They weren't specifically amused that the king's little sister had been reduced to such a state. No, they simply enjoyed the fact that someone more pathetic than them was cowering and weeping.

If the goblins had known who she was, they would probably have treated her even worse. Goblins made no attempt to hide their jealousy or grudges. The girl knew full well that she had sunk into a dark pit where these monsters' lusts raged unchecked.

There was no help.

There was no salvation.

All was lost, all had been stolen from her, all debased.

And yet, the goblins still intended to take every last vestige of what she had.

They'll never be satisfied. I'm sure of it.

She could apologize, cry and beg, but it wouldn't be enough for them, even if she died.

The only way they might be distracted was if they tired of her, or forgot about her, or if their interest was drawn by some other poor victim.

"Ooh... Ah... Ergh..."

In light of that fact, she had resolved, at the very least, not to plead for forgiveness. Not because of a desire to resist the goblins, or out of pride. Simply because she didn't want to sink so low, and because she knew pleading wouldn't do any good anyway.

She was under no illusions: the goblins would steal that resolve from her, too, and probably in just a matter of minutes.

"GGBGBG!"

"GRB!"

The goblin leader lifted his staff—it was a dried-out hand—and waved it around, giving his subordinates some kind of order. There was a flurry of wet footsteps as the dirty monsters came closer, full of greed.

The faces of her dearly departed mother and father flashed through her mind. Then she saw her older brother.

Was he angry at her? she wondered. Worried about her? She could only imagine.

All she wanted, the only thing, was to go home.

But she never would. Not without a miracle…

§

"I attempted to investigate at the temple, but their tattoo is of a kind I myself have never seen."

The elevator bore the adventurers downward silently. If it weren't for the floaty feeling under their feet, they would never have thought they were in a moving box.

High Elf Archer frowned and flicked her ears, whereupon Lizard Priest advised her, "Swallow." She did as he said, and the discomfort in her ears seemed to vanish.

"However, I strongly believe they have a spell caster with them."

"A goblin shaman, right?" Priestess said.

"I can't say for certain," Goblin Slayer said, causing Priestess to blanch a bit. She was well past the point where she might go limp with fear, but such an enemy was not one to be met without anxiety. She gripped her staff and took a deep breath. Then another. Fill the lungs, then let it out.

High Elf Archer patted her rising, falling shoulders.

"…Doing all right?"

"Yes," Priestess said, smiling bravely. "I'm fine."

She glanced over at Goblin Slayer, who was talking to Dwarf Shaman and Lizard Priest. Planning and calculating, no doubt. It helped her relax to see them going about business as usual.

"I think we can assume these are the same goblins who have been causing trouble in the area lately. He would be their chieftain," Goblin Slayer said.

"If you're right about that, then…taking down the spell caster first would be the obvious way to go," Dwarf Shaman replied with a stroke of his white beard.

"Nay, but I think it would depend on the number and equipment of our opponents," Lizard Priest argued. The cleric, a member of those most renowned warriors, the lizardmen, turned his long neck this way and that, vigilant. "In any event, were we to be ambushed when these doors opened, it would be something of a duck hunt."

"Projectiles, then," Goblin Slayer grunted. "How troublesome."

"Hey, Long-Ears," Dwarf Shaman said grimly. "Can y'hear anything below?"

"Just because I'm an elf doesn't mean I can hear *everything*, okay?" High Elf Archer frowned and closed her eyes, her ears working up and down. Everyone instinctively fell silent. Only the soft sounds of their breathing filled the space.

After a few moments, High Elf Archer opened her eyes again. "…Hmm. There's a lot of them, I think," she said, but she didn't sound very sure. "More than ten, I'd guess? Maybe even twenty. I hear a lot of footsteps. I can't figure out what they're wearing, though."

"Anything else you noticed?" Goblin Slayer asked. "Anything at all."

"Not a sound, but—" High Elf Archer twitched her nose. "There's some sort of weird smell. From down below."

"Do you think it's poison gas?"

The answer to his question came from Lizard Priest. "No, I should think they are performing a ritual of some kind. Burning some sort of incense would be natural enough."

"Whatever it is, I guarantee it won't do us any good to breathe it in," Dwarf Shaman said. He *humphed* thoughtfully then clapped his hands as an idea occurred to him. "Say, Beard-cutter. Do you have those—those things we used once? The cloth-and-ash things that filtered out bad air."

"Those were improvised out of need. Given enough time to prepare, it would be better to soak a cloth in antidote." Goblin Slayer pulled a bottle with a string wrapped around the neck from his item bag. "I'd rather not use a potion now, but I suppose this is the time for it."

"Oh," Priestess said, raising her hand, "then let me...!" The party turned to look at her. She blushed, not quite used to being the center of attention. "Er, I just, ahem, thought maybe we could open with Holy Light like we usually do..." She sounded more apologetic the longer she spoke. "I thought maybe that would be... the safest thing to try..."

Goblin Slayer did a quick mental calculation of their remaining spells. Three, and this would mean using one on entry.

If the captive was safe—meaning alive—she would almost certainly ask for healing.

That would leave them with one miracle. Was that "just one miracle," or "one whole miracle"?

He shoved the potion back in his pouch.

"Handle it."

"Right!"

His response was simple as could be, and Priestess nodded vigorously, her face lit up.

"Very good. Mistress Priestess shall make our opening gambit, while I shall, I suppose, be on the front row." Lizard Priest made a strange palms-together gesture, looking positively excited. "Thankfully, I've been able to conserve the miracles that I can ask from my forebears. What of you, master spell caster?"

"Lessee, here... I've two more spells—no, make that three, but..." Dwarf Shaman dug through his bag of catalysts as he spoke then grinned. "How about it, Beard-cutter? What d'you want?"

"A source of light," he replied without even thinking. "The rest is up to you."

"You got it. That'll be me, then."

"And I'll just do what I always do," High Elf Archer said, restringing her bow and feeling out how many arrows she had left. "You mentioned projectiles. That means shooting. I'll stay loose. In case the dwarf falls over or anything."

"I won't fall," Dwarf Shaman said, glaring at her. "As long as no anvils stumble on top of me!"

Huh! High Elf Archer went red and shot back something in kind, and then they were off and arguing, as usual.

Lizard Priest, who seemed to find the sight relaxing under the circumstances, rolled his eyes in his head. "After that, the key will be...flexibility."

"...You don't mean just act at random, do you?" Priestess said with a wry smile.

"No," Goblin Slayer answered, shaking his head. "Flexibility is something goblins aren't capable of."

§

"O Earth Mother, abounding in mercy, please, by your revered hand, cleanse us of our corruption!!"

Thus came forth Purify.

A sacred wind swept through that place of filth and pollution; Priestess's prayer, offered in loud voice, broke through the elevator doors like a miracle.

"I swept away the miasma!"

"Perfect!"

The adventurers jumped out into the room, now free of the choking fog. The rusted alarm, which had once been a trap, jingled once and then fell silent.

"GGOBOGOB?!"

"GORO?! GOBOGOR?!"

Goblin jabber, words most likely of blasphemous import, sounded in the gloom. Dwarf Shaman, who could see in the dark, frowned and immediately grabbed some coal from his bag.

"Hold your torch up, give us light, will-o-the-wisp, burn in the night! Onibi, I call on thee, give a little light to me!"

He flung the coal into the air, where it burst of its own accord into a blue-white flame. The thing he had called forth with Control Spirit shone brightly in the dungeon.

The space it illuminated turned out to be a burial chamber in the truest sense of the words. A pair of doors in the distance must have been the elevator to the depths that former adventurers had sought. There were signs of furious battle all around the dim stone room, along with shattered steel, tattered armor, and bits of skeletons in black outfits.

If this had been any normal dungeon crawl, it would have been a place of absolute solemnity.

But now, it was inhabited by goblins. The very heart of this dungeon was piled high with goblin junk, filth, and food scraps.

By the walls all around were those who had tried this dungeon without a plan, or perhaps who had lost to the goblins...

"That's awful...," Priestess said, involuntarily putting a hand to her mouth at the horror of it. Goblin Slayer grunted softly.

Several corpses dangled there, suspended by meat hooks dug into their flesh, like strange, hideous fruits. It was all too easy to imagine that being hung by their skin was the last stage of untold tortures.

"GOROBG!"

"Ohh... Ah..."

At that moment, among the confused shouts of the goblins, a soft, weak cry could be heard. It was the hostage—the princess, up on the altar.

A goblin dressed in elaborate clothing, likely their leader, had her by the hair and was pulling her up.

She's alive!

"One staff. Five swords, five clubs, two spears, seven bows, no hobs—twenty in all!"

One of the adventurers was wearing grimy leather armor and a cheap-looking helmet; on his arm was a small, round shield, and at his hip, a sword of a strange length.

Goblin Slayer, who had flung the torch from his left hand into the room, quickly assessed the situation.

"As we expected. A shaman is—"

"No...!" Priestess interrupted.

Her joy at the princess's survival was fleeting; now both her eyes were open wide. She was looking squarely at the goblin with the staff, tattoos all over his body.

Was it fear? Past experience? No. A sharp tingle ran along the nape of her neck.

A handout!

Priestess correctly interpreted the revelation from the munificent Earth Mother and exclaimed, "That's a *priest*!"

Apostle of the heinous gods of Chaos! Non-Prayer to the rightful and just gods!

"GBOB! GOROBGGRB! GOROBG!!"

As if in response to Priestess, the goblin's prayer echoed through the room. He waved his staff and gibbered in his bizarre tongue, and a hazy, sinister light began to gather around the altar.

"That son of a...!"

Far be it from High Elf Archer to let him get away with that: she loosed an arrow at the goblin, meaning to take him before he had time to react—but the arrow bounced away with a dry clack.

"No way...! Protection?!"

The goblin cultist gave them a vile grin, and they perceived a wall of pale light around him.

Goblin Slayer knew well the strength of that light. He had relied on it more than once.

It certainly wasn't that he hadn't thought of this possibility. His battle with the goblin paladin on the snowy mountain had been close to a year before, but he still remembered it vividly.

But a goblin believer?

In the whole world, there seemed few things less amenable to each other than goblins and faith.

Now he clicked his tongue at himself to realize he had been making this unconscious assumption.

"Try this, then!"

There wasn't a moment of hesitation in Goblin Slayer's words or actions. He was not fool enough to throw away the advantage of surprise.

No sooner had he spoken than he flung a cruelly shaped blade into the darkness.

The knife, its blades bent like broken branches, went flying to one side.

"GOBO?!"

It traveled with a sound like a buzzing bee, until it found a goblin archer who was outside the protective barrier. Dark goblin blood spewed into the low light; the headless corpse tottered and fell over.

The head, meanwhile, rolled into a corner of the chamber, there to rot for the next hundred years.

"That's one! Take out the archers. We'll have to do this hand to hand!"

"Ha-ha-ha! Understood!"

While he shouted, Goblin Slayer pulled on the string he'd tied to his knife; meanwhile, Lizard Priest jumped into the fray.

The powerful lizardman was a master of unarmed combat.

"O sickle wings of velociraptor, rip and tear, fly and hunt!"

But he didn't need to stay unarmed: his catalyst, a fang in his hand, swelled and grew until he was holding a polished blade.

Then Lizard Priest, breathing hard with the excitement of battle, stood solidly with his legs apart, his breath coming like steam from his jaws.

"GOROBG!"

"GOROOBG?!"

"Eeeyah!!"

From their own back row, the goblin archers loosed a volley of arrows, but Lizard Priest swept them aside with his tail and launched a kick. "Goblin arrows are like a spring shower!"

He proceeded to use his Swordclaws, one in each hand, to eviscerate the nearest goblins.

One, two. The bravest goblins—or rather, the ones who had been pushed forward by those behind—lost their heads. Who would willingly challenge such a terrifying beast? So much easier to target the little cleric girl standing near the back, or the elf alongside her.

"GGBGR! GOROGOBOGOR!"

The evil goblin priest rained abuse on his followers as they recoiled then issued new orders to his archers.

Get up there. Shoot for their soft back row.

But the archers, having observed the demise of their late comrade, didn't budge. In fact, they tried to squeeze in behind the wall of Protection themselves.

"GOROBG!"

"GOBOGOROB?!"

The goblin priest, enraged, kicked his archers out from behind the barrier—literally. An instant later, one of the foolish monsters had High Elf Archer's arrow through his eye.

"Too easy!" Her long ears flicked triumphantly as she scanned for her next target.

Fortunately, there were a great many bodies and remains to stand on. Not that she was eager to perch on a corpse.

High Elf Archer made one graceful leap after another, loosing her bud-tipped arrows in midair in quick succession. They pelted down on the goblin priest at the altar, but the invisible barrier refused to give way.

It was just too tough. High Elf Archer frowned. There was no way that beast could be as devout as their girl.

"Clean them up—I'll cover you!" she said.

If she couldn't take out the leader, then she would change focus. As she pulled out her next arrow, she kicked off the wall in a wall jump.

In response, Goblin Slayer raised his shield and moved forward. He let the howling Lizard Priest serve as a distraction, while he closed in on the altar where the archers were standing. "Currently four. Sixteen left. Five of them archers...!"

"GGOBOGOG! GOBOROOBG!!"

"GOROB!"

The priest, with his bird's-eye view, was not so blind as to miss Goblin Slayer's approach. He spat an order to his spearmen, who tried to keep the adventurer from getting closer.

Goblin Slayer didn't have time for armed combat. He simply pounded the throwing knife into an enemy spear.

"GOROBG?!"

The broken blades entangled themselves in the haft of the spear, which broke. The goblin's dirty eyes widened in amazement.

Goblin Slayer let go of his weapon and brought his shield to bear.

"GOROOOGB?!"

"Five!"

The sharpened edge of his shield split the goblin's skull. He kicked the creature as it tumbled backward, sweeping down with his hand to grab the spear off the ground.

"Six!"

"GOOBOGORO?!"

He pulled his shield out of the fifth goblin's skull, using the momentum to propel his spear into the sixth goblin's neck. He let go of the polearm amid a geyser of blood and drew his sword.

"Fourteen left!"

"GOROBG!!"

The goblin priest, rather than blame the fact that his choice of orders was poor, excoriated his subordinates for their stupidity.

The archers were looking this way and that, trying to decide whether to target the elf, the lizard, or the human. One of them hesitantly readied an arrow, then recalled that in fact there was a dwarf protecting a human girl, and aimed his arrow in that direction.

"GORG?!"

An instant later, though, something pierced him through the neck, and he died choking on his own blood. His arms flopped and the arrow shot off, pinging off the floor in an absurd direction.

It was simply impossible to escape the aim of an elf. Now there were four goblin archers left.

"Ho! Not bad for you, Long-Ears!"

Speaking of Dwarf Shaman, he was indeed protecting Priestess, as the goblin had seen. He had a hand in his bag of catalysts even as he unleashed a flurry of ax blows to keep the goblins away.

Thankfully, Beard-cutter had taken care of the handful of spear wielders. Goblins with clubs and swords he could handle, somehow.

"GGOROGB?!"

"GOOBG?!"

One goblin, and then another. Goblin Slayer, Lizard Priest, High Elf Archer, and Dwarf Shaman each cut down monster after monster.

"............"

But Priestess, observing the melee from the back, couldn't shake the sense that the hairs on the back of her neck were standing up again.

I wonder what's causing this weird feeling...

She was the only one with the opportunity to calmly evaluate what was happening. It was her role to take advantage of that.

A battle was raging around her, and she was only standing there holding her staff. She desperately tried to keep her heart from racing at the thought.

The goblin priest waved the relic in his hand, giving orders—if they could be called that—to his followers.

He gave the captive princess one vicious kick, then another, in retaliation for what was happening.

Priestess couldn't imagine his heart was here. Couldn't believe he was truly praying to the gods in heaven, or whatever equivalent he had.

So why doesn't the protection vanish?

Was she to believe that the evil gods were so compassionate? No, it couldn't be.

For a miracle... For a spell... One always had to pay a price. Give something in exchange for twisting the very logic of the world.

It could be the soul, shaved away by a prayer; it could be a spell committed to memory; a catalyst; one's vitality.

—?

Suddenly, Priestess looked down at the blood pooling by her feet. A flash of insight rushed through her mind.

She looked up and shouted: "Goblin Slayer, sir—she's a living sacrifice...!"

That was all it took.

Goblin Slayer's helmet moved even as he slashed the throat of the goblin in front of him.

Red lines ran along the floor, visible against the goblins' dark blood. Red-black lines forming a pattern whose channels led back to the altar.

It looked familiar to him.

He himself had helped with it on the farm more than once.

"He's bleeding them!"

Indeed: the source of the blood was the goblin corpses—and the bodies of the adventurers hung on the wall.

It was bad enough they had been tormented in life. Now the goblins would continue to take from them even after they were dead.

The blood dripped from the corpses, flowing toward the altar, where it brought power to the deities of evil.

"GOROGBG! GOROBOGO!!"

The goblin priest cackled viciously. Priestess's vision went red, and she felt something hot.

This is unforgivable. Where had that thought come from?

In the back of her mind, she saw... She saw her comrades from that very first adventure.

How could there be salvation for anyone if they were to be the goblins' playthings even after they were dead?

"I'll do it!" she shouted, raising her sounding staff. The adventurers all glanced in her direction then nodded.

"Take care of it!" Goblin Slayer shouted, and Lizard Priest howled, "Be not hesitant!"

A goblin archer was trying to load a third arrow, but before he could manage it, Lizard Priest's massive body was hurtling through the air. He landed with his tail pounding the floor and slammed into the archer, practically breaking the monster in half.

"Ha-ha-ha-ha-ha! Know this, vermin: you have no escape!!"

"GOROBOGO?!"

"GBBGOR!"

The two remaining archers flung down their bows and tried to run. It was an uncommonly wise decision for goblins—or would have been, if there hadn't been an enemy directly behind them.

"Thirteen... Fourteen!!"

In less than the space of two breaths, the goblins found their heads split open and their brains splattered on the stone.

Goblin Slayer gave the club in his hand a casual flick to get the gore off.

"GOROBGOR?!"

"GRR!"

The five surviving goblin foot soldiers began to close in on the center of the room. The goblin priest was jabbering behind them, but they felt no obligation to listen to the likes of him. The goblins, each planning to put himself first in the fight that was to come, raised their weapons and charged at Priestess.

There was no thought in their minds of taking her hostage. They just wanted payback, somehow; they wanted to take her and hurt her in revenge.

"...!"

Priestess, stiff, nonetheless stared down the oncoming foe. Dwarf Shaman inserted himself between them, and from a distance, High Elf Archer was taking aim.

She could see Lizard Priest, too, and even *him*, all at once. There was nothing to be scared of.

She filled her small chest with a deep breath, let it out, and then shouted: "*O Earth Mother, abounding in mercy, please, by your revered hand, cleanse us of our corruption!!*"

The great and venerable Earth Mother once more responded to the devout supplication of her follower, touching their world with her sacred hand.

An invisible wave spread out from Priestess like a caress, washing over the chamber. The flowing channels of blood were transformed before their eyes into streams of pure water.

This spell is intended to protect, not to harm...!

That was why Priestess was sure the Earth Mother would permit her this usage.

"GGBOGO?!"

The goblin priest yammered in shock, and his voice scrambled Priestess's cleansing wave. Untainted water, though, was not fit for a living sacrifice to the evil gods. The barrier protecting him vanished instantaneously, and the goblin priest was left defenseless.

"GROBOGOG!"

"Uhh... Ahh..."

Well, not defenseless, exactly.

The evil priest of the goblins grabbed the girl he had taken for the sacrifice by her hair, using her as a meat shield.

One lone adventurer strode boldly toward him.

He wore grimy leather armor and a cheap-looking metal helmet, with a small, round shield on his arm and a club he had stolen from a goblin in his hand.

"Hmph." Goblin Slayer glanced back over his shoulder.

High Elf Archer's arrows, Lizard Priest's fangs, and Dwarf Shaman's ax had destroyed the goblin forces.

Priestess was safe.

Goblin Slayer looked forward once more.

The goblin priest, terrified, held the princess up desperately, struggling to protect himself. A mocking smile hung on his filthy face.

Goblin Slayer said, "This makes twenty."

He kicked, sweeping the goblin's legs out from under him, and where the creature fell, the club came down.

Then it was done.

§

With the battle done, a staggering silence fell over the burial chamber.

The only sounds were the ragged breathing of those left in the room, and the gentle scraping of equipment. High Elf Archer kept an arrow loosely nocked in her bow as she looked around, but then finally, she exhaled.

"Is it over…?"

"…Looks like it," Priestess said, the two companions sharing a relieved sigh. Then Priestess went up to the altar.

What can I say to her?

It wasn't far, but that question made the journey feel immense.

Should Priestess be happy the girl was safe—meaning that at least she had her life?

Should she be angry the girl had stolen her mail?

Neither felt quite right to her, and she reached the girl without having come to a conclusion.

"…Oh."

Priestess could see her own confused expression in the eyes that stared vacantly up at her.

The girl could hardly be called fortunate. And yet, it was because she had been chosen as a living sacrifice that she was still here. Wounded and heartbroken, her clothes torn, but not covered in filth.

Even at that very moment, Priestess still couldn't find the words. She looked this way and that as if searching for them.

Then she spotted something.

A bit of booty the goblins had stolen from an adventurer then tossed aside. It lay almost randomly on a pile of junk: some cheap mail, the kind that could be bought anywhere.

It had been repaired repeatedly, so much that it might have been better to simply buy a new set. She would have recognized it any-where: this mail was hers.

"…!"

Priestess grabbed it and pulled it close, and then she gathered the princess's slim body into a hug as well.

"Thank goodness…," she whispered, the voice squeezing out of her.

Was she glad to recover the mail, or the child? Even she wasn't sure. But she doubted it was just one or the other. If she had retrieved the mail, but the princess had been dead, or if the girl had been alive and the mail lost, she couldn't help thinking that it would have left a sting in her heart.

That was why she hugged them both.

She didn't know how to put it into words. But there was no question.

"Ooh, ah… Ah…!" It was all the princess could bear. She clung to Priestess and wept openly.

"It's okay," Priestess assured her. She rubbed the princess's back as the girl kept repeating "*I was so scared. I'm sorry.*"

Goblin Slayer took this in with a sidelong glance then let out a breath.

"Oh-ho," Lizard Priest said, rolling his eyes as he detected the sound. "Are we relieved?"

"…" Goblin Slayer thought for a moment then nodded slowly. "Yes. Because she seemed a bit unsteady. I mean her."

"Well, if she's feeling better now, no need t'ask why, I suppose."

"But if one were to ask, I might suggest this." Lizard Priest's long neck turned, and he scuffed at the pattern carved in the floor. "What do you think of it?"

"I should venture to guess that this place must have been intended to resurrect some dark god."

The channels created strange, complicated geometric patterns and were clearly some variety of magic. Then again, if this burial chamber was the heart of this dungeon, perhaps they were intended to summon some follower.

"So that's it for the job, right?" High Elf Archer said, her ears drooping tiredly. "We can get out of here?" She glanced in Priestess's direction.

But Goblin Slayer shook his head. "No. There are still goblins left above us. We must kill them all."

"*Ugh,*" High Elf Archer said, sounding profoundly disgusted, but Lizard Priest chuckled, "A most fearsome road home."

"Nothing to it but t'do it," Dwarf Shaman added, taking a drink of wine. Priestess was still holding on to the princess, who had finally calmed down.

Hence, what happened was not on account of anyone's lapse in vigilance.

Call it a roll of the dice, if you must.

It's just the way the pips come up sometimes.

"G..."

The goblin priest clung to life, despite his smashed skull. His brain whirled with even darker and more awful thoughts than before, and he reached out for his relic, his magical item.

"GOR...B..."

The priest had one selfish idea in his mind: *After all I've done, they can't fail to save me.*

Yes, it was self-centered. It wasn't faith. Right or wrong, it was not a thought offered to the gods.

So there could be only one answer.

"GOROBOG?!"

It burst forth.

Like a seed in spring. Like a sprout pushing through the earth.

The goblin's back swelled and exploded as it grasped its way into this world.

Splattered with the goblin's blood and guts, spreading out like a hideous flower, was a grotesque five-fingered hand.

"Hrm..."

"Wha...?!"

The adventurers were struck speechless by a sight so unholy they had to check to see if they were still sane.

Goblin Slayer was instantly ready to fight, and Dwarf Shaman reached for his bag. In the blink of an eye, High Elf Archer had taken a handful of her few remaining arrows.

But Lizard Priest—and Priestess. The two of them understood what this was.

The goblin's twitching limbs stretched out on the altar, scraping through the filth.

It was a pale arm.

An arm bigger, wider, more massive than a tree.

An arm that had appeared from thin air, just a pulsating limb with twisted, grasping claws.

The fingers, stained with goblin blood, reached out like serpents seeking their prey.

Amazement? Terror? It was impossible to say.

But Priestess would not let them threaten the girl she had clasped to her chest any more.

She held the princess fast as her trembling lips formed the words.

"A greater demon's hand...!"

Then came a blast of immense sharpness, and the young priestess screamed from the unendurable pain.

CHAPTER 9

Goblin Hand, Sign of Destruction

Faith can mean more than selfless prayer.

An offering to placate rampaging gods, a cry for the help you just happen to need—that's faith, too.

What, then, was in the goblin's heart? It was too late now to know.

"Ngh, ahh...!"

Priestess writhed with the pain, but her very breath froze in the air, tormenting her further.

The dim world of the dungeon was already painted over with white, the freezing snow of the blizzard so sharp it seemed to cut her skin.

The Onibi fires vanished in an instant, even the last smoldering flames of them winked out of existence.

Priestess, though, refused to move from where she was. She had in her arms a frightened, trembling, yelping little girl who was curling herself up as she tried to run from the terror. Priestess held her close in her thin arms, stiffening up and protecting her with all the strength in her little body.

"Hrr—rrooahhhh...!"

If there was to be a response, then, it would come from Lizard Priest, the very first party member to notice and react to the aberration. With his breath coming as steam, he jumped forward, unleashing a roar that reverberated around the burial chamber.

"Ah, you who have survived the white destruction! Maniraptora! Behold my deeds in battle!" He placed his massive body to shield them from the brutal cold emanating from the greater demon's hand. Frost formed on his scales. His skin froze. Snow collected on his claws and fangs, causing his body to pitch.

Priestess blinked—her eyelids threatened to freeze shut—and adjusted her grip on her sounding staff with fingers that felt they might never come loose from it.

"We...need...a miracle...!"

"I am...afraid...not!" Lizard Priest looked toward Priestess, his usual lecturing tone undiminished. "I, as it happens, can no longer... use mine...!!"

Yes: be it magic or miracles, such feats demand a certain amount of strength to twist the very warp and weft of the world around one. Lizardmen were not built for the cold to begin with. Now Lizard Priest's eyes were nearly closed, as if sleepy, betraying how near he was to the end of his endurance.

Thus, it would not do for Priestess to use the last of her precious miracles here and now. The young woman bit her lip and swallowed any objection.

"Scaaaalyyyy!!"

Lizard Priest's intervention, though, did little to turn the tide. They were still in real danger of complete destruction.

Dwarf Shaman was shouting, and High Elf Archer was hugging herself, calling a warning. "Guys, this... This is bad...!"

There was no time even to acknowledge her. Goblin Slayer was on the move.

Blocking the sleet and hail with the round shield on his arm or letting it bounce off his helmet, he made a beeline.

"You are alive?"

"...I am, at least, not dead yet."

Then, pointing his sword at the hand of the greater demon that was causing this snowstorm, Goblin Slayer supported Lizard Priest as if carrying him on his back. Goblin Slayer just managed to hold up the great weight of that body and work his way backward.

It was too late now to advance at a run. He didn't have the equipment necessary to deal with the frozen floor.

"My thanks," Lizard Priest said, to which the only answer was, "It was nothing," after which Goblin Slayer looked around behind his helmet.

"Make a wall...now!"

"A wall, he says...!" Dwarf Shaman replied, his beard crunching as he moved. "You mean the snow!"

The dwarf slammed a palm down on the snow piled on the ground. He was just visible in High Elf Archer's peripheral vision as she started running. For an elf, connected to nature as they were, a bit of ice was no real obstacle. "...This way, quick!"

"Right...!"

Priestess crawled along, supporting herself with her staff and covering the princess with her body; the cleric, too, was clearly at her limit. Her skin was pale and bloodless, and her sweet lips were turning purple. Her teeth chattered ceaselessly.

High Elf Archer had scant protection from the cold herself. Even so, she shielded the girls as best she could with her small body as they retreated. Her long ears were shaking.

"Orcbolg, hurry up...!"

"Y-yes...!"

It had only been twenty or thirty seconds, just a single turn. But to the adventurers, it seemed to take forever to collect themselves. The sight of them all huddling behind the stubby dwarf was almost comical.

"Ice Princess Atali, now, I call you, give this hero a dance, like the blowing flakes of snow through the air prance!"

At this moment of crisis, though, his craggy form looked as sturdy as a cliffside. The snow sprites he directed with Spirit Wall danced around the adventurers. Before the party's eyes, the blowing, piling snow became a wall to protect them.

Fight snow with snow. It could even block out the cold.

"A simple snow cave... How about it?"

"...It'll...have to do..." Priestess touched Lizard Priest's freezing body—he was panting hard by now—and made a quick decision. She was no healer, but as a cleric of the Earth Mother, she knew a thing or two.

"Give me a healing—no, a Stamina potion!"

"All right." Goblin Slayer pulled two bottles from his bag and tossed them to Priestess. "You and that girl should each drink as well."

"Got it!" Priestess scrabbled at the stopper with stiff fingers. She doused a cloth from her item pouch with the contents and pressed it to Lizard Priest's mouth.

His consciousness was fading, and trying to pour a potion down his throat might have choked him. Priestess watched Lizard Priest suckle at the cloth, and meanwhile, she drank from one of the half-frozen potions herself.

It burned as it went down her throat, and then she let out a breath of relief as she felt a heat in her stomach.

"Beard-cutter, Long-Ears, you drink something, too." Dwarf Shaman, who was taking a gulp of wine as if to say his work here was done now that the spell was active, tossed his bottle to the others.

Goblin Slayer caught it and poured some of the wine through his visor. Then he passed it to High Elf Archer. "Drink. It will warm you. If you don't move, you will die."

"…You know I'm not good with this stuff. But I guess this isn't the time to complain." The elf took the bottle in both hands with a look of disgust then licked daintily at it. Then she poked her head up over the wall of ice to see what the greater demon's hand was up to.

The hand, which had popped out of the goblin's flesh like a flower pushing through the earth, was still up on the altar. After invoking the snowstorm, the "trunk"—cords of muscle bulging out—writhed and twitched.

It was a terrible sight, one High Elf Archer wasn't eager to look at, but she was a scout. It was her job.

"…Looks like it can't reach us here," she said.

"Then we were successful," Goblin Slayer answered. "How is the girl?"

"…She's getting weaker," Priestess said, gently giving the girl some of the potion from which she'd taken her sip. "I don't think we can stay here long."

"What do you think?" Goblin Slayer asked. He clicked his tongue when he saw how hard Lizard Priest was breathing. "...Never mind," he corrected himself. "We must attack, or we must retreat." Then he stashed his sword in its scabbard and let out a breath.

He looked around at his party. Dwarf Shaman had one spell left, Priestess a single miracle. Lizard Priest must already be at his limit.

The goblins were dead. The girl was rescued. There were still goblins above them.

The snowstorm was getting stronger. That was obviously the hand of Chaos, and yet...

"There is no reason we must destroy it."

There was only one conclusion.

"True enough," High Elf Archer said with a hint of a smile. "You're right. To borrow a phrase, it's not a g—"

But that was as far as she got.

The wall of ice shattered with a roar, and High Elf Archer's body went flying through space.

"Hrgh... Agh?!"

She slammed against the wall of the chamber with a sound like a breaking branch, and blood dribbled from her mouth.

What had happened? The answer was simple.

The greater demon's fist had twisted up those ropelike muscles and *jumped.*

A blow from that fist, as large as any giant's, was more than enough to punch through their wall.

The adventurers were showered with shards of ice, buried, and unfortunately, it was their scout who had taken the direct hit.

Priestess cried out, shouting the name of High Elf Archer, who was crumpled like a dried leaf.

"I'm...f...fine..." Her voice came in gasps, tiny and weak. When the metal helmet looked at Priestess, she nodded tearfully.

Goblin Slayer let out a breath. It was all right, then—not critical. If it had been, she wouldn't have been able to hide it.

"So the bastard can move…!" As he rose up, clearing away the snow, though, Goblin Slayer was unable to act immediately.

In front of him was the greater demon's hand, like a snake raising up its head.

Can it see me?

He seriously doubted it. Perhaps that meant it had some form of extrasensory perception or the like.

An old deer-hunting technique flashed through his mind: Put snow in your mouth, become a part of the scenery. Then go for the kill.

"What's the plan, Beard-cutter?!" Dwarf Shaman had Lizard Priest's massive body across his shoulders as if he were hiding under it. Priestess was crawling along, still holding the Princess, and giving High Elf Archer a shoulder to lean on as she got drunkenly to her feet.

Goblin Slayer didn't know what to say right away.

It was not a goblin. So what should he do? It was not a goblin. This was no goblin.

This was not like that monster (whatever it had been called) that they had battled. This was different from the thing in the sewers, the dark elf, and even that ocean snake.

He realized with surprise how few things he actually had experience of.

Goblin Slayer thought. That was something his master had told him. *All you can do is think.*

You have no talent. No smarts. No skills. But you have guts. So think!

He thought. Would an icicle come crashing down or a snowball come flying?

What did he have in his pocket? In his pocket, he had…

"A hand." He finally squeezed the words out. "…Let's do it."

Even he could hardly believe the sound of his own voice.

"Yes, sir!" came an answering shout, without an instant's hesitation.

A young girl was looking directly at him, clutching a sounding staff in her frozen fingers and heroically trying to keep her body from shaking.

It was a demonstration of Priestess's—yes—faith.

§

The greater demon's hand was starved and withering.

A goblin's flesh and soul—how much nourishment could there be in such things?

Adventurers.

It had to kill the adventurers, the Pray-ers.

The poor fools must be preparing themselves to die. Their lives. Their souls. Their despair.

The hand gently stroked the air, seeking these things.

There.

The senses of a greater demon, the thoughts of such a monster, were so far removed from those of the adventurers that they could not hope to fathom them. In the end, it was simply impossible to imagine what he—or she?—might be thinking.

But there was the dwarf, working his way slowly back with the liz-ardman, the elf girl, and the human sacrifice. The way the muscles thrashed when the monster recognized that dwarf had to be inspired by something we could call joy, or at least greed.

The muscles of the greater demon's hand squeezed and bulged, the entire thing pulsating.

Then it leaped—at which exact moment a stone came flying from one side.

The hand stopped as if it had been slapped, the wrist turning this way and that.

"Over...here!"

It was just a rock. Sling or no sling, the girl's slim build was not going to be enough to do any damage.

But there she was, a girl standing there, fighting back the fear and the cold.

When it spotted her, the movements of the greater demon's hand became shockingly fast. It twisted toward her, its hideous fingers skittering along the floor like spiders.

"...Eek?!" Priestess exclaimed at the terror of it. It was moving fast, probably too fast for her to deal with. It would catch her, clasp her, twist and break her, squeeze and choke her. Her flesh and bones would be reduced to mush, her innards to a bloody soup; she would be utterly shattered before she was even dead.

"As if I would let you…!"

"—?!"

Priestess never shut her eyes as the hand closed in on her. And then the instant before it grabbed her, the arm was thrown sideways.

Was it because of the icy floor? No. Magic, then? No.

"Some call it Medea's Oil. Others, petroleum. It's gasoline."

There was an adventurer with a cheap-looking metal helmet, grimy leather armor, a round shield tied to his arm, and a sword of a strange length at his hip. Even a beginner would have better equipment than this man, who now threw a small bottle on the floor.

A viscous black substance ran across the ground.

"———!"

The monster couldn't keep its footing (or was that handing?), slipping and struggling.

"Goblin Slayer, sir, fire…!"

"We can't, it's too cold," he said sharply. "Fall back and go!"

"Yes, sir!"

Priestess ran as gingerly as she could, taking care not to slip on the ice as she made for a corner of the room. Goblin Slayer moved to cover her retreat, reaching into his item bag.

"'*Never leave home without it*,' eh?" He whispered the words Priestess spoke so often and pulled out a grappling hook.

He sent it flying toward the hand scrabbling along the ice and oil. He felt it set with a bite; surely not enough to cause pain, but…

"Hrm…!"

When he pulled it taut, the gigantic arm went sliding on the gasoline, slipping around. This would help make up in some small way the great gulf in their strength and weight. It was not enough to turn the battle in Goblin Slayer's favor, obviously, so he had to be careful what he did.

"Come…!" He gave the rope a jerk as if directing a cow that refused to listen to him. He looped the rope around the hand several times as it continued to struggle with the gasoline.

Making the floor slick was well and good, but it would be pointless if he was caught in his own trap. He slid his feet along to maintain his balance. He dropped his hips, put his strength into his legs. If he survived this, he would have to put cleats on his boots—or perhaps cover them in fur.

"—!"

The enemy, however, was not about to simply let Goblin Slayer have his way. The greater demon's hand twisted its wrist powerfully, as if swatting an especially annoying fly.

"Hrah…?!" Goblin Slayer was lifted into the air.

A moment later, he slammed into the wall of the chamber like a toy on a string being wielded by a careless child.

"Hrgh?!"

He heard his armor crack, but he didn't let go of the rope.

He dropped to the ground, slapping the floor just before the impact to soften the fall. He was all right. Nothing hurt enough to be broken.

"Goblin Slayer, sir!— Goblin Slayer!!" Priestess, heading deeper into the room, turned back and let out a cry as if she might burst.

"There is no…problem…!"

With a click of his tongue, Goblin Slayer stood up.

Yes, I can still do it. It's dangerous, but possible.

He was still in better condition than after the beating that whatever-it-was had given him beneath the ruins. Perhaps that had been a higher-level monster than he had realized.

Then again, it was always possible that his own level had increased.

Whatever. The point is, the difference between his power and mine is not absolute.

He snorted, finding his own thought comical, then supported himself unsteadily.

"How are you doing over there?"

"G-good!" Priestess said, quickly turning back toward her own objective. "I'm…almost there!"

When Priestess reached the double doors resting at the far side of the burial chamber, she pulled out an item.

The Blue Ribbon. The thing Sword Maiden had given him, and he had given her just now.

Priestess tied the Ribbon around one hand and pushed on the door.

When she did so, lo and behold, a blue light began to glow beside the door, and a row of symbols carved itself in the air.

It was a mysterious light, once lost. Priestess bit her lip as it shone upon her.

I knew it, Priestess thought, recalling Sword Maiden's words. She put a hand to her small chest. *This is the key to this place…!*

Priestess quickly ran her slim fingers over the keyboard. It was all right. She could do this. "Anytime!"

"I see…!" Goblin Slayer pulled on the rope with all the strength he had left.

There was an answering *snatch!* as the hand grasped at the floor, fighting not to move.

It was a tug-of-war—for an instant.

"Hrn…?!"

Unexpectedly, the hand went limp, and Goblin Slayer took a tumble. The greater demon's hand, which had ceased to resist him, worked its fingers even as it slid toward him.

"—Eek?!" Priestess let out an involuntary cry. She felt like the burial chamber was suddenly several degrees colder.

Magical energy swirled around the greater demon's palm, the air creaking.

Another blizzard…?!

Priestess's past battles flashed through her mind like an inspiration.

The gigantic ogre.

The upraised arm.

The swirling magic—conflagration.

And him, standing with his back to her.

Before, she had used up everything, hadn't been able to move.

But now.

Now…

"Goblin Slayer, sir!"

"Orcbolg!!"

A sufficiently advanced skill is indistinguishable from magic.

Like High Elf Archer's archery.

She lifted one leg up to support her bow, off to the left, drawing the string with her teeth. It was bizarre, and yet, beautiful. And as for the arrow she had readied...

"O sickle wings of velociraptor, rip and tear, fly and hunt!" Lizard Priest used the modicum of strength he had regained to invoke Swordclaw. "What is this great destruction of yours? If you wish to make corpses of us, bring forth the fiery stone fallen from heaven, and do it that way!"

The flame of his life force, once guttering, had begun to burn a bit more brightly. The help for this last vestige of his consciousness, which he could not otherwise have maintained, did not come from his ancestors.

Because, of course, he was not alone.

"Dancing flame, salamander's fame. Grant us a share of the very same!"

It was thanks to Dwarf Shaman, who had used some coal as a catalyst to cast Kindle.

With the renowned hardiness of his people, Dwarf Shaman had gotten them to just in front of the elevator. Now he grinned knowingly and took a sip of fire wine.

"Do it, Long-Ears!"

"Hhhh—rahhh!!"

A very un-elf-like bellow filled the room, and there was a flash of light.

Dragon fangs, her companion's fangs, slammed into the greater demon's hand.

"—?!"

It was not, of course, enough to cause serious pain. They were just the shots of a dying elf (no matter how superb an archer she might be) against a high-level greater demon (be it only its palm). It would be enough if they even pierced the skin. And yes, it was enough.

The fangs of the fearsome nagas were powerful enough to stop the hand from summoning its magic. It reeled from the impact, the vortex of magical energy disappearing like water sloshed over the edge of a cup. The twisting air snapped back into place and, at that moment:

"Yaaah...!"

Goblin Slayer would not miss this opportunity. The grappling hook, which he had pulled out by sheer force, along with the oil on the ground, sent the greater demon's hand sliding.

"—!"

Now.

With the threat sliding directly toward her, Priestess didn't hesitate for a moment: she began tapping the elevator's keyboard.

The doors opened without a sound. The greater demon's hand slipped inside, literally.

"—!"

Beyond the doors was nothing but a hole leading to a very long drop. No creature alive could survive the fall—but the greater demon's hand would not take the plunge so easily.

Even as it slipped and slid on the gasoline, it spread its fingers, trying to catch itself on a wall or crawl along. It looked like some kind of bizarre spider, a creature otherworldly and fearsome. It might not escape the fall, but it was bent on at least taking this girl with it.

If the greater demon had any personal awareness left, such was most likely its thought.

All the more reason to...

"O Earth Mother, abounding in mercy, by the power of the land grant safety to we who are weak!!"

All the more reason to play her part, here and now.

Her prayer, a prayer that shaved away part of her very soul, reached up to heaven and earned her a miracle from the all-merciful Earth Mother.

The invisible barrier of Protection spread out to either side, like a lid, to shield her devout follower.

"Hrgh...!"

The greater demon's hand, rebuffed, pounded angrily against the barrier, causing Priestess to wince each time as if she herself were receiving the blows.

But that was all.

Not long after, the hand began to slip away, and even though it dug its nails into the walls, loath to give up the fight, it was drawn inexorably back toward the pit, until it fell into the dark.

There was a long, silent moment. Finally, High Elf Archer's ears twitched, and she let out a breath. "Did we...do it?"

She didn't sound sure herself.

Priestess, though, didn't answer. Indeed, she couldn't answer. The tingling in her neck still wasn't gone.

This isn't over…!

"——!"

There was a deep *thud*, and a hairline fracture ran along the barrier of Protection like glass about to shatter.

"Ah, ahhh…?!"

The greater demon's hand had flexed every muscle it had to leap upward and launch its fist against the barrier. Priestess yelped with pain as if she herself had been struck and dropped to her knees.

Thud! A second hit.

"Ugh… Hrgh…?!"

Priestess's vision clouded as a shock wave went through her solar plexus. She couldn't breathe. She fell prostrate and groaned.

"Hrrr… Ahh…"

A third blow. It felt like it was tearing out her insides; she was flung back up to her knees.

But…I can't…!

She forced back down the bitter fluids that threatened to come up, staring fixedly straight ahead.

I can't give in… This isn't over… It isn't…over!

It wasn't that she had some special assurance. She simply believed. Believed she must not be defeated here.

The goblins. The stolen mail. The rescued girl. Her rescued self. Sword Maiden. Her friends.

The thoughts swirled in her mind. Was this what it meant for one's life to flash before one's eyes? No, no. This was no time to be getting lost in memories.

Goblin…Slayer…sir…!

"It's coming!"

His words sounded to her like a benediction. She clung to them, supported herself with them, stood with them.

The greater demon's hand stiffened. It was pushed up from below, shoved against the holy wall.

Why—how?

Somehow, Priestess felt she could understand the hand's confusion. It brought a smile to her pain-racked face.

"This is…an elevator," she said. "And you're going up…!"

It was the "box," rising up from below, that had the critical effect. The greater demon's hand was caught between the metal structure rising rapidly toward the surface and the Protection barrier…

"—!—…!!!!!!!!!"

It survived for several long seconds before, with a disgusting squish, it was reduced to hunks of meat.

With the cursed connection gone, the body of the goblin the greater demon had been using virtually melted. It ran down past the elevator in hideous, reeking black rivulets.

A moment later, Protection disappeared, its job done, and the elevator's incongruously cheerful *ding!* sounded in the burial chamber. The doors slid open without a sound. They were the entrance to a bottomless pit, to the very abyss.

Everyone was breathing in hard, ragged gasps, and for a time, nobody spoke.

"…A hammer and…an anvil…" Priestess managed at last. She almost stumbled, using her staff to support herself. She put her free hand against her throbbing stomach.

This was the absolute limit. They were out of prayers after fighting all this way from the moment they entered the fortified city.

As Priestess's slim, elegant body pitched forward, she felt herself supported by a rough, gloved hand that casually clasped her and drew her close.

"That's right," Goblin Slayer said. "You did well to remember."

"Because you…" Priestess smiled, her face sweaty. "Because you… taught it to me."

"…Is that so?"

"Yes."

Goblin Slayer fell silent then, supporting her shoulder as they walked. One step, then another. They worked their way along a floor covered with oil and ice and blood and flesh, one step at a time, ever forward.

In front of the elevator—so close, yet so far off—she found her companions supporting one another as they waited for her, as she had known she would.

Just the opposite of another time I can think of, Priestess thought suddenly and smiled.

Nobody acted like they were taking pity on her, yet she appreciated the gentle walking pace they took. And then suddenly, she noticed something. Something that might have been minor, trivial.

He's never…supported me as we walked before.

Priestess thought she could feel heat rising in her cheeks and looked down. She saw his boots and her own feet side by side.

So not all firsts were bad.

That was her little insight, here in the heart of this dungeon.

§

Of course, none of that meant it was all over.

"He's…going that way!"

"Oh, for—!!"

More goblins were waiting for them when the elevator arrived at the first floor.

"GROORB! GBOOROGB!!"

"GBBOROOROB!!"

There were fewer than before, to be sure. These must have been the remainder of whatever they hadn't destroyed earlier, or else monsters come up from lower floors.

"GOOBOGB!!"

"Why…you…!" Priestess swung her staff as hard as she could, keeping the goblins with their hideous expressions at bay.

High Elf Archer loosed arrows nonstop—but compared with her normal shooting, her movements looked as dull and slow as a Porcelain's. She had run out of bud-tipped arrows, too; now she relied on the rusty metal ones she stole from the goblins.

"It…hurts…!"

"GOOBOG?!"

And yet, it was enough. The goblin stumbled backward with an arrow through his eye and collapsed.

"Five!"

Almost instantly, Goblin Slayer jumped on another enemy.

"GBBOOGB?!"

He used his shield to stall the upraised club, deflecting the impact and pushing his foe over before closing in. Restraining the creature's futile resistance with the shield, Goblin Slayer stabbed out with his sword at the monster's throat before twisting violently.

"GOO?! GROGB...?!" The goblin died choking on his own blood.

"That's six," Goblin Slayer muttered. Priestess and High Elf Archer, both breathing hard, looked at each other.

The room was full of goblin corpses, including those from the earlier battle that hadn't been cleared away. Goblin Slayer stepped on the bodies as his metal helmet turned. "How's this area?"

"All good," High Elf Archer said with a weak flip of her ears. "I think. I'm not as sure as I'd like to be."

Her voice was thick with fatigue. She leaned her left shoulder against the wall to compensate for her right arm hanging limply at her side.

"...I'll call the others, then." Priestess spoke bravely, but although she was uninjured, she looked much like High Elf Archer. She was so tired she was dragging her feet, tottering as she approached the door; she gave a little shout as she summoned the strength to open it. "It's okay now," she said.

"Ah, sorry 'bout that..."

From beyond the door Priestess held open emerged Dwarf Shaman, his face slack. He had Lizard Priest's massive body across his shoulders, along with the much smaller form of the princess.

"Many...apologies... If I could only make my body...work a little more..." Lizard Priest's voice was muddled as he tried to apologize. He had gotten a little of his strength back—but just a little. His movements were obviously impaired after surviving the blast of freezing magic. Not to say someone other than a lizardman would have done any better...

"No... I'm sorry I don't have more power," Priestess said, shaking her head. She meant both physical strength and the power of her faith. If only the goddess would grant her a more effective healing miracle...

If only she'd still had the focus and vitality left to maintain a deep prayer connecting her soul to heaven.

Perhaps Dwarf Shaman understood what she was thinking, for a tired smile came over his bearded face. "I wonder if you could carry these two no matter how much strength you had."

"But..."

"Human muscles and dwarf muscles just aren't the same, lass, no matter how many of them you've got."

In other words, this was his moment to shine.

Even in light of his advice, Priestess couldn't help but be stung by her own weakness. Still puckering her lips, she checked over Lizard Priest and the princess. It was the most she could do at that moment.

Lizard Priest had always had plenty of life force, but the much weaker and more drained princess was in danger. Priestess touched the girl's cheek gently, and the princess seemed to whisper something in response.

"Thank you" and "I'm sorry."

She murmured the words over and over, as if she were talking to herself, and sometimes Priestess could make out *Big Brother, Father,* and *Mother* as well.

Priestess looked at the princess. They were almost the same age, or perhaps the princess was even a little younger than her. Priestess, about to turn sixteen, closed her eyes as if to suppress something.

A year and a half ago, she had been just like this. Ignorant, innocent, powerless, and above all, stupid.

She's...me...!

Priestess hugged the princess's battered body to herself.

What had she been able to do since then?

Was there anything she could do for the girl now?

Could she be any use to him at all...?

"Nothing is useless." The low voice caught her by surprise, and she looked up. Goblin Slayer was looking around vigilantly, but he was standing near the wall. It was unusual, for him. "You must simply work with what you have."

"...I think what he means is, don't worry about it. Though he could stand to learn to express himself a little more clearly." High Elf Archer, despite her pale, sweaty face, had her usual reproof for Goblin Slayer. She would stiffen from time to time, press a hand to her side. Hopefully it was just bruised. Because if it was broken...

"You two," Priestess said, struggling to steady her shaking voice. "Are you both okay?"

"Yes," Goblin Slayer answered with a nod. "I can go on."

"Oh, I'm fine," High Elf Archer added, but then she closed her eyes and looked down.

Fine was not a word that appeared to describe either of them.

So Priestess simply said, "Okay," and was quiet.

After a few minutes' rest, with no signal from anybody, the adventurers got to work once more. They couldn't afford to stay here very long.

Nobody spoke. But all of them knew what was waiting for them next.

They turned a corner of the corridor, heading up the stairs one step at a time, as if filling in spaces on a grid, heading for the surface. They fought as they went; the charge only took them twenty or thirty seconds. Despite their rest, though, it felt like it took an hour or two.

And then finally, at last, they reached the top of that long, long staircase, where...

"GOOROGB...!"

"GOOBOGR! GBOG!"

"GRROOR!"

"GBBG! GROORGB!!"

Goblins. Priestess shrugged, her face a mixture of fear, resignation, and readiness.

The courtyard in front of the dungeon was filled with greenskins. They smirked at Priestess and High Elf Archer, obviously imagining how they were going to bring low the women and the other adventurers. They held weapons of every kind— How many were there? Twenty, thirty? Forty, fifty?

"...Welp, that's par for the course," Dwarf Shaman said without much enthusiasm. "We weren't very subtle about how we dealt with that greater demon's hand. Otherwise, we might've gotten out of here unnoticed."

"...It's the opposite of normal," High Elf Archer said with a dry laugh. She had the same expression on her face as when they had been swarmed by goblins in the sewers. "It looks like *we're* the ones who are going to get slain…"

"Dungeons for a dragon, tunnels for a troll, and an abyss for adventurers! Heh-heh-heh!"

"This makes good sense," Lizard Priest said and got up from Dwarf Shaman's back unsteadily.

"You in one piece, Scaly?"

"When I meet my death, it shall certainly be on my feet," Lizard Priest replied. He made a wild gesture with his jaws, baring his fangs. It must have meant he was ready for anything—indeed, lizardmen were always ready for anything. His people always saw it as a good day to die. "So, have we any plan, milord Goblin Slayer?" He sounded downright pleased; his eyes spun in his head.

During all this, the goblins were advancing on them step by step. It was clear they had no intention of launching a sudden charge. They were enjoying the sight of the adventurers drawing back toward the dungeon entrance. It was an absolute pleasure seeing them in the goblins' accustomed place, looking this way and that. It was a balm to the heart, seeing those who normally hunted them reduced to such pitiful circumstances.

All the more reason this was the perfect chance to teach them a lesson, to hurt them, impregnate them, eat them.

Those women didn't look very meaty. They would die quickly. That or enjoy them while they lasted.

No, they could be enjoyed dead as well as alive. Just wring their necks and have fun with them after that.

Wait, bury them up to their necks and see who can send their heads flying the farthest with the swipe of an ax—that would be fun.

"GOOBGBOG!"

"GRROOR! GRBB!"

"GGGROORGB!!"

The goblins drew closer, the hideous smiles still on their faces.

Goblin Slayer didn't say anything.

"Goblin Slayer, sir…?" Priestess slid closer to him, looking up at his helmet.

She felt she should say something at this moment. But she didn't know what. There were too many thoughts, too many things she wanted to say; it was all she could do to push back the feeling that it was all going to overflow.

So finally, she just looked up at that helmet with wavering eyes.

It was a cheap-looking thing of metal.

It was impossible to see the expression hidden behind the visor, but...

"The nation will not act in this matter, nor will the army."

"...Right."

Goblin Slayer sought his footing, his attention never lapsing. He checked the width of the dungeon entrance, sank into a deep stance, and readied his weapon.

He had found a place where the goblins would be unable to use their numbers to their advantage.

He intended to meet them head on.

He had not given up.

"Presumably, they don't even wish to be informed that a family member was kidnapped by goblins," he said, and his helmet moved ever so slightly. His gaze turned toward the princess.

Right. Priestess gave another small nod.

There was a clicking sound. It came from her sounding staff: her hands were trembling. She gripped it tighter, but the sound didn't go away. Her teeth were chattering, too.

"Goblin Slayer...sir...!"

As foolish as it seemed, she felt she had to do it.

She reached out her small hand toward his rough, gloved one, almost as if clinging to him.

He didn't push her hand away.

Instead, still looking at the goblins, he said, "This is goblin slaying."

The goblins were coming.

High Elf Archer readied the very last of her arrows.

The goblins were coming.

Dwarf Shaman gently set the princess down and drew his ax.

The goblins were coming.

Lizard Priest spread wide his hands and tail, striking an imposing stance.

The goblins were coming.

Priestess bit her lip and stood fast, her sounding staff held in one shaking hand.

The goblins were coming.

The adventurer—the one in the cheap-looking metal helmet and grimy leather armor, with a round shield strapped to his arm and a sword of a strange length at his hip—said, "But if not…"

The goblins were—

§

"Lord of judgment, Sword-prince, Scale-bearer, show here your power!"

§

—the goblins were blown every which way.

"GOOROGB?!"

"GBB?! OROG?!"

A purple flash of electricity.

The air boiled as the blade of judgment swept down from above upon the goblins, sweeping them away. The sky, which had been enveloped in dark clouds, suddenly shone like midday, a Thunder Drake growling overhead. It was almost no sound, just enough to make their ears tingle—true divine majesty.

"Wha…?"

"Well, now…"

High Elf Archer could only gawk, while Dwarf Shaman gave a bit of an exasperated sigh.

"I see—the hammer and the anvil," Lizard Priest said with a shake of his head. "So this is what you meant."

"GOOROGB?!"

"GBBOOG?!"

The goblins, struggling to flee, were struck one after the next by lightning bolts that fell like rain.

In the midst of it all, Priestess was looking directly at *her*.

"Everyone, the goblins are not our enemy."

Her, standing atop the walls of the city, silhouetted against the pale blue of the dawn sky.

"Not they, but the foul fellowship, the Non-Prayers who seek to usher the Demons of Chaos into this realm."

A beautiful woman, accompanied by a white alligator, a holy beast.

The flesh of her voluptuous body was only just covered by her thin white garments. Her golden hair gleamed in the sun. The staff of the sword and scales, which she now held in reverse with the blade facing upward, was the sign of righteousness and the justice of law.

If one were to picture the Supreme God as a female deity, she might well look like this.

The only possible blemish was the dark sash wrapped around her eyes. And yet, it did nothing to mar her beauty. In fact, perhaps the sash only accentuated how stunning she was.

"A certain adventurer told me thus." To her bounteous chest she clutched a piece of paper bearing an unsightly scrawl as if it were holy writ. "Judge each and every one of them while they yet lived."

A great answering cry came from the city gates. Then the warrior priests came on like a tempest, literally trampling the goblins underfoot. The sword and scales moaned, and the monsters were induced to repent—when their skulls were smashed in.

"*O goddess of battle! Grant us victory!*"

"*O Earth Mother, abounding in mercy, by the power of the land grant safety to we who are weak!*"

"*Lord of judgment, Scale-sovereign, Sword-prince, let there be light…!*"

"*My god the roaming wind, let all on our road be good fortune!*"

"*Watchman of the Candle, shine a humble flame into the shadows of our ignorance! May darkness never fall!*"

The onrushing figures, calling upon the names of their sundry gods, were certainly neither the army, nor adventurers.

They were simply the fighting strength of the temple, who jumped to obey at a single word from a single great cleric.

The outcome of this battle was no longer in doubt. One of the heroes who had fought the Demon Lord was present now. The deepest and most awful dungeon in all the world could hold no fear. A handful of goblins, so much the less so. There was no way the adventurers could lose.

The goblins, who had thought they'd had their foes surrounded and now found themselves enveloped, began to shout and run. Perhaps they had it in mind to flee into the dungeon. But *he* met them with weapon in hand, as ever.

"Yes, I told her," Goblin Slayer said. He sounded somehow as if he were looking at something very bright. "But the rest was up to her."

Oh...

Priestess blinked.

She was sure, now, that she could see it. She shouldn't have been able to see it, yet there was.

The sword and scales held up by Sword Maiden were trembling.

Her lips were moving ever so slightly, her teeth striking against one another time and again.

The reason she was leaning on that alligator was because she didn't have the strength to hold herself up.

But...

But there she was.

With the morning sun at her back, its color mingling with the gold of her hair, she truly looked like a goddess. Weak with fear, hardly able to stand, terror tinging her expression—and yet, she confronted the goblins.

Priestess realized that Sword Maiden's unseeing eyes were focused directly on *him*.

That was the answer; that was the reason.

Priestess noticed that her hand was still clinging to his and blushed. She made to disentangle her fingers—hesitated—brushed his hand softly and, finally, pulled hers away.

She was humiliated, pathetic, pitiful...and yet.

I want to be...

...a source of strength to him.

That day, she stored up the smallest of prayers in her heart.

One day, she swore, she would be.

"Well now, that is *quite* the plan!"

"Oh, you're too kind."

They were at the house of a noble, which stood beside the river that flowed through the capital. It was so late at night that even the moons had hidden their faces.

Two men sat drinking at a table in a parlor whose luxury befitted a high official.

One of the men wore clothes cut to accommodate his portly frame; he was part of the nobility of this nation.

Across from him sat a man bearing a strange holy mark in the shape of a single forbidding eye; he was one of those who followed an evil cult.

In short, this was one of those events that had been held time and again since the very founding of the world, a banquet between companions in evil.

"Controlling the goblins using the fiery stone from heaven, causing them to kidnap the princess and sacrifice her to resurrect the greater demon…"

"If we could crossbreed the greater demon with the thing from beyond the stars, we could create a true horror," the cultist concurred.

"It could impersonate the princess, but it would be under our control, so we could manage the king somehow." The nobleman gave a belly-shaking laugh. He didn't seem to have any doubts about his ability to control an unknown entity from another realm. "If even one of those plots succeeds, well and good. But even if they all fail, if we spread a rumor that the princess was violated…"

Then no one would want to marry her. The power of the bloodline would wane, the king's royal glory would be overshadowed, and the scales of the Court would tilt dramatically.

"Why should that whelp of an adventurer run the government just because he's got a few drops of royal blood in him?" the nobleman said, shaking his head in intense displeasure. It was a gesture overflowing with pity for the world, with righteous indignation, completely characteristic of the great many high-class people in town. It said more about who *he* thought was fit to control the government than a thousand speeches ever could.

"…As for myself, I'm perfectly content to let His Majesty sit on the throne, so long as my faith continues to spread," the noble follower of the God of Wisdom said pleasantly. "The knowledge of him is good for my profits, after all."

"But what's to be done about the hero?"

"Easy enough. She's a sweet little girl whom we can wrap around our little finger with a bit of fawning: *O Platinum!*, we'll say. *O great hero!*"

The first nobleman allowed the cultist to pour him more wine. He wiped away a few red droplets with his sleeve.

"If she plays along with us after that, then fine," the cultist continued. "If not, we find some convenient excuse to send her on a suicide mission."

"I can't see myself getting along very well with her type."

"Nor she with you, I suspect. How I would like to see her and her friends begging pitifully for their lives."

The nobleman smirked at the nasty image in his mind. The cultist, picking up on his amusement, chuckled and sipped his own drink. It made scant difference to him what happened to some so-called hero, or sage, or sword saint, women all.

But if his spawn were to gain their powers, what a thing that would be. Yes, that was all he cared about.

Knowledge was power, and power ruled the world. Few could truly understand what a sweet and beautiful thing that was.

That thought might have prompted, in some sense, a small factoid that flashed through the cultist's mind and then disappeared.

"…I was thinking, it's been some time since I heard any rumors of that interloper."

"Heh-heh—what, do you believe what people say? Don't make me laugh. That's just the idle fancies of peasants."

That was when it happened.

The quake, the wind, the thunder.

For a moment, they thought perhaps it was the sound of the river grown especially violent, but then came the roar.

It was, quite literally, the sound of a battering ram at the castle gates, the prow of a ship striking a wall.

Bursting through the wall of the parlor came, indeed, the prow of a ferryboat.

"Wh-what is the meaning of this?!" the nobleman and the cultist shouted.

An answer came, likewise, from the ferryboat: "It's been a long time, you scum."

The sculler existed more as a small, dim silhouette than anything—judging by the lines in the figure's black clothing, might it be a young woman?—but this spy was not the source of the words.

Instead, the speaker was a man, standing beside the sculler with a dignity that seemed out of place. He looked down at the astonished villains and growled derisively, "It's been a long time, you scum. Have you missed me?"

Look—yes, look—at his glittering accoutrements. Shining brightly even there in the dark were his armor, his shield, his helmet, and his gloves, as well as the sword that hung at his hip. He carried enough magical items to astound any onlooker: a blessing of Healing, an Evil-Banishing Light, an Anti-Freezing charm, a Primal Flame, and a Whirling Wind. And his name was…

"The Knight of Diamonds…!"

He was supposed to be nothing more than a myth, a fairy tale passed around among the common people. A phantom about whom whispers had spread in the city these past few years. A man who hid his face and punished evil by darkness, a true knight of the streets.

But he couldn't be real; there was no one that crazy.

For starters, slaughtering crooked merchants and nobles and cultists of one's own accord—didn't that make him a simple murderer? How could that boy playing at being king, with all his talk of righteousness, allow such acts to go unchecked?

Yet, there he was, right in front of them. But who exactly was he? Or what?

He must be a simple deviant.

Thus the nobleman seemed to think. He had either remembered his own station and honor or had concluded that his visitor was a simple ne'er-do-well. Feeling he had a better grasp now on his own position, he said forcefully, "Impudent fool! Whose residence do you think you're in? Remove your helmet, at once!"

"Oh-ho. So you want to see my face, eh?" The Knight of Diamonds sounded almost amused; he laughed with a sound like a lion bearing its fangs. "I'm happy to oblige—but I don't think you're going to like it."

With that, those glittering gauntlets reached up to his visor, lifting it without a sound.

Then his face stood revealed. The nobleman and the cultist alike felt their eyes go wide.

"Wha...?!"

"It—it can't be...!"

That was all they could say.

They were witnessing something that could not be. Something unbelievable, something that shouldn't exist—but the knight's was a face they knew all too well.

Their knees went weak, and they gasped for breath, forgetting themselves as they babbled, "Come! Come forth!"

The shouting brought armed men of the noble's personal guard running. The cultist, meanwhile, warped space as he summoned fiends and ghouls from another realm. The fact that the guards didn't flinch at this was proof enough that they were coconspirators of the men.

Gods. The Knight of Diamonds groaned.

Yes, one had to be broad-minded enough to accept all kinds of people, but that was no reason to turn a blind eye to evil. And there was no arguing with men like this; they would simply try to twist everything to their benefit. On top of that, considering how personal the stakes were in this instance, everything seemed tailor-made to put the knight in a bad mood.

The young woman in the shadows, seeming to sense the knight's thoughts, let out a breath of simultaneous exasperation and resignation. The Knight of Diamonds ignored her completely, laughing out loud.

"It looks like you're far beyond talk. Your fate is sealed."

Still looking at the pitiful noble in front of him, the knight lowered his visor once more and drew his sword.

The blade was all blinding flash, the stroke so violent and so precise that even the wind from the passing sword could have beheaded a man.

As if to emphasize to the men that they couldn't flee from before his blade, the Knight of Diamonds declared, "On behalf of heaven, I claim your lives!!"

Here, now, there was no place for mercy anymore.

CHAPTER 10

O My Prayers, Have You Reached Heaven?

"So after all that, he didn't accept a reward?"

"No!" High Elf Archer pounded the table, making the dishes jump. "Can you believe it?!" She had been grievously wounded not long before, but after a few days' rest, she was already back on her feet. That was an elf for you.

Guild Girl glanced, a little discomfited, at the others at the table but, nonetheless, still smiled. Witch enjoyed a sip of her wine with an innocent expression, and as for Priestess, she looked much the same.

For those gathered around the table, each with their own thoughts, High Elf Archer's fit of temper was nothing new.

Everything had been more or less as normal in the frontier town while Goblin Slayer and his party were away. Adventurers drank, laughed, went on adventures, fought, and came home—or, occasionally, didn't.

It was just daily life, Priestess thought, that they had come back to.

"I have to point out," Guild Girl said, "he *did* take a reward."

"Yeah—for *goblin slaying!*" High Elf Archer's ears bounded up and down in absolute frustration. She looked thoroughly drunk—except that the stuff in her cup was grape juice. Evidently, she was in an exceptionally bad mood today.

"Well, that's just who he is," Guild Girl said quietly. She leaned on the table with a *what can you do.* "Even if the person he rescues is a young noblewoman…he simply sees goblin slaying as goblin slaying."

And for him, maybe it is.

"Maybe," Priestess concurred.

She said nothing else, partly because there was nothing in the statement to disagree with, partly because it was true, and partly because she felt the same way.

"I heard there was a real ruckus in the capital, too," Guild Girl went on. "Another of the evil cultists' bases was destroyed or something. But I wonder who this Knight of Diamonds you hear about sometimes really is." Guild Girl cocked her head.

Priestess didn't know the answer. It was true: for the person she was thinking of, goblin slaying was just what he always did.

But…

But even so, she could tell that maybe there were more worldly ways to go about it.

He *had* saved a daughter of the royal household, even if it was "just" from goblins. He might not have been able to demand anything he wished, but surely, he would have been permitted a significant request.

Like in a fairy tale, he could have married the princess and lived happily ever… Heh! Well, maybe not.

But he might well have asked the king to take sterner measures against goblins, or requested a promotion to Gold rank, or asked for some discreet royal support, or…

Maybe he should be dreaming a little bigger…or not.

It was a flippant thought. Yes, Priestess saw that.

But *he* simply said, "This is goblin slaying."

No more and no less, and that was enough.

Goblin Slayer…

That was what he wanted, and that was what he kept doing.

"Ahh…"

"Well, now… What's this, sighing?" Witch, ever perceptive, immediately picked up on the little exhalation. "Today, you said something very, cute…about not wanting to go, home." *Did something happen to upset you?* Witch's eyes ran over Priestess, full of concern, and the younger girl looked at the floor as if to escape.

"No, not really…"

Not *really*, but… Her voice pinched, and she shook her head ambiguously.

But what can I do to be more like you?

She couldn't possibly ask such a childish question.

She wanted to be outstanding. Beautiful and strong, giving, always mellow, knowing anything and everything, elegant and refined… That was the kind of person she wanted to grow up to be.

Like Witch—like Sword Maiden.

After everything was over, after Sword Maiden had come rushing to the city, he and she parted without so much as a word. Sword Maiden had been busy dealing with the aftermath, and Goblin Slayer had withdrawn quickly.

Was that really all right?

But something must have passed between them, something they could communicate without speaking. Even if she didn't know what it might be.

For Priestess, though, the adventure that had begun with Sword Maiden's quest concluded without ever really feeling to her as if it had ended.

What had she been able to do? Indeed, could she do anything?

Priestess brushed a hand over her garments, feeling the mail beneath, covering her small chest.

She wanted to be a source of strength.

That was what she had prayed for, but there were no sudden, eye-opening changes. She was still a novice adventurer with just a year or so under her belt, still an inexperienced Steel rank.

Suddenly, she was moved to glance around: She saw Rookie Warrior and Apprentice Cleric quietly celebrating something. At a table across the way, Heavy Warrior's party was seated, Female Knight making some bold pronouncement.

At every turn, the tavern was filled with adventurers who seemed to sparkle.

And…what about me?

"It's…hard, isn't it?" The words, coinciding with her thought, came spilling out suddenly and quietly.

"Hmm?" High Elf Archer said, drawing a circle in the air with her finger. "What's hard? Tell your big sister elf."

"I mean…getting stronger?" Priestess put a finger to her lips, thinking for a moment, and then said, "…Or maybe just growing, I guess. I was just thinking, it's not so easy. It's…just a little overwhelming."

"Well, sure," High Elf Archer said as if none of this were any surprise. "Even a tree doesn't grow up overnight. If it did, man, that'd be a shock!"

Her words held the kind of knowledge and wisdom only an elf could have possessed, but they were expressed with a very un-elf-like attitude. The disparity caused Guild Girl to laugh, the tinkling in her voice like the ringing of a bell.

"Well, worrying about it won't get you anything," she said.

"Right…"

"And no one will trust you if you just go off on your own and then come back claiming you've done a bunch of training."

Guild Girl must have seen others like Priestess before. Her knowing advice was so gentle and kind it made Priestess want to cry.

"Come to think of it," Guild Girl added, "I've got good news. Good news for you, at least." She clapped her hands and winked—maybe she had noticed how Priestess was feeling.

"Good news…?"

"The royal princess, I've heard, has converted to a devout belief in the Earth Mother. Er, not that she's joining a nunnery or anything."

"That's…" Priestess, completely at a loss for what to say, looked at High Elf Archer.

The elf was all shrugs. It seemed there weren't many people she could discuss this with.

She found an image passing through her mind, of the girls who had gone to the Temple after their first adventure. Their bodies had been mostly unharmed. It was their hearts that were most concerning. Priestess knew all too well how easy it was to break a heart, to shatter a mind.

It was no good.

She had been no good. Again.

"It seems she had a chance encounter with a cleric of the Earth Mother."

"What...?"

Thus, these words that followed caught Priestess completely by surprise. She looked vacantly at Guild Girl, who had the look of a child sharing a secret.

"Allegedly, she said, 'I don't know what's going to happen in the future, but I want to grow up to be like her.'"

"_____"

Now Priestess was well and truly speechless.

"Like her"?

Was she being too presumptuous to think that "her" was...well, *her*?

"Wha— What...?"

Unexpectedly, she found her vision blurring. She blinked, rubbed her eyes. It didn't get any better. And her cheeks were so hot.

With no idea what to do, Priestess sobbed a little and let her face become tear streaked.

She had to get herself back under control. She was supposed to act cool and collected.

If that poor girl were to learn about this, it really might break her once and for all. This wasn't the end of anything, but for Priestess, it was everything.

And yet, for some reason, the world stayed misty and the words remained stuck in her throat.

"...Hey, that's great. That really is good news," High Elf Archer said softly, gently. Witch patted Priestess on the back.

Guild Girl stayed silent—whether because she understood or not, it was impossible to tell.

Really and truly happy to the depths of her heart, Priestess fought to open her mouth to say something.

At that moment, the tavern doors swung open, and Padfoot Waitress went rushing past Priestess.

For adventurers, the night was still young.

§

©Noboru Kannatuki

The twin moons shone chill in the night sky.

His breath fogged, mingling with the moonlight.

Goblin Slayer walked down a small road outside town with his usual nonchalant stride.

Nothing had changed.

He had accepted the quest, gone to the location, killed the goblins, rescued the captive, and come home.

That was everything.

That was his duty.

Just like the way the dry grass crunched under his feet, he knew.

Nothing had changed up to this moment, and nothing ever would.

The road went ever on and on, endless.

Words High Elf Archer had spoken to him once upon a time suddenly came back to him.

Look only at what's in front of your eyes.

His master had said something similar once. Though he had added, *Because you're too stupid for anything else.*

Just focus on what's in front of you, take care of it, then go on to the next thing.

Keep looking forward; move your feet. Stand up and proceed.

That way, everything in the world will be taken care of. If you don't do it, nothing will change.

"……"

Goblin Slayer found himself thinking:

I cannot walk the same path as those girls.

Unlike Sword Maiden, standing upon those walls; unlike Noble Fencer, fighting ever on; unlike even Priestess, who always kept moving forward, Goblin Slayer did not believe in the gods. He had never properly prayed. He didn't see the point.

But for exactly that reason, he was deeply impressed by those who could and did believe.

He felt that way about Lizard Priest, too, and Dwarf Shaman. Even High Elf Archer and Guild Girl.

He wasn't sure what Spearman believed. Heavy Warrior, though, he was confident. Each and every one, everyone…

Goblin Slayer stopped and looked up at the heavens. Two moons hung amid an uncountable number of stars.

He grunted softly, almost a groan. Then he shook his head.

He hadn't known what was right, but he knew what he ought to do. There was only one thing.

He picked up his foot, stretched it out, and took a step. Then he raised the other foot, stretched it out, and took another.

Walk. Move forward. Don't think about whether you'll get there or not. To keep walking, that was everything to him.

"Oh, welcome home!"

He raised his helmeted head when the voice came.

There was a warm light, not too far distant. It must have been seeping out a window.

He spotted her right away, leaning out the window, her red hair blowing in the night breeze.

"It's dark already," she said with a smile and a wave. "It's dangerous to just stand there staring into space!"

He caught the scent of boiling milk on the breeze.

"Yes," he said at length, squeezing out the words. "I'm home."

Even though she could hardly have heard him, the girl grinned, "Uh-huh!" and nodded. "Dinner's ready, okay? Come on in!"

"…Understood."

He thought.

Nothing has changed.

He went on adventures and killed goblins.

That was who he was.

That was what he had chosen.

And if the result of that choice was that nothing changed?

He spent no more time thinking about it but went into the house, closing the door slowly behind him. The sound of it shutting echoed warmly through the cold night air.

Autumn was nearly past, and soon it would be winter.

AFTERWORD

Hullo! Kumo Kagyu here!

Did you like *Goblin Slayer* Volume 8?

In this volume, goblins showed up, so Goblin Slayer had to goblin-slay them.

I put my heart and soul into writing it, and I would be thrilled if you enjoyed it.

But look, this is Volume 8. Volume 8! I feel like I've gone all the way from Analand to Mampang and back.

They've had me put out a second spinoff, and I'm even writing the story of Ujizane Imagawa.

All this is only possible because of all the support everyone has given me, for which I'm truly grateful.

By the time this book comes out, I think you should be able to "run" in the newest version of the city shadows. Yippee. Plus, the animated version should be broadcast by the time you read this. Incredible, huh?

Pretty much anyone who wants to be an author dreams of winning a big prize, getting published, having their work adapted as a manga and then as an anime. I didn't win any big prizes, but I've checked all the other boxes…I guess? I 100 percent expect to wake up in a hospital bed sometime soon. Honest.

Let me tell you about the anime: the art, plotting, music, and acting are all spectacular!

I hope you'll take a look if you're interested.

Anyway, on to the acknowledgments.

As ever, my thanks go out to everyone who has bought and read my books. And to those of you who have been cheering me on from the web-novel stage, I hope you keep supporting me.

To all my creative friends, thank you for all your advice and just generally putting up with me!

To my gaming friends: I managed to write another one! Thanks!

To all the summary-site admins who have given me their support, thank you once again.

Kannatuki-sensei is back this volume with yet more fantastic illustrations; thank you, Sensei!

To everyone in editorial, writing is the only thing I can actually do, so I really appreciate your saving my neck from everything else.

And to everyone else connected with *Goblin Slayer* in any way, thank you so much.

I plan for Volume 9 to be a story where goblins appear, so Goblin Slayer has to go slay them.

I'll pour my heart and soul into it, again, so please do look forward to it.

Thanks, and see you again!

SLAY THEM ALL

GOBLIN SLAYER

He does not let anyone roll the dice.

Watch it on FUNIMATION | NOW

FUNIMATION.COM/GOBLINSLAYER

©Kumo Kagyu·SB Creative Corp./Goblin Slayer Project.